Table of (

DON'T **LIE** TO ME

STACEY LYNN

Lyrics from The Nadas, "Only Love is Real," were used with permission. For more information on The Nadas' music, you can find them at www.thenadas.com. They rock!

Cover designed by Regina Wambe with Mae I Design and Photography. You can find more information about her at www.maeidesign.com

Ebook formatting by: Mayhem Cover Creations

Paperback formatting by: Angela McLaurin, Fictional Formats

Dedication

To Aaron

Thank you for your encouragement and support.

I couldn't travel this journey without you, your laughter, or your love.

One

I sang along to the music playing from the kitchen docking station while I sautéed a pan of bok choy stir-fry. I peeked at the clock before dancing across the kitchen to prepare a salad for dinner knowing I had ten minutes to finish up before Jack would be there, promptly.

It was how he lived everything, controlled, alert, and dispassionate—except for a successful closing on a new business property. Jack McMillan was CEO and President of McMillan Holdings, a real estate investment company his grandfather started. He took control of the company when his dad died in a car accident ten years ago.

At the age of twenty-two, he had recently graduated from college and was just beginning to be mentored into eventually taking the helm of his family's vast empire. Overnight, he became CEO and within the last five years grew the internationally renowned company from a multi-million dollar corporation into multi-billion dollar empire. He possessed power and control at every single moment I saw him.

As his personal assistant, housekeeper and personal cook, I saw a lot of him.

He was respectful and kind, but always from a distance. He wore his confidence like a perfectly tailored suit like he was made for his job and his position, and people bowed to him daily.

He expected perfection and was fierce with anyone who didn't deliver, but he was never cruel or angry. In fact, besides a slight smile or low chuckle, he rarely showed any emotion at all. It was as if he lived inside a perfectly carved wall of stone where nothing penetrated him. Some days it unnerved me, but I had seen just a few glimpses over the years of his kindness and generosity, and even playfulness, that made me want to see more.

Because for the last two years, I had lusted after him fiercely.

I wanted to watch his eyes light up in the throes of passion and to see him lose control, if even for a brief moment. I suspected long ago I was attracted to him simply because he was the most gorgeous man I had ever laid eyes on, but it went deeper than that.

I inwardly sighed every time he brought home a new toy, or video game for my son Logan, who often accompanied me to work on the days he didn't have school. As a single mom, my opportunities for dating were infrequent at best. Plus, I hated leaving Logan, even if my best friend, Macy, constantly offered—and sometimes demanded—I go out for a night out.

Jack was affectionate with Logan, often treating him like a niece or nephew, even though he didn't have any of his own since he was an only child.

I was lost in the entertaining sounds of my new Mumford and Sons album, dancing along by myself in Jack's impressively decorated kitchen, lost in my thoughts of him, when I heard a throat clear behind me.

Whipping around at the noise, my long blond hair flying out behind me, I froze when I saw him.

Jack stood in the doorway, hands clutching the top of the doorframe, impeccably dressed in his black Armani suit, with his dark red tie loosened around his neck and the top button of his grey shirt undone. There wasn't a wrinkle to be seen and he looked just as perfect as he had when he left for work in the morning.

It was also the most casual I had ever seen him look, and a warm feeling instantly began spreading through my lower stomach. I couldn't make out the defined muscles I knew hid under his designer suit, but I knew they were there.

There was a hint of amusement in his eyes along with the wide smile he flashed directly at me.

"Jack," I breathed out hoarsely. Whether breathless from the sight of him, or the dancing, I didn't know.

"Enjoying yourself?" He asked as he pushed off and walked towards the stovetop where his dinner simmered. He lifted the lid and inhaled. "This smells delicious."

"Thank you. It should be ready in five minutes," I said flippantly, but took a few steps away from him and towards the counter because I was feeling anything but flippant. I turned around and pretended to finish the salad, even though I was really just fluffing it with the salad tongs.

Mostly I just needed a minute to compose myself and hide the embarrassing blush from getting caught wiggling my ass in his kitchen.

"How was your day?"

I watched him out of the corner of my eye as he walked over to the fridge and took out a bottle of water. We had this conversation every night when he got home, on the nights I was still there. But lately, to my own ears at least, it sounded more personal, his voice a bit softer. It was probably my overactive imagination running away from me again.

"It was good. I confirmed your appearance with Jessica for Saturday night at the Opera. She's looking forward to it." I bit back my own grimace. Of course she'd be looking forward to a night out with Jack. The only thing that stopped me from wanting to gag is that I knew she was almost at her three-date limit. Then I'd be scheduling appearances, dates, and rsvp'ing on his behalf for other women.

I rubbed my hand across my forehead, and sighed. Either I had to get over this ridiculous obsession soon or I'd have to quit. Maybe I could go back and finish school. The thought alone made me snort.

Like I could handle law school and Logan. That ship sailed years ago.

"Something wrong?" he asked casually. I stopped pretending to finish the salad and removed my apron.

"No." I shook my head, still clearing my thoughts from my dream that would never happen. "I was just thinking."

He regarded me thoughtfully as if he expected me to say more but when he realized I wasn't going to, changed the subject. I was glad.

"Big plans for the weekend?"

I scrunched my nose up. "I have a date tomorrow."

"I see. Someone new?" His voice was clipped, with maybe a hint of irritation, but I chose to ignore it, based on my thirty-second resolve of getting over my feelings for Jack. I couldn't spend the rest of my life reading into words he said when Jack had never looked at me with anything except professional respect in his eyes.

"Macy set me up on a blind date." I didn't bother hiding my annoyance at the idea of blind dates. I loathed them. The only thing my date tomorrow night guaranteed was an attractive man to look at while enjoying a glass of wine in a restaurant that didn't come with paper kids' menus and crayons. Macy loved me too much to subject me to someone who didn't meet her idea of handsome, and she had great taste. Her own fiancé, Tate, looked like he should appear on the cover of GQ Magazine.

"You'll be safe."

I halted at Jack's words. They sounded like a rough command and while I could brush off the irritation earlier, this was definitely not a kind suggestion.

"What?" I turned and asked him.

"You'll be safe. He's a stranger, and you're …" I froze as his hand reached out … to touch me? I wanted him to. Screw getting over the obsession with him. When Jack McMillan was within five feet of me I simply couldn't think straight anymore.

And now I was imagining him touching, no, caressing my cheek softly out of concern for my safety. I needed a drink.

As if he saw the surprise and confusions swirling in my mind, his hand snapped to his front pocket and he took a step away from me.

"I'm what, Jack?"

"You're a woman in the city and you need to be careful." He sounded even bossier as his dark brown eyes pierced me. He also sounded irritated. I just didn't understand why. Regardless, he didn't need to be condescending, and it annoyed me that he thought I was some helpless woman alone in the big bad city.

I sucked in a small breath through my teeth letting my irritation show, and then put a lid on what I really wanted to snap at him. After all, he was still my employer. "Have a good weekend, Jack."

I left the kitchen to go pick up Logan from the servant's suite room before heading home. My room in Jack's place was small, and it was an interior room so it lacked windows, but I was thankful for the space anyway. When Logan was a baby, Jack let me bring him to work since I worked alone almost all day long. It allowed me to stay with Logan most of the day, only needing daycare for longer nights or special events, and it had everything I needed—a small bed and an even smaller bathroom. Now we used it as Logan's playroom on the days he came to work with me.

I stepped over a handful of Legos and told Logan to put them away while I got ready to go home. It only took a few minutes and we were ready to make the short drive back to Lincoln Park. I looked at the time on my phone on our way out to the entryway. It was almost six thirty, but our brief conversation put me a little bit behind than I wanted to be. Oh well, the only thing I had planned for tonight was a game of UNO with Logan that I promised earlier and a glass of wine.

Jack stood in the entryway when we reached it, his hand clasped firmly to the stairway banister. He smiled and bent down to give Logan a small hug that made my heart flutter. When he turned his eyes to me, he looked just as angry as he did when I left the kitchen.

"What do you know about this guy?" He demanded as he walked towards us, his hands clenched into fists at his side.

Why was he so angry?

I shook my head. "What's gotten in to you? It's a date—dinner, a drink - and that's it."

"Where is he taking you?"

In five years of working for him, Jack had never pulled the overprotective big brother card, and while I liked it—evidenced by the warmth in my lower stomach—I knew he wasn't angry because he was jealous. I just didn't know why he was doing this. The entire conversation was frustrating.

He frowned at me; growing impatient by my lack of response. I sighed. "Frenzio's. Happy now?"

"No. I'm not happy about this." He spit out the words with as much frustration as I felt inside of me and took two quick steps toward me leaving almost no space between us. I backed up a step so I could look at him.

Standing at his full height, he towered over my five foot seven inch frame. He was well over six feet tall. The top of my forehead didn't come close to his chin and when he stood so close—which he had never done before—I had to crane my neck up to see him. He narrowed his eyes and ran a hand through his short, dark brown hair, somehow making it look even more perfect than it did before. He opened his mouth to say something and then shut it again, moving back and putting space between us. The entire conversation left me feeling baffled as we stood there watching each other.

"Mr. Jack, can I play your Playstation next time I come over?" Logan's smile broke our silence and I watched Jack's hardened eyes soften when he turned to him with a smile.

"Sure thing. Maybe I'll get a new game for you to try."

Logan's smile stretched ear to ear. "Awesome. I want Paper Mario!"

"Logan …" I admonished him. "It's rude to state what you want like that. Mr. Jack doesn't have to buy you anything."

He made a pouty face that made both Jack and me laugh; momentarily breaking the tension I could practically feel reverberating off him.

"Nonsense." Jack squatted down in front of Logan again and gently rubbed his blonde curly locks. He may have been speaking to Logan, but his eyes never left mine. "If you don't tell someone what you want, you'll never get it."

His words implied a double meaning, only I didn't know what on earth he meant and his darkened black eyes left me feeling too unsettled to want to stay around any longer to try to figure it out.

I simply nodded my head in the direction of the kitchen while I reached for Logan's hand. "Enjoy your dinner. I'll see you Monday."

He said nothing as he held the door opened for us, waited in the doorway until the elevator came, or before he shut it when we stepped inside. His silence left me more rattled than his words and my head spun in circles trying to figure out what had just happened.

I almost hated Macy for setting me up on a blind date with Dean. My lip curled in mock disgust for the hundredth time since I agreed to go out on this date. Dean. It was an arrogant, cocky name. The name sounded like he'd be some guy who grew up with a silver spoon in his mouth, a trust fund the size of Texas, and spent his days hanging out at the country club, golfing, playing tennis and hitting on the various Chicagoan socialites.

I didn't know any of this for sure, but based on the fact that Dean and Macy met at the golf club where her parents were members, I didn't think my assumptions were too far off. Ironic that most of the closest people in my life enjoyed the same type of lifestyle. Macy grew up in an extremely wealthy family in Chicago. She just never lived like it, or even admitted it to anyone really. Maybe I was being too judgmental of this Dean guy.

I sighed and set down my mascara. I didn't even know why I was doing this. Maybe it was because I was desperate. Five years of being a single mom, dropping out of my first year of law school and a full time job as a personal assistant slash housekeeper and cook for business mogul Jack McMillan didn't allow much time for a personal life.

I sighed again at the mere thought of Jack and the unsettling way he spoke to me the night before. I had yet to figure out what caused all the tension between us, I only hoped it was gone by Monday.

That was a total lie. If I was honest with myself, I would totally admit that if there was one person I wanted to be on a date with tonight, it was Jack.

Brushing the pointless thoughts of Jack McMillan out of my head, I finished getting ready for my dinner with Dean. Maybe Macy was right and I needed this.

There was no point in trying to get out of the date anyway. If I did, Macy would kill me and an angry Macy was someone no one wanted to see. She may have looked innocent and naïve with her just over five foot stature, but I laughed silently remembering all the guy's asses she verbally kicked when they tried to take advantage of her, or the way she stood up and defended me after Marcus took off.

The very name sent shivers down my spine and not in the pleasant way it did when I thought of Jack. Shaking off my anger at the mere thought of his name, I smoothed out my short black skirt, made sure the red belt on my silk blouse sat perfectly around my narrow waist, and tossed my blonde hair over my shoulder.

I looked good. I'd rather be playing UNO Attack and lounging around in my yoga pants with Logan for the night, but dinner, wine and Dean would have to do.

I wrinkled my nose again at the name, slipped on my grey peep-toe pumps and headed out to kiss my boy goodnight.

"Hey kiddo," I said as I leaned down to give the most perfect little boy a kiss on the nose.

"Mo-om …" He moved out of my reach and added an extra syllable to the word, expressing his severe disinterest in my public display of affection. I chuckled to myself before ruffling his mop of blonde curls.

I pointed my finger at him with a smile on my face. "Be good for Macy, okay?"

Logan simply nodded before going back to his Legos. The kid could build houses and cars from his Lego sets for hours, which was incredible, except for when I stepped on a lone one that hadn't been put away. Those tiny pointy toys hurt like hell.

"And make sure you clean your toys up tonight."

After fishing my keys out of my purse, I narrowed my eyes at Macy and pointed my key fob in her direction. "If this sucks, you're never going to hear the end of it."

She simply rolled her eyes and shook her head. "He's great. And fun. Trust me, if you can relax, you might actually enjoy yourself." She looked quite pleased with herself as she sat on the couch, scrolling through the screen on her smartphone. Her short jet-black hair was pulled back into a ponytail and her designer clothes were replaced with my preferred clothing—yoga pants and tank top.

I doubted it, but I didn't bother telling Macy that. She'd just roll her eyes and explain, again, how good it would be for me to get out into the dating world again and find something to do just for me. Apparently, ogling Jack and playing infinite games of UNO didn't count as a successful personal life to her.

"Then you date him," I said teasingly.

"Yes. Tate would love that." I laughed with her. Obviously, her fiancé wouldn't like it.

"So what do you know about him again?"

"He's been working in DC for the last few years and just moved back to Chicago. And Tate likes him." She smirked at me victoriously.

If anyone was more protective of Logan and me than she was, it was most definitely Tate. He was great with Logan, always taking him to baseball games in the summer, the parks, and even coached his little league soccer team last fall. Which was hilarious considering he didn't know a thing about soccer, but it had been a great six weeks watching him take the time to be so devoted to a boy he wasn't related to at all.

Tate was awesome, and had come to be like my brother in every way that mattered ever since he and Macy got serious last year.

So he had Tate and Macy's approval. Maybe he wouldn't be so bad after all.

"And what did you tell him about me?"

"That I had a sexy friend who needs to get laid because she's way overdue for a night of hot lusty sex." Her face was completely serious, but her dark brown eyes sparkled with mischief.

I looked down at my sleeveless grey silk top that didn't allow for a single inch of cleavage. "Perhaps I'm overdressed then?" I asked with mocking sarcasm. "If I'm playing the easy slut I should probably change."

"Shut up. You look great. I told him you're beautiful, intelligent, and you work too much and need to get out for a night of fun." She glanced down at her watch. "And you need to get going or you're going to be late."

I ran back to Logan, gave him one more kiss goodnight, accompanied with an 'I love you' and let Macy push me out the door.

"No ice cream after dinner this time, I don't need a kid on a sugar high when I get home tonight." I arched a brow at her accusingly.

She didn't rise to the bait. "Whatever. He'll be fine. Go have a drink and impress the pants off Dean." She wiggled her eyebrows suggestively. "Literally. I mean it."

She shut the door to my two-bedroom apartment on me and I sighed. It's just a dinner and a drink or two. How bad could it be?

Two

My nerves increased with every minute I spent in my Altima on the short drive to meet Dean at Frenzio's, a delicious and locally owned Italian restaurant in Lincoln Park.

It was a place I had wanted to try for years, but since my dates were few and far between, I hadn't gotten around to it yet. I wondered if Macy had put forth any suggestions for where he should take me. If she hadn't, I had to at least admit the guy had good taste in food. Frenzio's made the Chicago Newspaper Entertainment section almost monthly as one of the most delicious places to dine for genuine Italian cuisine, and reservations were difficult to come by.

I parked my car on the street and made the short block walk to the restaurant, the humid summer air instantly made my skin feel hot and sticky. Chicago was a great city to live, except for the summer humidity and the lake effect snow and arctic wind blasts we got in the winter. Basically, spring and fall were perfect.

I checked my watch; only five minutes late. I hated being late, but tonight I planned it. I'd rather have to find someone in a restaurant on a blind date versus being the person sitting there, waiting to see if I got stood up.

The delicious aroma of Italian food flooded my senses in the best way possible when I opened the door to the restaurant. I breathed in deeply, enjoying the smells in the air and listened to the soft clattering of utensils and opera music playing softly through the restaurant's speakers. As I looked around, I noticed white tablecloths spread over all the tables giving off a romantic feel, but the lighting was just bright enough to be casual and friendly. My mouth watered as I savored the aroma of basil and other heavenly spices. The company could potentially suck, but my belly would leave full. The thought brought a slight smile as I reached the hostess stand.

"Hello. I'm meeting someone … is Dean Neilson here?" As I spoke, my eyes surveyed the small restaurant, trying to see if I could spot him myself. I did almost instantly. A lone male sat at a table on the left of the restaurant, the perfect distance from the kitchen entrance and restaurant entrance so we wouldn't be disturbed by traffic from customers and workers, but central enough to not feel too intimate.

"Never mind," I said, turning back to the hostess. "I think I found him."

Dean smiled and rose from his seat when I reached the table. A pleasant smile appeared on his lips. I didn't bother hiding mine. The first thing I noticed about him was his pale blue eyes, or light gray. I couldn't tell in the light but whatever color, they were some of the lightest, almost crystal clear eyes I'd ever seen. His smile and shaggy blonde hair that curled just a bit at the ears made him even more attractive to me instantly. He looked playful, but yet still polished; the perfect blend of casualness and wealth. I groaned inwardly at the thought that I might actually have to admit to Macy that this date was a good idea.

I shook his hand when he extended it. "Dean Neilson. Nice to meet you, Emma."

"You, too." I nodded and sat down as he pulled out the chair across the table from him before returning to his own seat.

"So …" we both started at the same time and laughed at our own awkwardness after our waiter left with our drink orders.

I waved him on. "You first."

"I was just going to say that Macy didn't do you justice when she described how beautiful you are, but I stopped when I realized how much of a perv that would make me sound like." He smiled sheepishly and I couldn't stop another laugh. His laugh was infectious and Macy was right, he was hot with his clear eyes and button down navy blue dress shirt that fit perfectly across his chest and broad shoulders when he moved his arms.

"It's a little pervy … I'll let it slide."

We clinked our glasses together and fell into a nice conversation. Dean had two brothers and a sister and was the baby of all of them. All four siblings helped run his family-owned corporate construction company until their dad retired and they could take it over fully. Based on how he described his family, they seemed like a Rockwell painting: perfect, normal, and a tiny bit old-fashioned.

"If you're so close to your family, why'd you spend so much time in DC?" I asked right as our server brought back a delicious plate of scallop linguini. I moaned softly to myself when I tasted my first bite, the scallops practically melted in my mouth.

He shrugged unashamedly. "I always knew I was going to come back someday and help run the business; I just wanted to stretch my wings a bit, first. I wanted to prove to myself that I was a good engineer and wasn't just using my parent's name."

I appreciated his candor and honesty and felt immediately guilty for judging him so harshly before. He noticed.

"Let me guess," he asked, "you assumed you were meeting a spoiled little rich boy who lived off his parent's wealth?"

"Sorry," I mumbled a little bit but relaxed again as he just brushed me off.

"What about your family?"

"I'm an only child. My parents live on a ranch in Texas."

His eyebrows rose slightly. "What brought you up to Chicago?"

I leaned back and smiled at the memory of the day I met Macy on our first day at DePaul. I was a naïve southern girl and she was a local, rich debutante and sorority girl extraordinaire while I was wide eye-eyed and completely blown away by all the things in the city. Fortunately for me, she took me under her wing, showed me how to get around the city and I never wanted to leave.

"Small town … farmers …" I wrinkled my nose in disgust teasingly. "I had to get away and see something more important than the Texas flag plastered on every Chevy truck in town. I got a partial scholarship to DePaul. Came here, met Macy, fell in love, and never left."

"Fell in love?" He asked and based on the sparkle in his eye when he asked, I knew Dean and I were going to be great friends. Macy gave the same look when she wanted the good gossip.

"I meant the city; but there was a guy, too. He left after I got pregnant."

"You have a kid?" He asked, shocked.

"Macy didn't tell you?" That was odd. She always told guys she wanted to hook me up with I had Logan just so I didn't have to tell them and have an awkward moment like this one.

He shook his head. "No, but that's great. How old is he?"

"He'll be five in a couple of weeks. His name is Logan."

Our friendly banter continued through dinner as I shared stories of Logan and heard about his nieces and nephews from his oldest brother and sister. He was great to talk to, and definitely easy on the eyes, but the more I got to know him, the more I felt like the chemistry between us was of the friendship variety, and not the I-want-to-jump-your-bones variety. I let him pay the check after we were finished before he walked me to my car.

"Would it be a horrible way to end the date if I said it feels like you're my sister?" I laughed, loudly, at his question when we reached my car.

"No … I was feeling the same way."

He placed a hand over his chest like he was wounded. I slapped it away with no pretense or stress of an actual date. "I didn't mean that you're a girl. Just that I feel like you're my brother or something."

He leaned in and gave me a quick kiss on the cheek. "I had a great night with you. Can we hang out again sometime?"

I kissed him back and just as I expected, only felt a friendly affection when I pressed my lips to his cheek.

What I didn't expect was to immediately hear the voice that caused butterflies on a daily basis to come from behind me.

Jack McMillan's voice sent shivers down my spine instantly.

I looked up at Dean, whose face had lost all friendly appearance and turned to Jack. He looked stunning in his black dress pants, perfectly pressed white shirt even though it was nearing eight o'clock at night, a dark purple tie I had just bought him that week, and short brown hair I almost daily wished I could run my fingers through.

"Hey, Jack." I said breathlessly. I couldn't help myself. I looked back to Dean and introduced them watching them size each other up as only men can do when they're in the presence of competition. Except I wasn't anyone's prize so it left me feeling confused.

Dean leaned in my ear and spoke quietly. "Call me sometime. We can double with Macy and Tate."

I smiled up at him. "Absolutely. I'll see you later. It was really nice meeting you."

"You too." He gave me another quick kiss on the cheek goodnight before turning around and walking to his car down the street.

I watched him walk away for just a second and took a deep breath before turning back to Jack.

"How are you, Jack?"

His focused gazed was still on where Dean had walked away. It made my insides swirl when I realized Jack was tenser than I normally saw him. Surely he wasn't jealous, was he? I brushed the ridiculous thought from my mind instantly, but not before a slight blush crept on my cheeks.

Jack noticed when he turned his eyes towards me. "Good date?"

The deep timbre of his voice made my stomach do flip-flops. What was wrong with me? I had worked with this guy for five years and I'd always found him attractive and completely sexy, but lately whenever he talked to me I felt like a girl getting ready for her first date; all weak kneed and stuttering with nerves. It wasn't like me at all, but something happened to me whenever Jack focused his dark brown eyes on me, much like he was doing now. I swallowed slowly.

"We had a nice dinner."

"Doesn't look like it went that well if it's over so soon." He spoke with the same tightness in his voice he had the night before. I felt just as unsettled as I did then, too. His masculine hands clenched into fists at his sides before opening and stretching. I wondered for just a second what those hands would feel like on me and brushed it away before I completely embarrassed myself. That was just stupid. Jack had never looked at me with any sort of interest beyond a professional capacity. He wasn't jealous or anything else towards me except maybe, protective like Tate.

Thinking of my date reminded me that he had one that night too. With Jessica. The very thought of the overly botoxed and breast implanted Barbie doll made me grimace.

"He was nice. How's Jessica, weren't you supposed to go to the Opera with her tonight or something?"

That time it was Jack who flinched visibly. "I ended it with her."

I smiled inwardly. Jessica had obviously reached her three date limit one date too soon. I simply nodded in understanding. I'd worked with him long enough to know that he didn't get close to anyone; except for maybe Logan. Jack was kind to him and I was thankful that besides Tate, there was another man in Logan's life willing to teach him about all the important boy things, like how to play video games. It was something Jack had been much more willing to do in the last year when he got home early and I wasn't done cooking dinner for him.

I smiled as I thought about how comfortable the two had looked together the prior week when I walked in on Jack teaching Logan how to play Madden NFL on his Playstation. One muscular arm draped around Logan's tiny shoulder as he described which buttons did what. I knew he meant nothing by it, just being friendly to him, but to me - and Logan especially - it meant everything.

I played with my hair nervously for a second before smiling and wrinkling my nose. "She was pretty bad, Jack."

A slight smile appeared on his lips, forming just enough to cause a dimple on his left cheek to appear. I loved that dimple.

"I know. I don't know what I was thinking."

I did. She came from a perfectly well-groomed family, was stunningly gorgeous and had a brain the size of a pea; the exact replica of all the other women I had seen him date over the last few years. I wanted to ask him why he always chose the women who were just after his name and his money but I bit my tongue. My job wasn't to advise him on his personal life, just schedule it.

He nodded towards an Irish Pub a few doors down. "I was going to head in for a drink. Want to join me?"

I hesitated for a moment as I tried to figure out what was going on. Ten minutes ago I was on a date with Dean, laughing about Logan flushing his Lego people down the toilet and now I was standing on the sidewalk, with Jack.

I glanced down at my watch. It was just after eight. Logan would still be awake and I knew Macy wasn't expecting me home, or at least hoping I wouldn't come home, for hours yet. I had no reason to decline other than the thought of spending time alone with him right now sent my nerves into overdrive.

I nodded and tried my hardest not to jump when his hand lightly touched the small of my back as he led me through the doors into the small and musty bar.

I scrunched my nose at him once we were sitting on stools at the small bar. "This doesn't seem like a place you would normally hang out at."

I eyed the traditional Irish decorations and beer logos all over the wall. There were bowls of shelled peanuts along the bar and booths, the floor littered with shell crumbs. It looked much dingier than the places I normally planned for his dates and nights out with clients.

He turned to the bar and raised two fingers to get the bartender's attention. "What do you want to drink?" he asked when the bartender walked towards us, white towel haphazardly slung over his shoulder.

"Vodka tonic, please." He eyed me suspiciously at my choice before he turned and ordered a simple bottled Budweiser. My stomach felt like a thousand butterflies had taken residence and I needed something stronger than the glass of red wine I had earlier with Dean.

"You're also not a Budweiser guy either." I didn't bother hiding my smile. I did all the shopping for Jack, and in five years, I had bought every type of alcoholic beverage you could imagine. Never was there anything on his list as simple as a Bud heavy.

The corners of his lips twitched slightly. "I can be a normal, hangout and drink a beer kind of guy."

"Sure you can," I deadpanned. I looked around the bar again and for the second time wondered why Jack would be in a place like this. It wasn't bad. Macy and I came here often with Tate, but it was just a long way from the Streeterville hi-rise where Jack lived. It was even farther from where the Opera was, and nowhere near Jessica's house.

"Why are you here, Jack?" I asked him after a couple sips of my drink.

He didn't answer. Instead, he took a long swig of his beer without removing his eyes from mine. He set it down, and wiped his lips with his thumb.

"I wanted to make sure you were safe." He sounded like he hated himself for his admission.

It irritated me, again. I leaned a bit away from him and crossed my arms. "So, you followed me?"

I watched as his eyes erased any emotion they previously held and went back to his typical professional indifference. He was starting to give me whiplash with his looks that looked like he cared, only to have them erased immediately.

He shrugged unashamedly. "You're important to me."

I had a sense there was something more to his statement, but I was too nervous to ask. If Jack cared about me for something other than my job, it would cause disaster. Because as much I was attracted to him, I knew his style, and I knew it wouldn't last. And if something happened, and then ended, it could be uncomfortable working at his place all day. The best thing for me to do, regardless of how much I wanted to be important to him in an unprofessional way, was to shake it off.

"I'm sure you could find another housekeeper." I rolled my eyes in a teasing way, hoping to break the ice. It worked.

Eventually, we fell into an easy banter, much like we normally shared during the week as we talked about a few new properties he was investigating. The man in front of me was a finance genius.

All things I could appreciate since I majored in finance and headed into corporate law before I dropped out of law school.

"So, your date tonight." He frowned and waved for the bartender to send him another drink.

I smiled as I thought about how nice Dean was. He was wholesome, the perfect boy next door. He was the guy every mom wanted their daughter to bring home. Unfortunately, he caused nothing to stir inside of me, unlike the man currently sitting in front of me.

"We will be good friends," I answered with a slight grin. I didn't miss the sudden tenseness that rippled across Jack's chest and shoulders as he shot to a straighter sitting position.

"Friends?" He asked after he took a sip of his beer.

I nodded. "I felt like his sister."

Something deep inside me enjoyed watching him relax. He was jealous. I never would have guessed before that very moment that the reason for all of his tension had nothing to do with Jessica, but something, whatever it was, to do with me.

"That tie looks nice on you." Instantly I wish I could take the words back, my fingers however were short in getting the message. They slowly reached out and played with the ends of the dark purple tie I bought for him just a week ago. Jack looked down at my hands, fiddling with the sharp point at the end of the tie and back at me.

"My assistant has good taste."

I rubbed my tongue across my teeth. This wasn't happening. I had known Jack too long to risk my job over throwing myself at my boss. The realization shocked me back to reality and I let the tie fall from my fingers. I needed to get a grip on myself, and quickly. I waved at the bar tender for a refill and drained my first drink, pretending nothing had just happened.

It didn't last long though because almost instantly Jack's hand was on my thigh, resting softly just above my knee.

He looked down at his hand and then back at me. "This is probably inappropriate isn't it?"

Fuck no … or yes. Good grief, what was wrong me? I took a sip of my re-filled drink, wincing slightly at how strong it was before turning to him.

"I'm not sure anymore to be honest."

Clearly I had drank too much to think straight. I wanted to smack my head into the bar and at the same time, grab his tie and take him … where? My place? Not with Logan there.

"If it helps, I'm glad the guy thought of you like a sister."

I swallowed, slowly, wondering if he was implying what his deep, lustful voice sounded like. His eyes darkened and he leaned closer to me, incrementally slow, as if giving me the time to back away. I didn't. Maybe I should have but I was in such shock over what was happening a bomb could have gone off and I still wouldn't have moved.

"We've been drinking."

He nodded. I could feel his breath on my cheek. "This is probably a really bad idea."

"You're my boss, Jack." Instantly, I wanted to take the words back because as soon as they came out of my mouth, his hand left my leg like my skin burned him. I shivered as I watched him bite the inside of his cheek.

He took another pull of his beer and set it back down on the bar. The haze left his eyes and he immediately went back to the calm, cool and collected Jack McMillan that I had seen almost every morning and night for the last five years.

I wanted hazy eyed, touchy-feely Jack back but I knew it was too late.

"I should probably make sure you get home safely."

I looked down at my watch. How could it be almost midnight? I imagined Macy doing a happy dance at the thought of me being out so late with Dean. If only she knew what was really going on.

"Yeah …" It probably was a good idea, but I didn't want to leave. Finally, after five years of crushing on Jack, he was here in front of me, and for all that I could see, he wanted me. I didn't want it to end.

His fingers touched mine as he took my half-emptied glass and set it on the bar. "Come on. I'll take you home."

He was still too close to me for me to think clearly because at the sound of the word home, an involuntary grin spread across my cheeks. I bit it back quickly, knowing he didn't mean anything by it, but the tension that was there earlier still lingered.

I simply nodded and stood up, wavering for just a second before I finally found my equilibrium. I held onto the hand that Jack offered and warmth flooded me instantly.

I looked up at him and smiled.

His Adam's apple dipped as he swallowed and breathed deeply. His white dress shirt flexed across his chest so I could see his muscles practically ripple. It caused my stomach to waver, and not in an unpleasant way at all.

I didn't like the frown line that appeared between his eyes. "You've had too much to drink."

Probably. Between the wine at dinner and now the vodka tonics I figured I would be sporting quite the hangover in the morning, but I was too proud to admit it to him. Not when he was looking at me so worried.

"I'll be just fine."

Jack simply grunted and pulled me towards the door. He opened the door to the silver Mercedes SLK that I had picked out just a few months ago and strapped my seatbelt for me.

"I can do that myself you know."

"I know." His worry line burrowed even deeper. "I just want to make sure you're safe."

He shut the door and a few seconds later was sitting next to me.

"My car is just around the corner."

He looked at me like I had lost my mind. Oddly, I felt the exact same way. Here I was, on a date with one guy, letting another take me home and I didn't feel the slightest bit guilty over it. What in the world was happening tonight?

"You've been drinking." It was a statement filled with such conviction it left no room for arguing. "I'll have someone get your car home for you tomorrow, but I want to make sure you get home safely."

"There are cabs for that you know." I wanted to lighten the mood. To ease his worry and the sudden seriousness that had struck as soon as he touched my leg.

Actually I wanted him to put his hand back on my leg, but wasn't brave enough, or drunk enough, to ask.

Instead of lightening the mood I just received a scowl. Was he mad I drank so much? He shouldn't be. I was with him the entire night except for the first drink I had with Dean. I wanted to point that out to him but his body was so stiff sitting next to me and his knuckles clenched so tightly around the steering wheel I wasn't sure it was a good idea to bring up Dean.

I gave him directions to my place and ten minutes later, he was dropping me off in front of my apartment building.

I didn't want to get out. I knew on Monday, we would both appear like nothing had happened, but something had. In the span of just a few minutes and just a few touches, I knew that Jack had ruined me for anyone else. I wanted him, job be damned.

I watched him get out of the car and come around to my door. When he opened it, he simply took my hand, not saying a word and interlocked our fingers on the way to my door. I opened the front door and he followed me upstairs. He didn't look at me, or acknowledge my presence in anyway, just simply walked like a man on a mission.

I wanted to be that mission.

When we reached my door, he let my hand drop back to my side. I gazed up at him longingly. I had had just enough of a taste of Jack McMillan for the night to want more.

And I knew he felt it. His pupils were larger than they should be and his breathing just a touch faster for a man who ran five miles every day.

I cleared my throat. "Thank you for making sure I got home safely."

His hand reached up and gently pushed a small piece of hair away behind my ear. "It was my pleasure, Emma."

His eyes moved to mine and I realized that I had my keys out, but hadn't moved at all to unlock my door. I was frozen. Completely enamored by the man in front of me. I didn't know what to say and he seemed in no big hurry to let me go through those doors, ending whatever it was that was happening between us.

Without any warning at all, his hand moved from my hair and wrapped around my neck pulling me close to him. My eyes widened just slightly before Jack's lips pressed down on mine. They were warm, soft and delicious. He kissed my top lip, and then teased my bottom, urgently seeking entrance. I opened my mouth and let his kiss deepen. My entire body melted into him and I grabbed the tie around his neck that I had fondled earlier and held on for dear life, pulling him closer.

My back hit the wall in my hallway, causing me to gasp into his mouth slightly. He didn't relent. Instead, he pressed up against me, his thigh pushing in between my legs that seemed to spread on their own accord. If I was able to think clearly, I mostly likely would have realized I was rubbing myself up against him like a dog in heat, but in the moment, I couldn't. My insides were throbbing as I wantonly moaned and tried to ease the ache between my thighs that being so close to him created.

With one hand on my neck, he pressed me up against the wall, and his other hand lifted my thigh so it wrapped around his waist. My blood felt like it was on fire, burning through me as I felt Jack's erection press against my core.

His lips moved from my mouth to my neck, as he rocked his hips into me again. I tipped my head up and moaned, giving him easier access to the soft skin on my neck. It felt so good, his large hands holding me firmly against him, his warm breath all over me.

"You taste so good," he whispered as he softly flicked his tongue across my skin. "And you're so beautiful, Emma."

My hands flew to his hair, holding him against me. This was really happening. All my fantasies about wanting Jack were coming true. I was too lost until in the feel of his hands and body pressed up against mine that I didn't even register the words he was saying.

I barely registered the loud slam of a door closing shut from somewhere down the hall, but it registered with Jack. He immediately froze against my body and then moved away just a fraction, his breath heavy against my lips. I shivered involuntarily, still caught up in the passionate moment we had just shared.

Jack didn't look me in the eyes, but focused his gaze on the floor underneath our feet, his jaw tightened in what was clearly frustration even as he struggled to slow his breathing. Something really good or something really bad had just happened. It took me all of three seconds to realize it was the latter.

My heart felt like it was on a runaway train, beating so fast it was almost completely out of control. I placed a hand over my heart as if that would settle the madness inside of me.

Jack took another step back as one of my neighbors walked past us in the hall, giving us both a smirk that told us he knew exactly what we were doing in the middle of the night, with me still pressed up against a wall.

It seemed to only frustrate Jack further. When he turned his piercing brown eyes on me, I wanted to wrench over in pain because I knew exactly what he was going to say. One of his hands fisted the back of his neck tightly before he shoved both of his hands forcefully into his pockets.

He took two more small steps away from me. The space between us suddenly felt as wide as the Grand Canyon even though he was only two feet away. I couldn't bring my eyes to him so instead I kept them fixed on the tie I had just grabbed so forcefully. It was wrinkled in the middle where my fist had held on to it, only minutes before.

"That shouldn't have happened." Regret filled his rough voice and it only increased the distance I felt growing between us by the second. "I don't know what got into me."

I nodded, but stayed silent, afraid my voice would show how much it hurt to hear. I knew Jack enough to know that once he made up his mind, he never went back on his decision. If he thought kissing me was a mistake, nothing I could say would change his mind.

I bent down to pick up the keys that dropped on the floor during our kiss and slowly raised my eyes to his when I stood back up.

"Thanks for the ride home," I said solemnly. Turning my back to him, I put the key in the door. Just as I heard the familiar click of the door unlocking, Jack's large hand covered mine.

"Tell me you're okay with this. I don't want this to make your job uncomfortable Emma." I blinked my eyes tightly together; feeling like a cold drink of water was just splashed all over me. Of course he'd be concerned about work right now. I suddenly felt incredibly stupid for even thinking he was interested in me.

I looked back to him, only to be shocked to see a look of sadness fill his features. "It's fine, Jack. I'll see you Monday."

He nodded once. "Just like normal?"

I blinked, his words shocking me even though I shouldn't have been surprised. Slowly, as I processed what he said, I pursed my lips together. I wanted to either yell at him or smack him, but knew nothing would change what had just happened in the hall. "Like normal," I replied and then opened the door without another word.

I made it inside the apartment and shut my door before sinking to the floor, resting my head against the wall. There wasn't going to be anything normal at all about showing up to work on Monday and I knew it. I had just had a taste of Jack, something I had wanted for years. And it would be my last.

Three

I moaned in pain when the shrill beeping of my alarm clock woke me up first thing on Sunday morning. My head felt like it was going to explode and even though I had brushed my teeth severely before crashing into bed the night before, my mouth felt like I had slept with a handful of cotton balls in it. I needed water desperately. And ibuprofen. And coffee. Definitely coffee.

Slowly getting up, I dressed in the pair of yoga pants I wished I could have stayed home and worn the night before and made my way to the kitchen for some much needed hangover relief. The delicious smell of coffee permeated the air and I smiled, knowing Macy was already awake.

I had cringed the night before when I saw her huddled up on my couch sleeping peacefully underneath a quilt my mom had made me for my high school graduation. It was old and tattered after years of use, and Macy's small body barely fit under it, but she was sleeping so deeply I didn't want to wake her up to send her home. I also didn't wake her up because I wasn't nearly ready to explain why I was getting home so late from my date with Dean.

I smiled just thinking about him, doing whatever I could to avoid thinking of the clusterfuck that had occurred between Jack and me. I also knew, as I hit the kitchen and saw Macy look at me expectantly, that my time of avoidance was now up. I couldn't hide it from her either. Years of trying to hide things from Macy had taught me that she always knew when I was lying. I completely sucked at it.

"So …" She started with a wiggling of her eyebrows. "I take it you charmed the pants off Dean, after all. How was he?"

I snorted and teasingly pushed her out of my way on my way to the coffee pot. She should know better than to try to get any form of conversation out of me before my first hit of caffeine.

She grew more aggravated by the moment as I slowly, poured my coffee, walked to my chair, pulled it out, and sat down, making the entire process take five times longer than normal. It was only then that I took the first, long, lingering sip of coffee. Macy was a half second away from exploding in frustration as I tortured her with my slowness. I bit back a smile when she slammed her hand on my kitchen table.

She narrowed her chocolate brown eyes at me. "You have two seconds to start talking before I call Dean and get the story from him."

I chuckled. Dean would have no idea why I was out so late.

"Dean and I decided after dinner that we felt more like brother and sister than anything more."

Her face fell in shock. "Seriously? He was perfect for you."

I shrugged and took another sip of the coffee letting it warm me and wake me up at the same time. "There was no chemistry and we both knew it."

"That was a really long dinner for you guys to not have any chemistry."

I exhaled slowly, wanting to prolong the moment where I told her the truth but desperately wanting to run from it. I set my coffee cup down and pinched the bridge of my nose with my thumb and finger. I wanted to erase the part that happened after dinner with Dean and just completely forget I had run into Jack at all. I didn't want the reminder of how horrible the night had ended, and how I felt like a fool when I had closed the door to my apartment. I looked over at the door, wanting to erase everything but knowing I couldn't, before looking back at the irritated little squirt sitting across from me.

Her fingers impatiently tapped the top of my table.

"We ran into Jack as we were leaving dinner and he invited me for a drink."

She was a stuttering, fumbling mess when she finally found her voice. "You … Jack … drinks?"

I laughed softly and did the best I could to dismiss the thoughts I knew were running rampant in her mind. She knew what kind of torch I carried for him. I tried to hide my embarrassment from her, knowing if she looked too closely she could probably still see how swollen my lips were from the scorching kiss he gave me when he plastered me up against the hallway wall.

"It was just a few drinks, no big deal."

She didn't believe me. I didn't realize I was actually touching my lips until she gasped and stared at me like she'd just solved the global warming crisis. Pure exaltation filled her face as she started wagging her fingers at me. "You kissed him!"

I cringed and looked at Logan's door, hoping her loudness wouldn't wake him up. I knew he was too young, but the last thing I ever wanted him hearing about was his mom's sexual escapades … not that there'd been any recently to share.

"He was up late—there's no way he'll hear us," she said, reading my mind and still bouncing up and down in her chair.

"Tell me. You have to tell me what happened."

I scrunched my nose trying to figure out how much to share. She worked for Jack too and I didn't know what was appropriate since we both worked for him. He also knew she was my best friend and we told her each other everything. Surely he wouldn't be too upset to know that I spilled what happened to her. It was a risk I was willing to take.

"I drank too much at the Irish pub next to Frenzio's and he drove me home. He kissed me when we got to my door."

"And … how was it?"

I looked back at the door, remembering how it felt when his large chest pushed mine against the wall, how hot it made me feel when he moaned into my mouth and held onto to the back of my neck with his strong hand. It was amazing.

"It was the best and absolute worst kiss of my entire life." I groaned in frustration and then dropped my forehead into my hands on the table. "It was incredible. Hot, passionate … I don't think I've ever had a more powerful, mind-blowing kiss in my life." I groaned again and shook my head, frustrated that I had allowed myself to get a small taste of Jack McMillan. After seeing the regret and remorse that filled his eyes when we finally pulled away, I knew he was never going to touch me again.

"Why was it the worst?" she asked softly. Surprised she wasn't digging me for more dirt on the good part, I slowly took my head out of my hands.

"You should have seen the way he looked when the kiss stopped." I opened my mouth and shut it again, not wanting to relive the worst part. "He told me to forget it ever happened and that he shouldn't have done it in the first place. I've never seen him look so sick to his stomach."

I got up from my chair and went to refill my coffee cup, replaying the scene in my head the entire time.

"Well that sucks. I've seen the way he looks at you when he thinks no one is looking. Personally I'm surprised it took him this long to make his move on you."

I shook off her ridiculous statement. Before last night, Jack had never given any indication that he was at all interested in me. But if not, then what the hell happened last night? He couldn't have been upset about Jessica. He never let a woman get to know him enough to care what they thought. Macy and I were potentially the only exception to that rule, and even then, he was always friendly but purely professional. Everything personal I learned about him was through Google and Macy's connections through the country club. Besides the small glimpses he allowed people to see, he kept his private life and past locked up tighter than Fort Knox.

"I think you're seeing things again."

"And I think he likes you. And he adores Logan. I don't know what caused him to finally make a move on you last night, but trust me; he'll realize it was a mistake to push you away."

I turned to her and smiled softly. "And what am I supposed to do then? How am I supposed to see him at his condo tomorrow, when I can still feel his lips on mine today?"

She shrugged simply. "Ignore him. Pretend it never happened just like he said. It'll drive him crazy."

"Maybe I should just forget it. I don't want to be just another three-date girl, and I have Logan to think about. He's crazy about Jack, and I'd hate to risk the relationship they have."

Macy bent down and picked up her purse before slipping her ballet flats on her feet. When she reached the door, she turned to me with a mischievous smile. "Maybe it could end up being a great, happily ever after relationship and the reward would be well worth the risk. Ever think of that?"

Ever since his lips left mine that was the only thing I could think about.

I wasn't about to tell her that.

My silence apparently spoke for itself because she simply wiggled her fingers at me and started walking out the door. "I'm going to go home and wake Tate up so he can cook me some breakfast. Have fun at work tomorrow."

She closed the door before I could tell her to shut up. Smart girl, I thought, and then frowned into my coffee cup. Ignore Jack and simply pretend last night never happened. I had been pretending for what seemed like forever that I wasn't interested in him at all. How hard could it be just to keep on pretending?

I set my coffee cup down on the counter harder than necessary and jumped at my own annoyance for letting him affect me so much. It was just one kiss with a guy. It's not like I hadn't had my share of kisses and hook-ups over the years.

Go to work and pretend it never happened. I could totally do that.

Two hours later once my laundry was finishing up, Logan had eaten breakfast and we had both showered for the day, I was bored out of my mind playing my fifth game of UNO.

"How about we play something else?" I asked him, trying to hide my boredom. It wasn't that I didn't like the game. And I did absolutely love that my son could spend hours playing cards, board games and with his toys instead of solely focusing on our video game system, but I just wasn't in the mood today. I needed something to take my mind off going to work the next day.

I laughed when Logan whined for just one more game.

"Puh-lease, mommy?" I couldn't resist his chubby cheeks and smile.

"Okay. One more, but then I want to go do something. The zoo maybe?"

Logan's face lit up like the Fourth of July fireworks. I took that as a yes, and dealt out seven cards to each of us for hopefully, my last game of cards for the day.

After he beat me in the last game, I sent him to his room to get his shoes on so we could head out to zoo. I was moving all the items from my clutch bag I used on the previous night's date to my bigger purse when I realized that my car was still parked several miles away outside Frenzio's.

As if on cue, someone knocked on my door. I opened it and smiled at Shane, Jack's driver.

"Hey Shane," I said politely.

He held out my key ring that I had given to Jack last night and smiled. "Mr. McMillan asked me to return your car today."

My smile fell at the mere mention of Jack's name. If Shane noticed, he didn't mention it.

"How are you feeling today?"

I frowned slightly at his question. Shane and I have known each other for years, and I was pretty sure this was the most we had ever spoken. Normally it was just the pleasant hello and good evening when we passed in the entryway to Jack's condo. I stiffened when I realized Jack must have said something.

"Fine …" I said slowly, suspiciously.

He smiled and handed me a brown bag in his other hand. I gave him a look, but then took the bag and opened it. Two gourmet cupcakes sat at the bottom of the bag. I knew with only a quick glance they were my favorite caramel apple flavored ones that came from the bakery near Jack's building.

"Mr. McMillan asked me to deliver these to you. Said he hoped they make you feel better." He arched an eyebrow in question as to what that could mean, but I didn't tell him.

My stomach soured at the reason behind the cupcakes. Was he still feeling guilty for the kiss and trying to placate me with cupcakes? Or was he concerned about the hangover he probably knew I would have?

Either way, the cupcakes were sure to be delicious, but now I wasn't sure if I wanted them. I thought about telling Shane to take them back, but that would raise questions and it certainly wasn't in line with our agreement of forgetting everything, so I thanked him and told him I would see him tomorrow.

"Hey Logan!" I called to my son who was still in his room, probably trying to teach himself how to tie his own shoes. "Mr. Jack brought you cupcakes!"

The easiest solution was to let Logan have both. He loved it when Jack spoiled him silly with delicious cupcakes and brownies from the gourmet bakery and he wouldn't look at them wondering what receiving them meant, much like I was still doing.

Logan ran out of his room, shoes untied and on the wrong feet. It didn't seem to slow him down any as he ran right up to me and took the bag from my hands before digging into it at the table.

"These are your favorite, mom." He voice came out muffled, his mouth full of yummy goodness.

"I know. But you can have them both today."

"You're sharing with me?" He asked in between bites, a large smile on his small little face.

"Yup. But just this once." I pointed a finger at him and winked. "Don't expect it to happen again, okay?"

Within five minutes, he had inhaled both cupcakes, I had fixed and tied his shoes, and we were in my car on the way to the zoo. Maybe watching Logan enamored with the monkeys would take my mind off my weekend.

Four

I was a complete moron to think it would be easy to ignore Jack and the kiss that never should have happened. After I dropped off Logan at preschool on Monday, I hurried over to Jack's condo to start cleaning and do the grocery shopping for the week.

When I arrived, he stayed in the doorway of the kitchen the entire time while he dictated to me everything he needed done for the week. He showed absolutely no sign of the friendliness we had always exchanged. Instead, he sounded frustrated the entire time, with his shortly clipped demands and one word answers to my questions.

I'm not even sure he looked at me … just sort of, through me. Or at a blank spot on the wall just to the left of me.

Monday night and the rest of the week weren't any different. I bit my lip to keep from snapping at him and answered every request with the same simple "Sure, Jack" or "Yes, Jack" that I always did.

Every conversation left me tenser than the one before, wondering when one of us would crack and just bring up the stupid kiss so we could move on, or worse, wondering if he would decide he could no longer work with me.

Thursday rolled around and I was cleaning his master bathroom, which was always surprisingly clean considering a male bachelor lived there. Jack was meticulous with everything he did in his life. Surely his grooming habits would be no different. I shouldn't have been surprised, but I always was.

I finished scrubbing the toilet and removed my yellow plastic gloves, when my phone pinged alerting me to a text message. It was Macy.

FYI; Jack left work in a rotten mood. Said he was going home. Thought you'd want the heads up.

I typed back a thanks for the warning message, snapped my phone shut and put it back in my pocket before picking up the cleaning supplies, wondering what he could possibly be in such a rotten mood about now.

It wasn't long before the front door slammed open. I jumped in the kitchen when I heard it crash into the wall behind it and then jumped again when it slammed shut. Choosing to do what I had done every night for the last four nights, I kept my back to the doorway, my focus solely on making the dinner salad in front of me. I knew when Jack stepped into the doorway without even looking. It had been like that for me for years, like there was a shift in the air current whenever he was around.

I ignored him and kept my focus on the salad, not wanting to turn around and see the frustrated face that had become so familiar that week.

His deep voice jolted me. "When are you going to yell at me?"

I turned around slowly, crossing my arms protectively in front of me and leaned back against the counter.

"I don't know what you're talking about," I replied, hoping my voice sounded much smoother and calmer to his ears than it did mine. My heart jumped at the mere sight of him and lodged a lump in my throat so large it made swallowing difficult.

He shifted uncomfortably in the doorway but didn't make a move to enter the large room. This was getting ridiculous.

"I have nothing to yell at you for, Jack."

"I took advantage of you. You should hate me."

I scoffed. I didn't remember it happening that way at all. "You didn't take advantage of me. I wanted …" I felt heat creep to my cheeks and I shut my mouth. The last thing I wanted was to let him know how much I actually wanted him. I closed my eyes and shook my head a few times to clear my thoughts. "You told me to forget it ever happened. I've been acting normally, just like we agreed."

He growled and took two steps forward into the kitchen for the first time in four days. I didn't bother trying to stop my eyes from wandering from his short messy hair, to his square jaw that was set like he was getting ready to demolish a competitor, down to his light blue button up shirt that had the top button un-done. He was missing his tie. I don't know why I noticed, but I did. He always wore a tie. But two things shocked me most of all, while my eyes travelled slowly down his body, appreciating every single inch of it. The first, was that he didn't make a move to stop me even though I was being completely obvious; and two, based on the tightness I saw along the zipper on his dark grey dress pants, he was clearly aroused.

I tried to swallow past the lump in my throat, but I couldn't. I tore my gaze away and took a sip of my glass of water that was sitting next to me on the granite counter.

"Did you forget?" he asked with a voice that sounded much rougher than it did earlier.

I rubbed my tongue across the front of my teeth. "Did you? You're the one that told me we should."

A frown line appeared in between his eyes as he narrowed his gaze at me. I had no idea why this was making him so angry. I could understand the regret if he thought he was taking advantage of an employee, but anger?

He moved his hands to his hips, never once taking his eyes off mine. He still looked angry when he said, "No. I didn't."

In all my fantasies I had had that week, and all the dreams I envisioned of this moment, I always pictured Jack looking lustfully at me, admitting he made a mistake before carrying me off to his bedroom and making love to me for hours. My stomach dropped to the floor as I saw a fire in his eyes like he hated me for not being able to forget one simple kiss. I instantly had the sinking feeling that nothing about my relationship with Jack would be the same again, and not in the good way it played out in my fantasies.

"Do you want my two weeks' notice then?" I choked the words out softly, barely audible and turned back to his salad, not able to bare another minute of seeing the anger in his stare.

I gasped when his hand grabbed my elbow, spinning me around and pinning me against the cold countertop. His arms blocked me in on the sides and the fire in his eyes burned brighter than before.

"I don't want you to quit, Emma." I cringed as he spit the words out vehemently. I felt his hot breath on my cheek from him standing so close. I wanted to tear my eyes away from him, but I couldn't. My heart was pounding in my chest with so much force I was sure it was loud enough for him to hear.

I was almost afraid at his forcefulness, but that feeling was tempered by the desire I had for him as soon as he had walked into the kitchen and allowed me to gaze on his arousal.

"Then tell me what you want because I don't want to keep seeing the regret in your eyes every time you look at me."

"I want …" He started and stopped. He closed his eyes and took a deep breath. When he opened his eyes again, they were softer than before; his voice gentler, much like they had been last Saturday. "I want to know what it is about you that suddenly makes me feel completely out of control. I want to know why, when I saw you lean in to kiss Dean on the cheek last week I wanted to pummel him for having his hands on you."

"I told you about Dean." I interrupted him, but he just scowled at me and continued.

"I don't get emotional, Emma, you know that. But ever since I touched your lips last week I feel like I'm a volcano ready to explode and I don't know how to handle all this shit I'm dealing with."

I made a face. He didn't make that sound like a good thing; at all. I didn't bother hiding my disappointment.

"Oh."

"That came out wrong." Slowly, one of his hands gently cupped the back of my neck. His hips leaned in just a little bit, just enough for me to know he was still aroused. Goosebumps flooded my body at the mere touch he gave me, making me crave more.

His thumb gently rubbed my bottom lip and he sighed. "I'm not good enough for you."

"You're intelligent, successful, and handsome. What else could I want?"

"I'm too old for you."

"Seven years isn't too big of a difference."

"I'm dark and scary and incapable of caring about people."

I scoffed. "You take care of Logan and me all the time. Quit cataloging your faults and tell me what you want Jack." My hand slowly moved up the planes of his stomach, gently feeling his abdomen tighten as I travelled farther up across his pectoral muscles and around to his neck, much like how he held mine. They moved on their own volition and the only thing I could think about was how I desperately didn't want him to push me away again. Not now. Not anymore.

He leaned down and rested his forehead on mine, then inhaled softly, and rubbed his nose into my hair. "You smell like peaches and cream and I haven't been able to get this smell, or the taste of your lips, or the feel of your hips out of my head. I feel like I'm losing complete control but I can't stop thinking about you, or wanting you."

"You make that sound like a bad thing."

"It has the potential to ruin me." With his head on mine, I couldn't look up and see the torment in his eyes that I heard in his wavering voice. I don't know what he meant by that, but I knew he wasn't talking professionally. Maybe he felt the same way I did about him.

Taking a risk and being with Jack McMillan would most definitely ruin me for all other men, and open the door to have my heart shattered into a million pieces all over again.

I should have been afraid. A part of me was. This was all coming from a man who had a three date limit. I didn't know if our drinks counted as one, or if this did, but regardless, I knew our time together was limited.

I moved my hands and slowly undid the first button on his shirt, and then the second. Taking that as a sign of my acceptance, which it most surely was, Jack's hands gripped my waist, picked me up and set me roughly down on top of the countertop. I immediately spread my legs, allowing him to move right up against me, his erection evident when he pressed into me. His mouth attacked mine like a dying man in search of water and I had no other choice but to take everything he had to give me.

He groaned deep in his throat and fanned the flame already building in my belly for him. I shifted closer to him, needing to rub myself against him and find relief from the pressure that was building faster than I had ever experienced before.

He tore my shirt and bra off of me before I could blink and then stepped back, just fractionally, and gazed down on my full breasts with almost completely blackened eyes. He was hungry for them and I leaned back on the counter, giving him a better look. His mouth moved to one, licking it teasingly. I moaned and shifted my hips again into his erection.

I wanted to remove his pants and feel him deep inside and let him devour me until I was fully sated. I lost all patience when his mouth covered a nipple, hardening it into a tight little bud. His other hand worked feverishly on my other nipple.

"Jack … I need …" I was seconds away from completely falling apart and he was still fully clothed. I didn't even know what I needed exactly. More pressure, more of him, faster, harder … I couldn't finish the thought.

He removed his mouth from my nipple and began torturing my stomach with light feathery kisses.

"I know what you need," he whispered into my stomach. The light vibrations sent shockwaves throughout my entire body. I tried to buck my hips toward him, showing him what I needed most of all but his large, and surprisingly soft hand clamped down on my hip holding me firmly in place. The more I wiggled, the firmer the pressure became.

"I'll take care of it, Emma. Stay still." He was mad if he thought I could stay still through this torture of his tongue teasing my lower stomach. He swirled his tongue deep inside my belly button and I arched my back into him, groaning his name loudly. I threw my hands into his hair pulling him closer, or pushing him down, I wasn't sure. I just needed him to move.

"You taste so good, Emma. I can't wait to bury my cock into you. Tell me you want me."

I moaned again, louder than before as his hands went to the waist of my pants. He began pulling them down but stopped, and looked me directly in the eyes. "I need to hear you say it."

His hungry voice was commanding. I had never heard him sound so absolute in what he needed before. This was much different from the professional tone he used with me during work hours or the friendly banter we exchanged with Logan. It left no room for me to back out or argue with him. Not that I wanted to. I wanted him desperately.

I nodded. "I want you." I wiggled my hips, hoping he would get the sign and remove the rest of my clothing.

He smiled a wicked grin, one side of his mouth quirked up slightly higher than the left. His eyes felt like they were piercing into my soul as he removed my pants. He sucked in a quick breath when he reached my black lace thong and lightly trailed his fingers across the edges, sending flames sparking through my entire core. He chucked lightly and kissed along the top edge of my underwear, soothing the bumps that prickled every inch of my skin, before removing them completely.

I sat up and removed his shirt, pushing it off his shoulders while he kept his hands firmly planted on my thighs, only moving them to shuck off the cuffs of his sleeves. When I reached for his pants to finish helping remove his clothing, he stopped me with a penetrating gaze. "Not yet. Lean back on your arms and open your legs wider."

I felt my wetness increase just by the words he spoke and the way he stared at me, almost daring me to disobey. I couldn't. I had never been bossed around so much before with a man, and certainly never thought I would like it, but every time Jack spoke and told me what to do, my body operated immediately; as if on instinct. It made me feel slutty and sexy all at the same time.

I gasped as he pulled me to the edge of the counter, nudging my legs further apart and gazing longingly down at my folds that were dripping wet.

"You're so fucking wet," he murmured before leaning down and with one long, thick stroke of his tongue, had me screaming his name.

"Oh god … Jack!" That one swipe almost had me falling over the edge of complete ecstasy and had it ended there, it would have been more than enough, but Jack wasn't done. He roughly inserted two fingers into me and moaned at my tightness. His tongue continued to flick against my clit, nipping it, devouring it all while his fingers pumped tightly into me.

My arms felt like they would give way at any moment and my entire body started shaking. My orgasm began building from a depth I didn't know existed.

"Come for me, Emma. I need to hear it." He went back to work on my clit, licking and sucking ferociously as my orgasm built higher and higher. "That's it baby, let it go. Now."

He made one final swipe against my core and applied pressure with his thumb, his fingers moved simultaneously inside me in a come-hither motion. I exploded, screaming his name. The walls of my vagina clenched, pulling his fingers deeper. My toes tightened, and my thighs tensed around him, holding him in place.

If I wasn't so completely out of my mind, I might have been embarrassed by my behavior but I was too far gone to care. I fell back against the countertop, the cold granite felt instantly cooling against my heated and flushed skin as the last of my tremors left my body.

Leaning over me on the countertop with his hands next to my head, he smirked. "You don't think you're done yet, do you?"

I laughed at his playful but still sexy tone and shook my head back and forth.

He took one of my hands in his and pulled me up so I was sitting flushed against him. My nipples hardened instantly when they rubbed against the soft hair on his chest.

"Wrap your legs around me."

I did what I was told because I was too satisfied to argue, and because the sound of his deep voice had my insides pulsing again. Good god, I thought. If I only got three dates with this man, I think he could potentially leave me sexually satisfied for life.

I leaned my head into the crook of his neck.

"Where are we going?" I whispered as his hands wrapped around my butt and he started walking out of his kitchen.

"To my room. Where I'm going to fuck you senseless." My cheeks flushed in response.

"I think you already did that."

He laughed and lightly tapped one side of my butt.

"Not even close."

Five

He wasted no time when we entered his room. I fell onto the middle of his bed and rested on my elbows; savoring every second it took for him to remove his pants and then his white boxer briefs that clung to him like a second skin. Tanned and toned to perfection, his lean muscles rippled with every move.

Sexiest thing ever.

I licked my lips and dropped my eyes to his impressive erection. My lips twitched a bit in surprise. He stalked towards me with a sexy, smug grin on his face. I swallowed slowly, letting his eyes gaze all of my body.

My breath was already increasing and I resisted the urge to press my thighs together to ease the burn that was already growing again. The man hadn't even touched me yet and I was slowly beginning to fall apart.

He slowly climbed up my body from the foot of the bed, kissing and flicking his tongue over almost every single inch of me. By the time his tongue darted out and licked along my collarbone, my nerves were wound so tight again that I thought I could burst at any moment.

He chuckled softly in my ear, his breathing faster than I had ever heard it. "You like this."

I murmured something indecipherable and wiggled my hips, wanting him to settle inside of me.

"Jack." He moved until he was directly over mine, we were just inches from each other and then his hands reached out, grabbing onto mine and plastering them to the mattress on either side of my head. I strained up to kiss him but he moved away and pushed his hips into mine eliciting another moan from deep in my throat.

He kissed me roughly and quickly and left me gasping for breath when he reached over and grabbed a condom from his bedside table.

Once sheathed, he grabbed my hands again and stared down into my eyes. I wanted to know what he was thinking when he furrowed his brow. It almost appeared he was thinking of something, questioning the decision to have me in his bed. But I had waited years for this and wasn't about to give him up.

I wiggled and bucked my hips against him, reminding him that I was still here waiting for him.

Between heavy breaths he sighed, his brown eyes focused on my blue ones. "You make me feel out of fucking control Emma."

I still didn't know if that was a good thing or a bad thing. I also didn't want him to leave me here like this, to regret what he had done and walk away from me again when I was already so close to peaking. And he hadn't even touched me yet. I shivered beneath him.

"You said you were going to fuck me senseless," I whispered breathlessly.

A wicked gleam appeared in his eyes. Without another word, his hips lifted off mine. I spread my legs further and tilted my hips, ready to accept his large cock.

I cried out, as soon as he thrust into me, harshly. It was harder than I expected, and he was larger and wider than anything I had taken before. My insides felt completely stretched and full. He left me no time to get used to his size or the fullness in me before slowly pulling out and thrusting even harder the second time. I moaned beneath him in equal parts pleasure and pain as he hit the back wall.

I bent my knees, bracing my feet against the mattress and closed my eyes, preparing for more, but I knew it wouldn't take much more of an effort for me to be thrown over the cliff. He stilled inside the second time and lowered his head to my shoulder.

"Christ you feel so fucking tight," he moaned deeply and moved his hips against my clit. I grasped him harder, my hands squeezing his hips, trying to pull him deeper. "Fuck, Emma. What in the hell are you doing to me?"

I didn't think he wanted an actual answer. I was feeling too close to being high out of my mind to come up with one anyway. He threw me higher and higher into ecstasy with each powerful thrust of his hips until we were both sweating. I wrapped my legs tightly around his waist trying to hang on for dear life.

I screamed his name once, my orgasm rocketing through every muscle, nerve and bone in my body and still he didn't stop moving inside of me; harder and deeper than before with my new position.

I had heard, and read about women having orgasms lasting as long as ten minutes but always thought the whole idea was full of shit. That was before Jack continued rocking into my body, a light layer of sweat covering both of us. I thrashed against his hands that still held mine, willing him to let me go so I could move them, hold him, and probably claw the hell out of his back but he just grabbed me tighter, sank his mouth to mine and swallowed my cries. I was almost at the point of screaming at him to stop, that it was too much, when finally, he thrust into me one more time, wrenched his mouth from mine and sank his teeth into my shoulder, his arms shaking above me.

"Fu-uck." At least that was what I think he moaned, but his breath was so shaky I couldn't be one hundred percent certain.

Slowly he rolled off me, removed his condom and tied the opening off before tossing it into a tissue and throwing it into a wastebasket.

He pulled me to him gently softly pulling me towards him so we were lying chest to chest. I stiffened for just a moment. Gentle was not a word I used to describe Jack and it threw me off after the incredible passion that had just exploded around us.

He smiled lazily, looking as sated as I felt. He drew a long tendril of my blonde hair, slowly pulling his hands through it, dropping it just over my uncovered breast.

"Your hair is softer than I thought it would feel."

"You thought about my hair?" My breath hitched a bit at the question.

"More often than I care to admit."

I laid there not knowing what to say at his admission. He didn't look comfortable admitting it to me. A slow awkward silence began to grow between us; or at the very least, I began feeling awkward. I had just had sex with my boss, Chicago's bachelor of the year who had supermodel gorgeous women on his arm monthly. I was just a law school dropout, single mother and essentially, housekeeper. I had never felt more uncertain.

Did I just add sexual favors, willingly, to my job description? I cringed at the thought.

I sat up quickly, looking around for something to use as a cover up. I suddenly felt much more vulnerable than I was when he laid me out all over his kitchen counter. Jack's hand grabbed me, just as my heart began to race in a panicking flutter.

"Tap it down," he barked harshly.

I snapped my head to him. "What?"

"You're worrying. And you're two point five seconds away from panicking and threatening to quit on me again. Knock it off."

His reminder of my job, my position, only upset me more. What in the hell had I just done? I ripped my hand from his and jumped off the bed. I took out one of his t-shirts from his dresser, one I had just placed there earlier, and threw it over my head and arms before I turned back to him.

When I did, his lust-filled eyes were staring at me. I flicked my gaze to the alarm clock behind him. It was almost five thirty.

I sighed in relief. "I have to get Logan from Penny's."

Penny was a high school student I paid to watch Logan just a few hours on the days he had preschool so I didn't have to leave work, pick him up and bring him back here with me.

Jack looked at the clock, back at me, and started walking toward me. He wiped his hair back from his forehead. "I'll go with you."

Not what I was expecting at all. I clamped my mouth shut, crossed my arms and tried, failing miserably, at plastering on a pleasant expression. "It's fine. I'll see you tomorrow."

He didn't buy it.

He dropped his eyes on me under half hooded lashes and stalked the rest of the way to me like I was his dinner. Except that was still cooking in the oven.

When he spoke, his voice left absolutely no room for argument.

"I'm coming with you. We're going to bring Logan back here and eat the dinner you have cooking, because I'm sure it will be delicious, just like everything else about you." I felt a heat creep against my cheeks when he gave me a knowing smirk. "And then we're going to work this shit out. Because I don't know what the hell just happened here today …" he wiggled his finger back and forth between us, "but it sure as hell isn't over yet."

I'm sure that was supposed to make me feel better, instead, all I noticed was an extremely gorgeous naked man in front of me, who was still hard.

Oh my hell.

He was still hard. How was that even possible?

The slow warmth on my cheeks blossomed into a furious heat all along my neck and upper chest. When I looked back up at him, his eyes and fierce expression were just about daring me to try to argue with him. I gave in with a reluctant sigh.

Jack's eyes switched from sexy serious to boyish in a split second. "Besides," he said and rocked back and forth a little bit on the balls of feet. I refused to look down. "I bought that Mario game Logan asked for last week."

"You're using my five year old to manipulate me into coming back here tonight?" I eyed him teasingly.

"Right now, I'll use whatever it takes." He turned from me and began pulling on his boxer brief and dress pants he had discarded on the floor earlier.

"Fine." I turned and went downstairs to find the clothes he'd ripped off me earlier. I set the oven timer to the 'keep warm' setting and then rested my head in my hands while I waited for Jack.

Logan was excitedly surprised in the best way possible when Jack walked through the door of my apartment. I told Penny we'd see her next week after introducing her to Jack and then looked around our small living and dining space, almost embarrassed that Jack was finally seeing my home for the first time.

He paid me well. He could afford it after all, and Logan and I had more than enough money to live comfortably. But we had a small two-bedroom apartment, in a turn of the century apartment building with only fourteen apartments and while it had charm, with the dark wood beams and floors and rounded doorways, it lacked the opulence and wealth of Jack's home. Our entire apartment could probably fit inside Jack's living and dining room area.

I looked at Jack, who had immediately been suckered into playing Legos with Logan and cringed. His tall and muscular frame exuded strength and power, even when he was sitting on my living room floor playing with my son. His mere presence almost overpowered the small space.

Logan adored Jack. It made sense. Jack never hesitated to purchase new toys or video games and systems, or books. He blamed it on being an only child and not having any nieces or nephews to spoil and while I appreciated it, and never thought twice of his thoughtfulness before, I did now.

What would I do when this time was done? Would we still be able to work together? If I ended up finding a new job, would Jack still have a presence in Logan's life?

The questions were too heavy and too daunting to answer in that moment. Jack looked up at me and smiled devilishly.

"Go pack a bag. I'm hungry."

My eyes widened. "A bag?"

He nodded confidently. "For the night."

A bag to spend the night? What had gotten into this man? Less than six hours ago he had shown up, practically begging me to yell at him for being an ass, and after two romps—albeit fabulous ones—in the hay for lack of a classier term he was expecting me to spend the night.

Logan's eyes lit up. "We're having a sleepover at Mr. Jack's?" His smile spread from ear to ear and I scowled at Jack before giving Logan my most serious mom look.

"No, sweetie. We're just going over there for dinner." I crossed my arms and glared at Jack, expecting him to argue with me. He didn't.

Instead, he whispered something in Logan's ear that I couldn't hear, patted him on the head and started walking toward me. His lopsided smirk increased incrementally with every step. There was no way in hell I was budging on this. Whatever sexual tension was released between the two of us today was going to stay exactly there - between us - and I wasn't about to let him manipulate me.

"I need to speak to you." I turned to Logan. "Pick up your toys. We'll be leaving in a few minutes."

I spun on my heels practically stomping down the hall to my room thankful Jack followed me. Although I noticed he was still smiling at me. I could practically see the cogs spinning in his head, planning something.

"What do you think you're doing?" I hissed at him once he closed the door to my room.

He didn't say anything for a minute. His eyes simply swept over every inch of my room, and stopped on my bed. It felt more intimate, him being here in my private place than it did when I was in his earlier. This was my private area, where I relaxed … and fantasized about the man in front of me.

His eyes moved from my bed, and slowly raked up my body making me feel as if I was still naked. I swallowed, roughly, trying not to let him wear me down even though my body had suddenly warmed from his stare alone.

Once his inspection was complete, Jack's eyes returned to mine. He simply shrugged. "You're staying the night."

I scoffed, "No, I'm not. I agreed to dinner and to talking."

He took several swift steps towards me, wrapping one arm around my waist and pulled me towards him. I ignored the tightening in my stomach. Good grief, he'd already given me two of the best orgasms of my life and with a simple hip wiggle I was instantly turned on again. I wanted to fight him off though. This certainly wasn't the time and I definitely didn't like the idea of being railroaded into making a decision.

With both of my hands on his chest, I pushed him off as hard as I could and took two steps back. "What in the hell is going on with you? Twenty four hours ago you looked at me full of disdain from one simple kiss and today you screw me and think it gives you the right to tell me where I'm sleeping?"

I almost wanted to smack the smirk off his face, almost. It was awfully cute.

"I told you I wanted to talk about whatever was going on between us."

I nodded and crossed my arms. "Which I agreed to."

"I do my best talking late at night, and first thing in the morning. In bed."

I rolled my eyes, but couldn't stop a smile from breaking out. "That doesn't sound like talking."

He crossed his arms and I watched his eyes darken. It was the same lust filled stare he gave me earlier and almost left me melting in a puddle on the floor.

"I told you I feel completely out of control around you. I can't explain it."

"Well rein it in," I said drily and pointed a finger at him. "I'm serious, Jack. I'm not doing this tonight; not with Logan there especially."

"Fine." But he didn't look happy about conceding. He almost looked wounded or hurt but I didn't want to spend the time thinking about why that could be. "Tomorrow."

I exhaled slowly and overdramatically letting him know how much his bossiness and assumptions were getting under my skin. "Logan has a sleepover tomorrow night," I muttered, mostly thinking out loud.

He grinned victoriously. I was frankly shocked he was asking me about the very next night already. That wasn't his typical MO with women he was with. I lightly grabbed his hand when he offered one out to me and let him pull me back to the living room.

"Are we going to Mr. Jack's now?" Logan asked when we reached the living room.

I shook my head. "Just for dinner."

He frowned and I was instantly annoyed that Jack had got my little boys' hopes up. But I was even more shocked when he answered Logan.

"Another time, little man. We can play Paper Mario tonight, though." I stumbled over my feet when Jack said it, spoken with such conviction and promise.

I turned to him and whispered harshly, "Stop getting his hopes up."

His eyes darkened in anger and I wondered what in the world he had to be angry about. I didn't have time to be dealing with someone, even Jack freaking McMillan, making promises to my kid, only to let him down in the future.

"I'm not." He spit the words out so forcefully, leaving me knowing that he fully intended to have Logan at his house. And what … with me? How long did he expect this little charade of ours to last?

My confusion from earlier bubbled to the surface all over again. My stomach tightened into a thousand different knots. This was going to be a really bad idea.

Jack's voice whispered in my ear as Logan went to find his shoes. "I told you to tap that shit down, Emma."

I couldn't help it. This could all just be a fun and wild game for him, screwing around with the young housekeeper for who knows how long, but this was my life. It was my career and my family and I had every right to be bothered by how fast everything had happened today.

"I can't help it," I said quietly to him. "I don't know if dinner is a good idea anymore."

This time there was no denying the wounded expression and even possibly, fear that flashed through his eyes. I shook my head and looked away to Logan who was happily skipping down the hall, shoes in hand, talking to himself about Mario. I couldn't tell him no.

I turned back to Jack, "Fine. I'll come tonight."

"Oh … you'll come."

And suddenly, I desperately wanted to.

Six

Watching Jack lounge in his media room, in his large comfy chairs and playing a video game had to be the absolute highlight of my day. Actually the entire night felt like a fantasy that I rarely bothered dreaming of. I was so young when I got pregnant with Logan that it effectively ruined my dating life for years. Guys in college, law school especially, didn't want the burden of caring for some other man's son. Even now it was difficult finding someone worthy enough to be around, knowing eventually it could lead to introducing the new guy to my most important little boy. The sacrifices were well worth it, but most nights, over weeks and years, it was a long and lonely road with very few supporters. Thankfully, I always had Macy, and then eventually Tate, and I guess even Jack to a degree.

Tonight I experienced the semblance of what normal family dinners would be like, talking about our day—at least the parts that were kid appropriate—laughing at Logan's jokes and antics while he talked about chasing girls around the playground. That had led Jack to give him a very serious discussion over manicotti about the importance of only chasing the girls that were worth it.

I had rolled my eyes. Jack didn't chase anyone; women fell at his feet everywhere he went. I had witnessed it first-hand. But now, he was mine.

The only question was for how long.

Watching Jack smile, laugh and have the patience of a Saint while teaching Logan how to play his new game only increased my yearning for something more. Something permanent.

I wanted that. I wanted a dad for Logan and a partner for me. Someone to stay up with on the long lonely nights when our child was sick and we could share the duty.

I wanted the hugs and kisses, the hello's and good-bye's every morning and after work at night, and I wanted to cook my favorite meals and not leave them behind at my job every day, knowing someone else would be enjoying them.

I sighed, loudly, frustrated at myself for letting my mind wander to the things that would ruin my night. It earned me a scowl from Jack and he instantly paused the game.

"You good with this?" He asked Logan and nodded toward a television larger than any person should possess in their home. It took up an entire wall and while it was great for movie nights, the turtles they were trying to jump on were so big they looked like they could eat us for dinner.

Jack sat his controller down, gave Logan his casual hair waggle, and nodded towards the door.

I met him out in his living room and plunked myself down on one of his incredibly soft chocolate brown sofas, and looked out over Lake Michigan. Jack's penthouse apartment sat along Lake Shore Drive in the Streeterville area of Chicago, just a few blocks off Michigan Avenue. His breathtaking view faced Lake Michigan. During the day, I would look out the windows and watch the rolling white caps and shipping boats and massive sailboats head out on the water. Tonight, with a lack of lighting, all I could see was blackness.

I sipped the most delicious Cabernet Savignon I had ever tasted and closed my eyes, trying to relax. It didn't help, though. Regardless of the amazing sex I had earlier, it had also come with too many questions, too many uncertainties and fears I had never anticipated in all my ponderings about what it would be like to actually *have* Jack.

"You're doing it again," he admonished me as he sat down on an oversized chair in the corner, facing me.

I stayed looking out the window, too unnerved at the thought of getting swept up in his gorgeous brown eyes.

"Every time you looked at me this week your eyes were filled with regret and disgust over our kiss last week. And that was just a kiss." I shook my head and took another sip of wine. "I'm waiting for the other shoe to drop."

"I can't promise you it won't."

I reluctantly dragged my tired eyes to his.

"I just know that I saw you today, and I had to have you."

Well, he did. A couple of times, and if I was being completely honest, I still wanted more. I also wanted more than sex and I wasn't sure he could give that to me. In fact, I knew he couldn't give that to me.

He leaned forward with his elbows on his knees and dropped his head into his hands, grabbing fistfuls of his hair before he looked back up to me. "I don't date."

I didn't say anything because I already knew that, and it only increased my resolve that whatever happened earlier in the day was temporary.

"And I don't get close to anyone, but you got under my skin a long time ago and I'm tired of fighting it."

Oh my shit. Startled, stunned, shocked, amazed, disbelief … just a few of the emotions that flew across my face at his admission. I clamped my mouth shut so it wouldn't drop to my knees. My wine glass shook a little bit in my hands. I held it in my lap so I didn't spill the red wine onto his luxurious sofa that probably cost more than my annual salary.

What was I supposed to say to that?

Apparently nothing, because he slowly stood up and joined me on the couch. Close enough to be intimate, far enough away to have my personal space.

I appreciated it.

I needed the small amount of space to think.

Except my mind went completely blank. Empty. I couldn't think of a single thing to say while he sat on the couch, both of us staring at each other. I bit the inside of my cheek, wanting to say something; anything, to erase the nervousness I saw flash in his eyes.

"Do you remember the day you showed up for your first day of work?"

I did remember. Macy had told him she had a friend who desperately needed a good paying job. She said I was intelligent, organized and a hard worker and everything he would need in his personal assistant. He hired me without ever meeting me.

I was fourteen weeks along in my pregnancy and on the tail end of my morning sickness. Still crying over the loss of Marcus, I had slept horribly the night before, and had thrown up three times that morning, barely making it to his penthouse on time. My hair was thrown into a disheveled bun and my eyes were red and swollen. It was the worst first impression I had ever made on anyone in my entire life. I was amazed he didn't fire me on the spot.

"I looked like shit that day."

"You were glowing and breathtaking. You looked so sad, but determined. I had never seen anyone be so brave considering all I knew you were dealing with. But you had your head held high, and I knew you were determined to be successful, to make something for yourself and your baby. Something gripped me that day, and all I wanted to do was protect you and help you and take care of you." He dropped his head a little bit while a thick silence grew between us. "I've spent every day since then trying to do just that but last week when I saw Dean touch you, I had to have more."

My head was spinning in circles, trying to figure out how this completely controlled man, could admit such things to me.

"So what happens now?" I asked tentatively.

He sighed heavily and leaned back against the couch. It was the first time I had ever seen him look so uncertain; so fragile, and I didn't know why.

"I'm going to fuck up. There's a reason why I don't date and let people in. I'm broken and damaged." He leaned forward slightly, resting one of his hands on top of mine in my lap and squeezed it gently. "But I still want to try."

I wanted to give in. To throw myself into his arms and bury myself in him. I wanted to fix whatever he thought damaged him. I wanted to see the confident and controlled businessman he always was, but I thought of Logan, and in the end, he was all I had. He was the most important person in my life and I couldn't jump into anything, regardless of how much I wanted it, without thinking clearly.

"We need rules," I said, without even realizing I was actually agreeing to take a chance on this man in front of me.

One side of his lips quirked up in amusement. "Rules?"

"You don't touch me while I'm working."

His eyes darkened instantly and he frowned. "I'm not sure I can keep my hands off you now."

I laughed softly and took another sip of my wine. "I'm serious, Jack. I need to keep a line between my job and whatever else happens. Otherwise …"

He gently took my empty glass of wine out of my hands, set it on the table behind him and pulled me onto his lap. I was straddling him and when he placed his hands on my hips, I remembered exactly what his hands had done to me earlier. I shifted against him and felt his hard erection instantly. How can he do this to me? One simple touch and I want to come apart at the seams.

"Otherwise, what?" He asked, his voice heavy with desire.

I frowned. "Otherwise I feel like you're just paying me for sex."

His eyes widened momentarily before returning to a softer haze. He nodded. "Fine. I get it. But your workday ends when I say it does."

I shook my head. "No. My workday ends at six and five on nights you don't need dinner; just like always. And no touching me around

Logan either."

He growled in frustration. I watched the gears in his mind turning trying to figure out a way to get me to change my mind. When he thrust his hips gently into me, I groaned and almost wanted to just give in and screw the rules.

Or him. Either one would work.

"Unless I need you for something else before then." A wicked smile spread across his lips.

I lowered my gaze to him, giving him the same look I gave Logan when I told him I wasn't messing around.

He threw his hands up in innocence and smiled roguishly. "Get your head out of the gutter woman. I meant any public appearances I need to make. You'll go with me."

"I will?"

"You will." He leaned in and kissed me gently. Our lips met in the softest, most chaste kiss possible before he pulled back.

"I will," I whispered softly against his lips. I suddenly didn't care about my rules, or about maintaining a safe distance. All I knew was that the man sitting beneath me, the same man I'd dreamed about for the last few years admitted to wanting me. I wanted to enjoy it for as long as possible, his warnings about being broken and damaged be damned. I was broken. We could be broken together, and maybe, somehow, we could find a way to fix each other.

I sighed regretfully, wiggled off his couch, and almost laughed at his frown.

"I need to get Logan home and put him to bed."

He stood up, holding onto my hips and then slowly let me go so I slid down every part of him. Once my feet were shakily on the floor, his hands moved to my waist and he pulled me to him, holding me softly against him and smiled down at me. I swallowed slowly, wondering if he was going to kiss me again, or potentially haul me upstairs to his bed, but he didn't make any other move.

"I'll see you tomorrow," he said roughly. "Bring a dress and pack a bag, because after six o'clock you're all mine."

His. It sounded good and left me speechless all over again, so I simply nodded before his hands fell from my waist.

I gathered Logan from the media room where he was still happily lost in Mario land and waved goodnight to Jack before we walked out the door. Tomorrow would change everything. I looked back at Jack's door, wondering briefly, if I had just made a huge mistake.

I was a walking contradiction.

I didn't want him to touch me. I wanted all working hours to be completely professional. I needed that clear line of boundaries.

Except all I could think about were his hands on my hips, and lower—pleasing me with his soft lips on my neck, chest, and stomach. I snapped myself out of my lustful daze and repeated the importance of boundaries. Then I kept repeating it for the rest of the train ride, as if merely thinking it over and over again would sear the thoughts into my brain.

I bounced my knee, tapped my foot, and ticked my fingertip across my front two teeth repeatedly only stopping when I noticed the other passengers shooting me annoyed looks. Normally I wouldn't care, but I didn't want Logan getting concerned there was something wrong with me.

I looked down at him and smiled. He was "reading" his first chapter book—which mostly just meant he was looking at the pictures. But he was totally enthralled in whatever Stanley was discovering on his latest adventure. I loved having a child who had a passion for reading from such a young age. I smiled at him again, and grabbed my own Kindle, hoping I could get lost in my own book to settle my nerves.

It didn't work.

It all flew out the door when I walked into Jack's kitchen after sending Logan to "our room" as he called it.

Jack was sipping his coffee nonchalantly against the counter in the exact spot where my legs had been spread out for his pleasure just the day before.

He grinned smugly. "Good morning."

He looked delicious dressed in a black suit, wearing the same purple tie he had the previous Saturday night. I flushed immediately and turned my head away.

Pushing off the kitchen counter, he slowly stalked toward me until he was just inches from my ear. The little hairs on the back of my neck stood up when I felt his breath on my ear.

"This doesn't count as touching, you know." He chuckled softly as he watched me visibly shiver beneath him.

I cleared my throat before I threw myself at him and took two steps away, drawing that clear line I so desperately needed and didn't want. I crossed my arms protectively against my stomach and turned to him with my most professional voice.

"What do you need done today?"

He quirked an eyebrow suggestively but when I rolled my eyes at him, he turned and set his coffee mug in his sink.

When he looked back at me, he was completely professional and friendly. It was the same look I had seen every morning for the last five years. I relaxed, knowing we were getting down to business.

"I'm hosting a business dinner next Friday night. I want it catered, but nothing fancy. I'm bringing on a new attorney in our mergers and acquisitions team and want to impress him. He has a lot of influence in town, but I still want it casual."

"He sounds important."

Jack nodded. "He is. He's young, but he's good. And his family is heavily political. I want that connection." I tried not to grimace. I knew a young powerful lawyer with a political family. The memory of him made me cringe and I brushed it aside immediately. It was a fleeting thought, and an even worse memory that I didn't want to relive right now.

I must have made a face because Jack looked at me hesitantly before continuing to rattle off a list of typical things he needed done and bought. I patiently took notes the entire time just as I always did.

Besides the teasing first thing, we acted like we had done every single day. This was a piece of cake. I could do this.

He walked out of the kitchen after telling me to have a good day and he'd be home at six. He gave me a pointed the look, but I said nothing, still determined to be completely professional. Then, he stopped in the doorway and leaned up against it.

"There's an invite on my desk for the Children's Hospital Charity ball in a few weeks. Respond plus one."

He turned and left without another word and I felt the color drain from my cheeks. Plus one, but no mention of me accompanying him. Of course there wouldn't be, the ball was weeks away. Surely our time would be done by then and he'd have me scheduling a new date with him for it.

I felt stupid immediately and emotionally drained from that realization alone and my day hadn't even begun. I helped myself to a cup of coffee, black, and took it to Jack's office and began responding to his personal emails.

I hadn't been working for longer than ten minutes when my cell phone dinged Jack's personal tone, alerting me to a text message. I grabbed my phone, reluctantly, but couldn't stop the grin from appearing on my face. I felt foolish all over again.

J: Would you do the honor of accompanying me to a charity ball? Three weeks from Saturday.

I laughed to myself and then responded.

You're asking me out on a date via text?

I stared at the phone, and smiled again when he responded almost immediately.

J: I told you I'd fuck up this whole dating thing. Say yes, anyway.

His playful tone—and lack of an apology—made me smile. And the fact that he used the word dating.

Okay. I can go with you.

I held the phone in my hand gently, almost willing it to ding again; wanting to know what he had to say. I was just setting it down on the desk when a new text came in.

J: I'll pick you up tonight at 6:00. Be Ready. Did you pack a dress like I asked?

Technically, he never asked me. He told me to bring a dress, but I didn't want to waste time arguing with him over a small technicality. Clearly he liked being a bit bossy, and I was discovering that I didn't necessarily mind.

Yes. Are you taking me out?

J: I am. And don't wear underwear. I want you bare for me.

Oh my god.

Oh. My. God.

I stared at the text for who knows how long reading the words repeatedly. And then I read it some more wondering if I mis-read it. Surely another message would come through any minute with a winking face, or something alerting me to the fact that he was just joking.

It never came.

But I was incredibly turned on by the whole idea. My hands were sweating and my heart was racing. He didn't mean it. Surely he didn't. My dress was short … it already barely covered my rear end and was by far the most provocative dress I owned.

When I called Macy the night before to ask her what I should wear, she told me to go big or go home so I decided to choose a deep burgundy, fitted, one shoulder-strap dress that brought out my blue eyes and showed off my legs. If I wore this tonight with Jack, with no underwear, it would be practically indecent. But even as I tried to talk myself out of it, I knew I would do it. Something in me wanted to do whatever Jack told me to do.

I struggled through the rest of the emails, blushing to myself, and glancing periodically for that 'just joking' text that never came. I spent the rest of the day distracted and turned on at the mere thought of what he had planned for our first date.

After lunch, Logan and I left the condo to make a run to the dry cleaners using the Audi A4 Jack provided for my professional errands. We stopped at the liquor store, an organic market where I bought all of his locally-grown organic fruits, vegetables, and meat; and then I drove back to Lincoln Park to drop Logan off for his sleepover.

"Be good!" I yelled after him when he ran off with his friend, Connor, as soon as the door opened. I sniffed at the thought that he didn't give me a good-bye hug or anything. Surely at not even five he wasn't too old for that now, was he?

After talking with his friend's mom, Peyton, and confirming that I would pick him up in the morning at ten, I made the drive back to the penthouse. My heart fluttered the entire time. I hadn't heard anything from Jack since that last text and the anticipation of not being one hundred percent certain if he was joking or not still had me squirming in my seat.

Seven

I made it back to work at five o'clock; thankful the Friday drive into the city was slower than normal. I had just enough time to shower in the bath off my servant's room and get ready.

I showered, curled my hair into loose waves so it fell halfway down my back, and applied my make-up, using enough eye shadow to create a romantic, smoky eye, but wasn't overpowering. I was just finishing applying a pale pink lip-gloss across my lips when I heard the front door open.

I quickly strapped on my gold high-heeled sandals, smoothed out my dress and turned back and forth in front of the mirror. The burgundy dress and eye shadow highlighted my bright blue eyes and the deep color accentuated my tanned skin. With a quick flip of my hair, I grabbed my clutch bag and was ready.

At least physically, I was ready, and in more ways than one.

With every step, my thighs rubbed together, giving me a reminder that I had followed Jack's directions. I felt smutty, but sexy. It was a heady combination and by the time I reached Jack in the living room my cheeks did not need that last flick of blush I applied earlier.

He smiled at me in what I could only describe as predatorily. His slow perusal of my body and my skin-tight dress only served to make my cheeks even more heated. By the time he turned his eyes back to mine, I was certain my cheeks matched my dress.

"You look ravishing," he said with a thick, aroused voice.

I quirked an eyebrow. "Is that a promise?"

He narrowed his eyes at me for just a minute, before reaching out his hand that had been behind his back. In it, he held one single calla lily. I took it and breathed in its delicate scent.

"Thank you."

He grinned that lopsided smile and clasped his hands together. "Someone reminded me today how much I suck at dating. I thought this would smooth things over."

"It does," I replied and took another quick breath from the flower. Really, I was just trying to calm my overactive heart. He looked even more breathtakingly handsome tonight with a slight scruff across his cheeks and chin. I didn't even want to know how it was possible for his hair and suit to look sexier at six o'clock at night than it did at eight this morning. It wasn't fair to those of us who fell apart by lunchtime.

Jack followed me into the kitchen while I searched for a vase thin enough to hold the flower. He filled it with water for me, and I set it out on the kitchen counter.

"Are you going to tell me where you're taking me?" I asked as he guided me out to the door of the penthouse to the elevator.

"No."

One hand stayed on the small of my back the entire time. The heat from his hand touching me there only reminded me of what I was missing beneath the dress. His hand moved lower on my back, just about to where my panty line would normally be. I moaned softly without realizing it. The slight tightening of his fingers against my back told me he heard it.

The door opened almost immediately. He pressed the button for the elevator and before the doors closed, pushed me up against the far wall. The gold colored handrail dug slightly into my back and my eyes widened in surprise.

He leaned in and kissed me roughly, and quickly, pulling back before

I had a chance to catch my breath. His lips were by my ear.

"Did you do what I said?"

His rough voice rendered me speechless. I nodded.

Slowly, one of his soft hands moved up my thigh. I tightened my muscles on instinct and his hand stopped moving. He massaged my thigh gently until my legs relaxed.

"Good girl," he whispered into my ear. My entire body almost exploded.

His hand continued journeying further up my leg, under my dress and along my already soaking wet center. I was too hot to be ashamed. This was torment and if it were any indication how our night was going to go, I would be a puddle of goo before we got around to the dinner part.

He moaned against my ear when his finger slowly, teasingly so, swiped along my burning center. I ground into his finger instinctually, wanting to feel him in me. I could hear my heart beating in my ears I wanted him so badly. How did he do this? I mewled when he denied me what I wanted, and instead, withdrew his hand completely, and inserted his now wet finger into his mouth.

With hooded eyes, he groaned and sucked my cream off his finger, only inches from my mouth.

I licked my lips and he smiled.

He leaned back towards my ear. "You taste so fucking good." And then, held his finger out towards my mouth, like an offering. Slowly, I flicked out my tongue, just barely touching the tip of his finger, but enough that I could taste myself on him.

I groaned, and had it not been for one of his hands holding my hip, I may have collapsed. He gently pressed his finger further in my mouth and I closed my lips around it, sucking it all the way in.

I would take whatever he would offer me, without shame, because somehow, he knew exactly how to turn me on and turn me into a quivering mess of need. I needed him. The thought was so powerful I almost gasped. But his finger tasted so good; the masculine taste of his salty skin, mixed with me that I couldn't stop myself. I licked and sucked his finger until I looked down and saw his erection pressed against the zipper of his dress pants.

I smiled. I had turned him on just as quickly as he did me, and I loved that feeling. Slowly I moved my hand down the front of his dress shirt, jerking him closer to me when my hand fisted around his belt buckle. It was just a quick jerk and I winked at him as my hand traveled further down and began massaging his erection through his pants. He placed both of his hands on the wall next to me, and thrust his hips into my stomach. The move practically pinned me against the back of the wall as the entire length of Jack's body pressed up against me.

I felt everything. And all I could think of was how I wanted his hands back on me. Anywhere. Doing anything he could to relieve the fire he so quickly started in me. How in the hell was I going to survive dinner?

"I can't wait to be inside you later. I want to watch you writhe in pleasure beneath me until you're so thoroughly fucked you can't walk tomorrow. I have big plans for you tonight Emma."

I closed my eyes and swallowed, imagining what those plans were. I was just about to ask him, but the elevator doors chimed and then opened. He pushed off the wall, grabbed my hand and smiled down at me as if we had just been discussing the weather.

I walked out following him wondering what in the hell had just happened. I glanced back at the elevator doors as we walked away only to hear Jack softly laughing.

Ten minutes later, we exited his Mercedes. He handed the keys to the valet and ushered me into Russalo. A hotel and restaurant that he owned.

"You're taking me to the hotel you own?" I hoped my voice didn't sound as breathlessly hopeful as it did to me. A ten minute car ride, with his hand high on my thigh, did absolutely nothing to extinguish the fire he lit for me back in his elevator. I was two thigh swipes away from exploding while I walked. I should have been embarrassed that he brought me to his hotel. But I wasn't. I wanted to grab him and rush him into the nearest available room.

"I'm taking you to the restaurant on top of the building. It's the best."

I frowned, disappointed. Next to me, he chuckled softly, clearly enjoying how worked up I was.

Every one greeted him as we walked into the building. The valet, the front desk concierge, the bellhop in the elevator. I bit back the urge to ask him if he came here often, but then all sense of humor left me as soon as we reached the elevator bank. I swallowed roughly and looked at Jack while we waited.

He didn't look at me. Instead, he stayed facing forward with one hand on my lower back and the other hand in his pocket. His posture was perfectly straight, and every feature on his face perfectly defined; straight nose, high cheekbones, square chin. He was mesmerizing, and he gave no hint of what was to come as soon as we stepped on the elevator. All I could think about was the taste he gave me earlier.

I snorted at the thought, since literally; I had had a taste … of me. And god help me, but I wanted more of him.

The elevator doors opened and I looked at Jack before stepping on reluctantly. I wanted some indication of what he had planned for me now. Was he going to throw me up against the back of the elevator? Was he going to tease me again and turn me on further? Was it possible for me to be turned on more than I was right then?

I wanted to ask him all of these questions as we stood close together without saying a word. His face was void of any friendly expression whatsoever and it was only then that I realized that the only words he spoke to me since leaving the elevator at his building was when I asked about the restaurant. Other than that, he hadn't said a word.

And then I realized, he planned this. I knew Jack enough to know that he planned and orchestrated every single minute of his day. At first I thought I had done something to upset him, but as I remembered what he said about me making him lose control, I knew this was his way of regaining it. He planned to have me bare and vulnerable for him, to make me uncomfortable for the sake of being completely aroused for him, and wanting him as soon as he gave the word.

His planned totally worked. I bit the inside of my cheek as I fought the urge to smile once I realized what he was planning. If this was his plan, I could totally play along. Perhaps I should have been angry that he'd use me like this, but I wasn't.

I trusted him. Completely.

If silence was what he needed to regain control, then I could play along.

I silenced my gasp as we entered Russalo's. The entire restaurant was a circular shape, and the walls were all windows. It gave us a complete panoramic view of the city of Chicago. Breathtaking didn't even begin to describe the gorgeous view. With the sun beginning to lower over the city, the entire sky was beginning to turn shades of purple and pink and orange, fanning out as far as the eye could see.

I wanted to grab his arm and proclaim my thanks for bringing me to such an amazing place. I wanted to kiss him and gush over the gorgeousness of what I saw. Instead, I bit my cheek again and remained silent; a small smile on my lips the only indication that I was impressed at all.

We didn't speak a single word to each other during our entire meal. The waiter came and he ordered a bottle of Chateau Mouton Rothschild. When the waiter returned to take our order, Jack arched an eyebrow at me as if allowing me the opportunity to order. I simply shook my head and nodded once towards him, silently giving him permission to order for me. And the entire time, over our two hour, seven course meal our table was completely silent.

We dined on an extravagant meal of brioche toast, mussel tart, and poached lobster with mascarpone sorbet. I wanted to 'oooh' and 'aaah' at the gorgeous presentations and even more delicious tastings. He was right. This had to be the best restaurant in Chicago and I was more than impressed. At one point, while I quietly moaned over my succulent lobster, a smug grin appeared from across the table. I lightly smiled back before going back to our silence, but I wanted that brief moment to show him how grateful I was for bringing me to Russalo's.

Our silence was not uncomfortable though. Instead, sexual tension permeated the space between us. Every time he raised his eyes to mine, he looked as if I was already naked and he was getting ready to enter me forcefully. He looked at me full of want and desire and by the time he paid for our check, I was one more predatory look away from coming in my chair. I could feel my wetness against my legs when he stood and pulled out my chair.

"Come with me."

God, yes. Please.

His sultry voice washed over me in waves and I almost fell apart right there as he firmly pressed his hand on my lower back possessively and led me out onto the terrace doors.

The view broke my vow of silence. "This is absolutely gorgeous, Jack."

I followed him, as he led me around a corner of the terrace. It was the middle of summer and the heat had been almost unbearable earlier in the day. When I had left the building to take Logan to his friend's house, the humidity was so thick I felt like I had walked right into a brick wall. I didn't know if it was because it was later in the day, or because we were up so high, but sixty stories up gave me a completely different impression of Chicago. The light breeze from the height cooled me off just enough so I didn't notice the heat or the humidity. The sun was now near the horizon. I had never seen a more gorgeous and peaceful looking sunset. The loud noises from cars were a muffled sound. I could barely hear the L-train from so high, even though I could see it clearly pass us by. I wanted to come back to this place every day just to escape the sounds and stress of everyday life. I felt completely relaxed on the terrace, overlooking the city with Lake Michigan in the distance.

Jack just quirked an eyebrow at me with a slight smile tugging at one side of his lips. Perhaps he was amused I had finally spoken. But he still said nothing as he walked towards the railing. We were completely separated from everyone else, and I noticed a brick wall behind us. It must have been behind the kitchen because when I had sat inside the restaurant, I was only able to see a wall of rounded windows.

He maneuvered us so he was standing directly behind me. I turned to protest, suddenly knowing exactly what he wanted. Surely he wouldn't touch me here, not when it was so easy that he could be recognized by someone.

He stopped me abruptly and turned me back around, pressing against my backside. I gasped as soon as I felt his large erection press against my dress that was barely covering my butt. All he had to do was raise it a few inches and he would have access to anything he wanted from me.

My body shivered at his touch immediately. He leaned over me, his hands on the safety railing just outside of mine and then he tapped the inside of my ankles, gesturing me to spread them further.

I obeyed. And I didn't even wonder why I was doing it. He wanted something from me, and I gave it freely. I had never done that before in my life, with any sexual partner. I was not someone who was willing to be bossed around, but with Jack, I simply didn't want to tell him no. I had wanted this—wanted him—for so long, the thought of refusing anything he wanted now that I had him, at least for a little while, was incomprehensible to me. And I trusted him to not hurt me—at least physically.

My heart, on the other hand, would be shattered into a thousand pieces all over my living room floor when he decided he was done with me.

I wasn't thinking with my heart at that moment. Pure animalistic desire filled me as his breath whispered along my ear and neck.

And when he finally spoke, it was like balm to my skin; instantly soothing me and healing any worry I had.

"Are you wet?" I groaned and nodded at his words. I wiggled my hips against him, eliciting a soft groan from him and I smiled. He may have been in control all night long, but that one sound told me he was as turned on as me. His tongue flicked out and licked the skin right beneath my ear. "You always smell so good, so sweet."

"Jack …" I stuttered. I was completely turned on but even more nervous.

One of his hands ran slowly up my thighs, outside the dress, and moved until he was gently caressing my breast. I leaned back into him, groaning softly as his hand massaged my breast. "Don't be nervous Emma. No one can see us but I can't wait anymore. Just stay quiet, but I'm warning you, it's going to be hard and fast." I shivered as he brushed a finger down my neck from my ear to my collarbone and then across my chest, all the way down my arm. My skin broke out into goose bumps, a trail of pleasure bumps following his finger, showing him how much his touch turned me on.

Without another warning, I heard him unzip his pants and the foil tear on a condom. I wanted to turn to see him, to see how excited he was at the thought of taking me sixty stories in the air but before I could turn my head, he pressed up against me, slowly lifting the hem of my dress.

He chuckled softly in my ear, briefly pausing his pursuit of me. "You're going to need more dresses like this." Without another word, he thrust into me so hard I thought he was going to throw me off the railing. I bit my lip to stay quiet like he asked, but a sound broke through my lips anyway.

One of his hands stayed clasped on to the railing while another one wrapped around my stomach and pulled me even more tightly into him. He gave me no time to prepare as he began thrusting into me, just like he promised—hard and fast. I threw my head back, tasting a slight metallic taste in my mouth knowing I had bit my lip too hard in order to stay quiet. I let go of my lip, bent down further and pressed my mouth against his forearm. I didn't bite, but I used it to hide the moans of pleasure fighting to escape.

"That's it, Emma. Stay quiet … .fuck you feel so good." His verbal praise sounded like heaven to my ears and the new position of me bent over increased the depths were he could hit inside of me. I had to focus on keeping my feet planted as my orgasm began building in me. My entire body began trembling with excitement. It was that moment where you're about to explode and it was taunting me, the ending just out of my reach. As if Jack sensed I was about to finish, his hand moved lower, and he roughly started rubbing my clit through the front of my dress.

As soon as his finger hit my tight bundle of nerves, I exploded. My interior walls clamped down on him more forcefully than I knew possible and I bit onto his arm and screamed in pleasure while he pushed two more times, quickly, into me. He leaned over me, panting as hard as me and groaned loudly, moving his hips in circles against me and wringing every last second out of our orgasms. We stayed there, coming down from our ecstatic highs in complete silence. Eventually he pulled out of me and I jumped when I felt a warm cloth pressed in between my thighs.

"Let me clean you," he muttered, almost reverently. And I let him, because I wanted to. It was more of an intimate act than anything we had shared yet as he slowly and gently wiped and cleaned my arousal from me. When he was done, he took off his condom and wrapped it in the handkerchief. I turned just as he finished re-tucking his shirt and watched him zip up his pants.

He smiled down at me, softly and held out his hand. "Let's go."

Eight

Jack led me to his room and my cheeks flushed as I looked at his bed, remembering what had happened on it yesterday.

It was then that I remembered my toothbrush and bag were in 'my' room downstairs. I turned to go get it but Jack grabbed my hand, his eyes questioning my sudden movement.

"I was going to brush my teeth. It's all downstairs."

"Stay here. I'll go get it." I stood back and let him go by, wondering if it was worth the hassle. I kept a spare set of bathroom things in my own bathroom and it felt silly to bring it up to his room.

When Jack returned, he took the bag to his bathroom and laid everything out on his counter. He looked tense again—frustrated—and I wondered what could have changed in the few minutes he was gone.

He must have noticed the worried expression in my eyes as I watched him nervously from the doorway to his bathroom. He looked at me through the mirror but didn't turn around.

"I don't want you using that room when you're here with me."

I raised an eyebrow, still questioning what he meant when he continued. "You're not my employee tonight. You're …" He stopped and I waited with baited breath for him to finish. I was what? A guest? A girlfriend? A date? A …? I think we were both confused at how that sentence should be finished, because I didn't have a single clue either.

"Mine."

Not what I was thinking he would say at all. Strangely, it didn't sound as offensive as I would have thought either. His eyes darkened marginally while he continued looking at me through the mirrored reflection. My lips turned into a slight smile, showing him I wasn't bothered by the word. In actuality, it turned me on, and I wanted nothing more than to climb into his bed and have his arms wrapped around me and simply enjoy being his for however long it lasted.

Without saying a word, but not removing my eyes from his, I took my toothbrush and began brushing my teeth. He stayed silent and still the entire time; only starting to do the same thing once I finished.

I smiled when he joined me in bed and pulled me to him softly. This wasn't the hard and fast move he gave me earlier on the terrace. My cheeks heated just thinking about how good that had felt and my body instantly wanted more.

"What are you thinking about?" Jack asked me quietly.

Too embarrassed to tell him how good it had felt to be taken so roughly in a public setting, I shared a half-truth with a small smile. "Dinner. It was really delicious."

His slight smile and softened eyes told he knew what I was really trying to say. He leaned in to kiss me. His lips were warm and soft as they gently teased mine. This kiss was different than any previous kiss. It was tender, and slow, and made my entire body slowly begin to increase in warmth.

Just as he began to deepen the kiss, and pull me closer to him, a shrill, angry scream started. Jack's hand on my waist tightened instantly and I knew he was not happy hearing whatever made that sound. I wasn't either.

He spit out a curse word and let me go immediately before reaching for his phone in his suit coat pocket. The angry screaming, which I now recognized as a Linkin Park song, grew louder when Jack removed it from his pocket and answered.

"What?" He growled into the phone and then turned from me and walked to the bathroom. With one hand roughly gripping the back of his neck, every muscle on his back tightened in anger. I had no idea who was on the other end of his phone, but whoever it was, clearly pissed Jack off.

I listened as he spoke in angry hushed tones to whoever was on the other end. He cursed and I jumped when he kicked the cabinets in his bathroom. I had never seen Jack like this. The man who controlled every motion was clearly rattled and all I could think was maybe his impenetrable wall wasn't as thick as I originally thought it was.

"Fine. But this is the last time … .I mean it, B." With that, he slammed his phone down on the counter and I watched from the bedroom as his hands tightened into fists on the bathroom counter. Jack bowed his head and I saw him taking deep breaths, his arms shaking in anger.

He turned to me, stomped out of the bathroom without speaking, and began throwing on his discarded suit. I had a sinking feeling I wasn't going to like whatever he was going to say.

"I have to go." He spit the words out like he was angry with me, and I flinched from his tone.

"Are you okay?" I asked quietly.

He calmed down, minutely, at my words and placed his hands on his hips. He had just gotten his pants on, but they were still unzipped and his chest was still bare. I scolded myself for taking the second to check out his perfectly chiseled chest and abs when he was so angry, but I couldn't stop myself.

"No. That was my brother. I have to go."

"You have a brother?" I didn't bother trying to hide my shock with my gasp or my widened eyes. In the five years I had known Jack, I had no clue and had never heard a single word mentioned about him having a brother.

His face morphed into a look of disgust. Whether it was from disdain about revealing personal information, or anger at his brother who he clearly hated, I didn't know.

I watched his hands tighten on his hips, as he walked towards me and sat down on his bed next to me. "I don't talk about him. Ever."

That gave me absolutely no information, but I didn't want to press. Instead, I moved to get off the bed to get dressed to go home.

"What do you think you're doing?" He asked roughly as I moved to get of the bed.

"I'm going home, Jack."

He pulled me back to him. "No. You're not. You're staying here so I can screw you again as soon as I get back."

I flinched at his words. It wasn't just his words that bothered me—but how angry he sounded when he spit them out at me. I wasn't going to stay here and be used by him to relieve whatever tension his brother created. I also knew better than to argue with him when he was clearly this upset.

"Is he in trouble?" I asked, changing the subject back to his brother in order to take his focus off me so I didn't lie to him.

Jack sighed deeply and removed his hand from my arm. "I told you I don't talk about him."

I arched an eyebrow, questioningly; knowing it was pointless to try to get information out of him if he didn't want to share. But it still hurt. He wanted to try this with me, he wanted to fuck or screw me senseless and have all this control, but the first time a personal question came up; he blocked me out.

I wondered if it would stay like this. Probably. I felt defeated as I realized that besides sex, Jack would probably never open up to me.

"Fine."

He gave me that look that said he knew exactly what a woman meant when she said 'fine.' That we were still pissed but weren't going to say anything, but we'd continue to stay pissed for as long as we wanted. I pulled his satin sheet up to cover my chest and wrapped my arms around me protectively.

"Fine?" He finally responded, questioningly.

I nodded, having nothing to say about it anymore. I felt stupid, rejected, and used.

Jack looked at me doubtfully as he left the bed and began buttoning his dress shirt. "You'll be here when I get back?" It was the first time he'd asked me a question, instead of demanding something from me. I didn't miss it. I didn't miss the look in his eyes that were questioning me, but I couldn't speak, for fear that he would know I was lying to him. His body was still filled with tension from the phone call.

I simply nodded again, but said nothing. He grabbed his keys and phone before walking away without looking back.

I waited a full thirty minutes, watching the clock next to his side of the bed tick by slowly before I got out of his bed. I got dressed, grabbed my bag and left his condo without a note. I had no doubt he didn't actually expect me to still be there when he returned from whatever it was he was doing.

When I got back to my dark apartment, I peeled off my dress, laid down in bed and cried. I cried until I drifted off into a fitful sleep, filled with dreams of Jack.

The combination of my cell phone exploding and a loud pounding jolted me out of sleep the next morning. I turned over in my bed, trying to place the noise and saw that it was only seven o'clock. With swollen, dry eyes, I rubbed my face wondering where the pounding noise was coming from. It didn't feel like it was the sound I heard in my head from a headache from drinking too much. I fumbled around on my nightstand, grabbed my phone to shut off the shrill sound, and grimaced when I looked at the screen. Jack.

Realization dawned on me and I sat up quickly, instantly regretting the quick motion. It only made my head hurt worse, but the pounding didn't stop because it wasn't in my head. I silenced the ringer on my phone and climbed out of bed as he shouted my name in the hallway. I had to answer the door before he woke up my entire building.

I threw on my ugly, large terry cloth robe that covered every single inch of my body and went to answer the door. I didn't want Jack seeing any part of me.

"I'm coming Jack!" I yelled back through the apartment so he would stop beating down my door before he broke it. The sound finally stopped but my head still hurt.

He looked panicked when I opened the door. Both arms braced on the sides of the doorway, his head bowed slightly, chest heaving, still wearing the same suit he threw on the night before. He looked like shit.

I didn't look at him when he raised his head. Instead I turned away from him, walked to the kitchen, and grabbed a cup of coffee, thankful I had remembered to set the pot to brew before I collapsed into my bed. There was a shitstorm coming, I could feel it, and I needed every drop of caffeine I could find. If I could mainline it into my arm, that'd be even better, but my mom always taught that me beggars couldn't be choosers.

"Do you want a cup?" I asked Jack, trying to ignore the pacing animal in my living room. He was seething in anger and I hated the tension that filled my tiny apartment.

My words stopped him instantly and even though I wasn't looking at him - in fact I was trying to look at anything else besides him as I sipped my cup of coffee—I could feel his darkened eyes on me.

"No, I don't want a fucking cup of coffee, Emma."

My own anger filled my body at his words. "Fine."

I spit it out at him just as angrily as he talked to me, knowing it would only piss him off. I didn't care in that moment. I was pissed, and my head hurt, and I could barely open my eyes. Plus, I knew that no matter what happened, he wasn't going to open up to me about anything. There was really nothing to discuss.

I ignored the anger rolling off him in waves and sat down at my kitchen table, gently setting the coffee mug down and plastered on the most indifferent expression I could fake. He came barging into my apartment early in the morning. He could speak first.

"I seriously fucking hate that word." He exhaled loudly and walked to my fireplace, looking at the pictures of Logan and me all over the mantle.

"Stop saying that," I scolded and drank my coffee. I meant the f-word, but he probably thought I was mocking him based on how quickly his head spun around and he stalked toward me. I refused to show him how angry and hurt and disappointed I was, though. "I meant 'fuck' Jack."

He stopped, and roughly ran his hands through his hair before he walked to the kitchen and poured himself a cup of coffee. I hid my smile at his concession for a cup of fucking coffee.

"You weren't there when I got home."

No shit.

I pursed my lips and raised my eyebrows slightly, looking at him from over the edge of my coffee cup that I held with both hands so he couldn't see them shaking.

"Did you really expect me to wait?"

He had the grace to look ashamed for even thinking I would still be there.

"I'm not going to wait around for you to screw me when you're pissed at someone else, Jack. I deserve more than that."

And there it was. I needed more than he could give me, and we both knew it. I watched his anger subside slightly and his tense expression soften. The muscles in his neck and chest loosened as he sat down at the chair across from me. He leaned back in his chair and silently drank his coffee. I was almost surprised he didn't just walk away right there.

Finally he set his coffee down and leaned forward, resting his elbows on the table. "I told you I'd fuck this up, Emma."

"You did. And I'm not as upset at what you said, it was how you said it and what you didn't say."

"I told you. I don't talk about Brian."

I lost my ability to bite back my snark. "He has a name today?"

Jack looked at me intensely. I couldn't tell if he was angry or frustrated. Whatever it was, it left me speechless. I shut my mouth and went back to drinking my coffee while I tried to ignore the gorgeous brown eyes and scruffy haired sexy man across from me. I chided myself silently. I was pissed at him, and yet I wanted nothing more than to gaze into those eyes for the rest of the day. I hated the contradicting feelings inside me.

I refilled my coffee cup, still ignoring the growing tension when Jack finally spoke. I froze instantly, not at all expecting his explanation.

"We're not really brothers."

I calmly set my hands in my lap, and waited, patiently for him to continue.

Jack reached back to his neck and rubbed it, not removing his eyes from me. He sighed heavily and I watched his shoulders sag. Whatever he was debating to say, was important. I stopped the hope in my chest from rising too far. I didn't want to get my hopes up that he would actually tell me something important only to have them dashed again. I simply waited.

"Steven McMillan wasn't actually my dad. I'm adopted." My mouth dropped to form a perfect 'O' shape in surprise. As much as I wanted to maintain my composure, nothing prepared me for that. I had absolutely no idea. "Yeah. Brian is Steven's biological son. We grew up together, but when I was thirteen, my parents died, and Steven adopted me because I was alone and he didn't want me going into foster care."

"I had no idea." My words were soft, along with my softening expression. This was more than I expected to hear.

"I keep it private. Mostly because it's no one's business but mine. After my parents died, I started getting into a lot of trouble at school and Brian got sucked into all of it with me. I was an angry kid, fighting and not caring about anything in the world. When we were sixteen, we got busted by the cops at a party. We were both drunk and high. Steven finally knocked some sense into me. He took me to my parent's graves and made me face them. Told me how pissed they'd be at me and how I was disgracing their memory and their love for me. It shook me up, but Brian was in so much more deeply than I was with drugs that nothing we said or did after that helped. He started hating me, blaming me for his problems, and that I was better than he was at sports and school. I grew closer to Steven, while he began to despise both of us. Slowly, our friendship completely deteriorated and he went off the rails with drugs."

I sat there, listening, while my mind spun with thoughts the entire time. I couldn't even imagine what it would feel like to lose your parents, and then your friend. There was clearly much more to the story than he had already shared, but it was enough. It was more than enough for me. The story explained so much about the man Jack was, and why he refused to get close to anyone.

"And then you took over his company."

I watched a look of sadness fill Jack's eyes. The look was so foreign on him I almost didn't recognize it. He took a drink from his coffee and shook his head slowly.

"I never wanted to take it from him, but he was so far gone by the time we went to college that Steven didn't have another choice. When Steven got sick, he told me he wanted me to take the company over one day. I always knew he wanted it to stay as a family business, so I changed my last name to his. Brian calls every once in a while when he's in trouble and I help him out."

"And that's what happened last night?"

Jack raised his eyes to mine, slowly. His silence was answer enough. I didn't need to know the specifics. Without him saying a single word, I understood. His guilt and pain written all over his face and in his defeated posture.

"No one knows except Martin." I smiled slightly at the mention of Martin. He worked for Jack's company and I knew he'd been around for years. He was Jack's mentor in the company when Steven died and was very much a father figure to him. I had met him several times and he was always warm and friendly with me. He reminded me of my own dad. "We promised Steven we would never let Brian - or his issues - be made public, so periodically we have to clean up his messes," he sighed slowly. "I've never told anyone any of this before, Emma."

It was equal parts a declaration at how much he trusted me and warning to never mention this to anyone again. I nodded in understanding.

"I won't say anything. To anyone."

Without warning, Jack's sad eyes disappeared. Instantly, the hazy look I was starting to know all too well replaced the sadness and regret. As much as I wanted to stay angry with him, I couldn't - not when he just opened himself up to me so much. I pretended to ignore the look of desire filling his eyes and pressed my thighs together.

He looked at the watch on his wrist, and then back to me. "We still have something else to talk about."

I cleared my throat and feigned innocence. "Talk?"

I watched as he licked his lower lip and nodded slowly. I felt the wetness between my thighs, just watching his tongue slowly wipe across his lips. The things he can do with that tongue.

Nine

Without a word, he came over to my chair. He crouched down and turned me toward him. My thighs opened for him automatically and a small victorious smile appeared on his lips.

But he didn't touch me; at least not how I wanted him to. Instead, his hands slowly rubbed up my legs, outside of my thick robe.

"This robe is the most hideous thing I have ever seen," he said softly, smiling right into my eyes. He slowly began untying the robe at my waist.

I chuckled softly in agreement, my voice breathless when I spoke. "Is this what we needed to talk about? My choice in sleepwear?"

"No, but now that you mention it …" his voice trailed off as he finished untying the knot at my waist. With his hands on my robe, he wasn't touching me at all, but my skin felt like it was on fire as his eyes roamed all over my chest, stomach, and completely naked body. "This is what you'll sleep in from now on."

Fine by me, especially if he always looked at me like that. Jack took my hand and slowly pulled me up so my chest pressed against his body. His erection evident as it pressed into my lower stomach. "We need to talk about you lying to me, and how it'll never happen again." His voice sounded ominous.

"Lying?" I choked the words out.

"You told me you'd be there when you got back. You lied." He continued without waiting for a response. Both of his hands framed my cheeks as he pulled back slightly, and earnestly looked directly into my eyes. "I'm going to fuck this up enough for the both of us, Emma. I need your honesty."

Without waiting for my answer, his lips fell to mine. Softly, teasing me, nipping my bottom lip, and then my top, and then moved to the corners of my mouth. I wanted a real kiss. Passionate and hard, like how he always kissed me but as I tried to move to take it, he pulled back.

"God I just fucking want you." Before I knew what happened, his arms went back to my waist as he picked me up. I immediately squealed and wrapped my legs around him. He carried me down the hall to my bedroom without saying another word. I buried my head into his neck, excited, and scared—still trying to figure out what he meant by punishment.

He stood me up on the floor right next to my bed and slowly let my robe fall to the floor.

"I'm sorry for lying," I whispered, my nerves increasing as he slowly scanned every inch of my body without touching me. I reached out to remove his suit coat, but Jack's hand gripped mine.

"You need to take that off." It was the same suit he wore yesterday to work, and then for our date. Essentially he'd now been in that suit for almost thirty hours, and it looked ragged.

Jack didn't move and didn't speak. Instead, he dropped my hand to my side and took one step back from me. I swallowed, slowly. His jaw hardened like it had last night in the elevator on our way to dinner. Was he doing the same thing again - staying silent to show that he was in control? Or was he trying to regain control? His silence unnerved me.

A slight twitch of the right side of his lip was his only movement. But as I watched his eyes, I didn't see any anger. I saw only lust, and a devilish sparkle in his murky brown eyes that told me he was planning something. I swallowed again, and resisted the urge to reach out to touch him, or myself. I was no longer afraid. His eyes told me he wouldn't hurt me; and the anticipation of what would come aroused me.

"Turn around and place your hands on the bed." The command was so similar to last night on the terrace I didn't hesitate to obey. If he wanted to take me hard and fast again, I would enjoy every punishing second of it.

I obeyed, and dropped my head just enough so I could see him standing still behind me. He had yet to move. I stood there, bent over at the waist for who knows how long until I finally heard the rustling of his suit jacket and then it dropped to the floor. His shirt, his pants, and the rest of his clothes followed it until he stood, in the same spot, too far behind me and completely naked. I pressed my thighs together to try to quench the heat in between them. The silence drove me crazy, not knowing what he was going to do, or say. He was so close, but so far away and the entire moment had my nerves crackling with a tension I didn't know possible.

"Don't do that," Jack scolded.

"Do what?" I asked breathlessly. I had no idea what he was talking about.

It took one second for him to reach me, I saw his legs moving towards me and then felt his fingers push into me smoothly.

"Don't tighten up. I like watching your pussy throb and your juices drip down your thighs."

Oh my god. That was the most vulgar thing I had ever heard, and yet at the same time, I had to resist tightening my thighs again. How can this be such a turn on? I had to move. I had to do something.

I jumped again when Jack's hand began rubbing my ass cheeks. The tender caress set off a humming of pleasure that only increased my arousal with every gentle brush.

Slowly, his fingers began moving roughly inside of me. I moaned with the instant pleasure of finally, having something there to take the edge off. I wiggled my hips, wanting and needing more. Much too quickly, he removed his fingers just as roughly.

I moaned again but this time, dissatisfied.

"You like that, don't you?" Jack was now so close, I could feel the heat of his body as he lined up behind me. "You like it rough."

I couldn't see him, but I knew from the tightness in his voice that his eyes were black from desire. I could picture his large cock, standing at full hardness. I licked my lips and nodded in answer to his question. My throat too dry to speak.

"Answer me with words, Emma."

"Yes. Apparently I do."

I felt the tip of Jack's cock lined up perfectly at my opening. I could feel myself throbbing, expectant at the pleasure that was sure to come. Soon, hopefully, because I was already so close to coming from the words he spoke to me. I needed him inside me.

With his hands on my hips to steady me, Jack pressed slowly into me, his cock taking the place of his fingers. He pulled me back onto him as he pushed himself all the way in and I felt the tip of his cock hit me all the way into my stomach.

"Ahh!" I cried out. In pain or pleasure, I didn't know. But he didn't stay long enough to let me figure it out either because just as my muscles began to relax around him, he pulled out completely. I groaned in frustration at the empty feeling he left inside me.

Silence filled the room except for the noises of my heavy breathing and a soft, amused chuckle from behind me. Jack enjoyed this game. It gave him control, and the power. I wanted him to have it, because I knew as soon as he released whatever he had planned, I would enjoy it just as much as him. But I still wanted him to hurry up and release it onto me.

"I have to pick Logan up in a couple of hours, you know." He laughed softly, most likely at the begging tone in my voice.

His hand lightly rubbed the back of my thighs causing me to shiver for his touch again. I leaned in to him, and he pulled away, just slightly. I could still feel the heat from his hand, but I needed it back on my skin. I stilled my legs from moving, hoping I would feel his touch again and it worked. Again, his hand moved along my thighs and I resisted the urge to moan, or move, or whimper. I bit my lip to stay quiet and still so I wouldn't lose that touch again. Slowly, his hand moved around to my front and I could no longer stay silent.

I moaned in pleasure and arched into his hand as he began rubbing my clit. The tight bundle of nerves pulsated against his fingers. I felt my orgasm beginning to build. I wanted to hide it from him so he would continue.

But I couldn't. I moved against his hand fiercely, craving the only contact with him that I had. Really, I wanted his body all over me, his cock pounding into me, and his arms holding me tightly but I would greedily take whatever he had to give me.

"Damn it, Jack!" I cried out as his hand disappeared from mine again right as I was beginning to come. I was panting and sweating and all sorts of turned on. I was annoyed and pissed and wanting. My head spun from the overflow of heat and emotions rushing through me. I wanted to scream at him, kick him out, and have him throw me down on the bed and screw me like he had threatened to do last night.

I did none of it. This was what he wanted, what he needed. As much as I hated the feeling, I wanted to give it to him.

"I'll never lie to you again, Jack." The words came out choppy as I spoke between my deep breaths.

"Promise me." I sighed when I heard his voice. It sounded soft and smooth and exactly how I wanted him to sound when he talked to me—kind and loving.

I nodded, but then remembered his earlier warning. "Promise."

His hands came down instantly and turned me around to face him. My painfully hardened nipples tightened even further when they pressed against the light dusting of hair on his chest. His kiss was rough and passionate and everything I wanted. I linked my fingers behind his head and pulled him towards me as I slowly moved onto the bed. Thanking whoever could hear me that he came with me, and crawled onto the bed above me, lining up his body and pressing it into me as I laid down on my messy covers.

"I could leave you like this. If I left you now, frustrated and so close to coming, you'd understand exactly what I felt like this morning when I got home, wanting to sink into you and finding you gone."

I shook my head. "Please don't."

A small gentle smile tugged at Jack's lips. "Do you want it fast or slow?"

I thought about it for a split second, loving that he was actually giving me a choice when so far, he's just taken me however he wanted it. I don't know why I felt a sense of pride and achievement that he was letting me have my say. We hadn't had sex slowly yet. It had all been lust filled and demanding and I wondered what slow sex with Jack would be like. He might have sex however I asked, but in the end, he'd enjoy it more if he was in the control of it. I didn't mind either way; I simply wanted him.

"I'll take it however you want to give it, Jack."

He exhaled slowly and lowered his mouth to mine. "Thank you for listening to me today," he said as he softly brushed his lips against mine.

Slowly, his hips leaned back and then forward, lining up at my opening. I widened my legs further and arched into him, once again feeling the tip of him against me. In one, long, drawn out movement, Jack inched into me. So slowly, I thought I might explode before he was fully inside me. If this was his idea of slow, it was more torturous than what he did before. I tried to arch into him, to take more of him, but he stilled and admonished me with his eyes.

"You said however I wanted it." I felt scolded, but only until I saw the amusement flicker across his eyes.

"You're killing me," I moaned as he pushed the rest of the way in, completely filling me.

"You amaze me," he said as he slowly pulled back out, and then quickly rocked back into me. Then moved again, out — slowly, in—as quickly as possible. By the third thrust, my insides were quivering and I was a mess of need and so close to coming. Every time he thrust into me, he spoke to me, his lips right on mine, but never kissing me, and never pulling away. It was the most erotic experience ever.

"You scare the hell out of me." So that one wasn't so erotic in words, but I knew what he meant because I felt the exact same way as him.

"You challenge my control."

"You drive me crazy."

"I've never wanted anyone more."

"You are so beautiful."

I fell apart as he pulled out from me, and on his last thrust, I grabbed the back of his hair and pulled him to my chest, screaming his name. My entire body started shaking, fluttering in pleasure, as he kept moving. But this time, his movements were more frantic; faster than before, but not rough. I could feel him grow even harder in me, as I pulsed around his shaft and I knew he was getting close. And just as he let go, calling my name, another orgasm rocked my body. I threw my head back into my pillow and wrapped my legs around him, wanting to hold onto that feeling for as long as it lasted.

I smiled once he rolled off me and my heart rate had decreased to a tempo slower than ready-to-explode. "You were right … you do your best talking in bed."

He chuckled softly and ran his fingers through my hair. It felt calming and comforting all at the same time. "What are your plans the rest of the weekend?"

"The usual. I have to get Logan and do all the work around here I usually save for weekends."

He looked confused.

I laughed. I knew Jack appreciated my work at his place, but he honestly had no idea what went on in keeping a house clean, clothes laundered, grocery shopping, cooking, etc. His naiveté humored me.

"Grocery shopping, laundry, cleaning … that kind of stuff."

"How long does that take?"

I scrunched my nose and thought about it. "Two or three hours if

I'm by myself; more if Logan's around."

"If I get him from his sleepover and take him to the park, would that give you enough time to finish before three?"

I looked at Jack questioningly. "You want to pick him up from his sleepover? Why?"

"There's a Cubs game tonight. I thought we could all go—my treat."

I only had to think about it for a split second before answering yes. And laughed at Jack's big smile. It wasn't the first time he'd taken us to games, but it felt better this time. "I'm surprised you'd do this." I said and then regretted it when Jack's eyebrows pulled together. "It's just … picking Logan up, the park … it's so very … domesticated."

Jack's mouth dropped in feigned shock. "I can be domesticated."

I snorted, completely unattractively, but I couldn't help it. "You are anything but domesticated Jack McMillan."

With a laugh, he pulled me over on top of him so I was straddling his waist and his already half-erect penis. "I'll show you domesticated."

I rolled my eyes and hopped off him. "None of that … you have to get Logan."

I scribbled down the directions to Connor's house, and then called his mom to let her know someone else was picking Logan up. I gave Jack one quick kiss good-bye once we were fully dressed and promised him I would be ready by three for the game.

Once he left, I sighed to myself. Going to a game with Jack wasn't anything different than we'd done for the last couple of years on occasion. But this felt different, especially with him picking Logan up and taking him to the park. It felt more like a partnership, something I'd wanted for myself—and Logan—for a really long time. I just still didn't know how long something like that would last with Jack.

Enough. I scolded myself and brushed the thought away before it could ruin my mood. It was a ballgame and a day at the park with Mr. Jack; Logan would be happy. I had the morning to myself and then an afternoon of fun planned.

Ten

Nothing entertained me more than a Cubs game in the summer. The warm weather, the hot dogs, and beer, watching Logan yell and fill out his scorecard along with the game … it always made me feel connected to the city and the people.

Spending the day at the ballpark with Jack changed the experience completely. Instead of overweight, sweaty vendors shouting 'Get your hot dogs' walking up and down the stairs, we had a private, air-conditioned room, and a fully stocked fridge along with someone to go get the food for us.

I didn't know which experience I liked more. I liked being pampered and taken care of. I also liked being independent and on my own. I got used to it when Marcus left after he found out I was pregnant. Being with Jack was hot and intense … and frustrating. I knew he cared for me, but I still doubted how long it would last and how comfortable I should become with the luxuries of his life—fancy cars, drivers for more fancy cars, suites for games and incredible food. He wanted to care for us. I wanted to fight it every step of the way while at the same time, finally just letting someone help carry my load with me.

"You're doing it again."

I slowly turned my eyes from the game I wasn't paying attention to, to the face of a man clearly annoyed.

I shrugged. Maybe I was, a little bit.

Jack placed his hand on my knee, and for the first time his touch didn't feel sexy—just comforting. I looked down at it, and then nodded to the bar in our suite where we could talk quietly and Logan couldn't hear. Although he was busy scribbling all over his program drawing the players he saw on the field so I doubt he'd hear us anyway. The kid could get lost in drawing for hours.

"You don't date and you've already said you're going to fuck this up," I said once we reached the bar and continued before Jack could defend himself. "And I don't trust easily … not since Logan's dad took off." I scrunched my nose up at the honesty and the reminder.

Jack looked at me for a while, just looked. A blank look on his face and then he cocked his head to the left and right, cracking it.

"So, you have issues."

I nodded, and flashed him a quick grin. "Probably not as many as you, though."

I relished the boyish grin on Jack's face, so different from the blank stare he had just given me, and much easier to deal with than the intensity his eyes usually held. I sighed deeply, feeling like I just exhaled the weight of the world from my shoulders. I had to be honest with him.

"You scare the hell out of me, Jack. I keep waiting for your three date rule to kick in and for you to send me packing when you move on to someone else …"

"That's not going to happen." Fire flashed in his eyes. I leveled my own serious gaze at him so he would stop talking.

"… and I have Logan to think about. He already looks up to you so much, and the only thing I can think of is what's going to happen to him when this doesn't work out."

"When?" He bit it out like a curse word. I almost wanted to take it back, but I couldn't. It was my biggest fear. "You sound so certain this will end already and we've barely just begun."

His eyes no longer held anger. Instead he looked disappointed with me. I turned from him and watched Logan, happily coloring on the baseball program. He was probably drawing the entire team, each uniform numbered and each player in their exact position as he saw them on the field. He was completely oblivious to the tension on the other side of the room and so innocently trusted me to take care of him and provide for him. Being with Jack involved so many risks—for my heart, my financial security, and for Logan. I could handle me. I hated not knowing how resilient he would be if Jack decided to end us.

When Jack spoke again, he was more relaxed, pleading with me to believe him. I wanted to. Desperately.

"I've wanted you for so long, Emma that the thought of you already assuming this won't work out kills me." He didn't take his eyes off me, but he roughly rubbed the back of his hand across his forehead, physically trying to smooth out the tension. "If you're unsure of me, of this … whatever is going on between us, I get it. But you need to walk away now, and I'll understand. And nothing will change when you come back to work on Monday. But if there's any chance you want this as much as I do, give me a chance to show you—and Logan—how much I want this."

I watched him giving me my out. I could walk away right now and go back to work, my heart intact and Logan completely safe. Except I gave Jack a piece of my heart years ago and I would never get it back. Not now. Not after all we'd shared in the last week and with his honesty laid out before me so blatantly.

I wanted him. I wanted to trust him.

So help me god, I stood there and realized I needed him. He stood in front of me, watching me, waiting for my decision and I saw him grow more tense and concerned with every second it took me to think about it.

I nodded. I was all in. No more doubts. I would trust him completely. All the tension in his features and shoulders relaxed infinitesimally before my eyes. He stepped towards me softly, not saying a word, but yet, speaking so much in his silence. He needed me to trust him. I sighed as his hand gently reached out and cupped my jaw and my cheek. He leaned in, never once breaking eye contact with me, and gently placed his lips over mine; barely touching me as he brushed them ever so softly.

"Thank you."

I melted into a puddle of lust and girly-ness and satisfaction just hearing those two words because I knew he meant so much more than he could say.

I returned his kiss just as softly, allowing him to deepen it—just barely—as his lips pressed more firmly into mine. My entire body flushed with pleasure at the simplest touch he gave me.

He stopped there, looked back at Logan and then back to me. I thought he was going to lean in for another soft kiss, but at the last second, he leaned in close to my ear and whispered huskily. "We're having a sleepover tonight, and you're not going to argue with me this time. I want you in my bed and Logan close by."

Yes, please. Amazing how I could go from wanting to protect Logan and filled with such doubt and one simple touch and look from Jack could erase it in a split second. I wondered briefly if our relationship would always be this mercurial and then stopped myself. Of course it would be, but I had a feeling the rewards would be better than the risks and I wanted to stop doubting and finally go after what I wanted.

Logan and I spent the rest of the weekend at Jack's penthouse. As soon as Logan went to bed Saturday night, Jack took me to his room and tenderly loved me until I was crying out his name in passion while he joined me shortly after. He held me all night long, my rule of him not touching me around Logan soon forgotten. I went home on Sunday night, only to grab a couple of overnight bags for Logan and me before we spent another night at Jack's house. Maybe I shouldn't have suddenly moved so fast, but I couldn't stop myself.

As soon as I gave Jack my promise to remove any doubt, and just let what was going to happen, happen; everything changed and I couldn't get enough of him. Based on how he continually had a hand on some part of my body—whether sexually or not—I figured he felt the same way.

We spent the rest of the week the same way. Jack kept his word and didn't touch me while I was working. That didn't stop him from sending suggestive text messages that left me wanting him—craving him. Once he came home those nights, we practiced christening every inch of his condo before I left to go home to Logan and I didn't mind in the least. The only thing I minded was being away from him at night. My body got so used to Jack in such a short time that I lusted after him, fantasized of his hands on me, touching me, bringing me to ecstasy every night I spent away from him. I had never been as satisfied sexually and knowing that Jack wasn't getting tired of me, gave me growing confidence that he really meant what he said. He wanted me and would do whatever it took to keep me.

Jack came back from work early on Friday to prepare for the dinner he was hosting with the new lawyer. I left the caterers in the kitchen to finish setting up dinner and decorating his formal dining room where they would eat, and met him at the door. Hungry for him.

He smiled at me with a predatorily grin as soon as he entered his home and I knew he wanted me, too. He stalked toward me and grabbed my hand, pulling me up the stairs without a single word. I was getting used to his control issues, and his need for quiet. It didn't bother me in the least that he said nothing. He just needed me.

"Shut the door," he said, seriously, as soon as I entered his room. His eyes glared at me as if he was angry and I watched him shove his hands in the front pockets of his dress pants, several feet away from me. Too far away from me.

I moved to take a step forward but stopped when he shook his head 'no.' This would be quiet, rough sex. My thighs clenched together automatically trying to stave off the feeling of lust bubbling inside me. Hell, it wasn't bubbling, it was growing closer to combusting every single second he stared at me.

I licked my lips instinctively, wanting this. When had I become such a sex fiend? I had him only twenty-four hours ago and yet my body acted like I had spent years on a deserted island, dying for physical attention. That was how Jack made me feel; completely starved and deserted when he wasn't around.

Was that even healthy? I had no idea, but as I watched him raise one eyebrow in warning to me, I didn't even care anymore.

I relaxed my thighs, embarrassed he had noticed through my short black skirt. I received a small smile in approval. It quickly changed back to a lustful grin as we stood there, just watching each other. My nipples hardened under his watch, just waiting for him to tell me what to do next. I knew this look. He wanted complete control from me and knowing that he needed that from me, left me fighting the urge to clench my thighs together again.

"Strip." He spoke as nonchalantly as he did when he told me earlier in the morning to have a good day. His eyes were anything but nonchalant while I slowly kicked my sandals off, and pushed my skirt down. I paused for a minute and let my eyes drag down his entire body. A seductive grin fell across my lips once I kicked my skirt away from him. I stood there, several feet away from what I wanted so badly clad in just a pink silk top and nothing beneath.

A low growl escaped Jack's throat when he saw me bare beneath the skirt. I loved knowing I challenged his self-control. I gave up feeling wanton, and embraced the control I had over him, too. I smirked at the thought and brought my eyes back to his. Then, I slowly, teasingly so, undid the top button.

"Hurry up before I rip your shirt off you," he commanded, a small grin on his lips.

I didn't listen. I took my time knowing that any second he was either going to throw me up against a wall and take me hard, or punish me for teasing him.

Either option sounded good to me.

I slowly separated one more button, thankful for my generous breasts that showed my cleavage now.

That one small glimpse of my skin was just enough for his control to break. Without any warning, Jack's arm was around my waist. He moved as quickly as a panther because in one blink of an eye he was too far away and then in another, I was up against his bedroom door. The cold wood pressed against the length of my body. Jack's entire body pressed up against mine and my already hardened nipples became unbearably uncomfortable.

"Jack …" I moaned. I meant it to be a warning not to actually rip my shirt off. There would be men downstairs when I left and I didn't want to be embarrassed. Instead it came out all breathy and husky and needy. I stopped caring about the shirt when he ground his erection into me.

Jack's mouth met mine forcefully. He swirled his tongue, not even waiting for me to allow him entrance. His hand moved from behind my back and grabbed one of my hands, holding it above my head. I arched into him and rubbed my bare crotch against his pants. I wanted him. Now.

My free hand reached out to his pants and I began fumbling with his zipper and belt. He moaned as I rubbed against his crotch and finally got the belt loose. With one hand, I unbuttoned his pants and slid the zipper down. I smiled into his mouth when I realized he was just as bare beneath his pants as I had been.

Hot damn, I thought as I released his gorgeous cock and fondled it in my hands. It pulsed in my hands and I instantly wondered what it would be like to taste him. What he tasted like. I never enjoyed doing that sort of thing to a man before, but who the hell was I kidding—I had never been with a man before Jack—just boys. And suddenly, I wanted to please him just as much as he always took the time to please me.

I pushed him away from my mouth and felt heat creep to my cheeks as I looked in his eyes and then back down to my hand. A small, embarrassed smile tugged at my lips.

I looked at Jack sheepishly. "I want to taste you," I whispered against his lips.

"Oh fuck, Emma." Jack answered, his voice as ragged as mine.

Without another word, I dropped to my knees in front of Jack and pulled his pants down with me. His cocked jumped right in front of me, and as I removed his pants from his ankles, I longingly took in the sight in front of me. Tentatively, I reached out and licked the tip of his cock and the drop of pre-cum that was sitting right at the tip.

I smiled when I heard a soft thump and looked up to see Jack's forehead resting against the door, one hand bracing himself up and the other softly rubbing my hair at the back of my head.

"Suck me," he ordered roughly. His eyes looked anything but rough though. He almost looked amused that I was down here on my knees in front of him, wanting to do this for him.

I turned my eyes from his before I lost my nerve and settled it back in front of me. I wrapped one hand around the base of his shaft and slowly pulled him into my mouth, sheathing my teeth with my lips. I swirled my tongue around his tip, surprising myself with how much I loved the salty and sweaty taste of him. Jack moaned above me and gripped my head tighter but still allowing me a semblance of control. I knew he was fighting it. He probably wanted to grab my head and take over but he resisted, allowing me this moment to take him how I wanted.

"Emma." That one word spoken with such lust and need moved me into action. I took him further in my mouth, until I swallowed all of him, the tip of his cock hitting the back of my throat. I moaned and hallowed my cheeks in order to relax so I could take all of him more comfortably. My hand went around and cupped his balls, squeezing them firmly and I relished the feel of his hand trembling slightly as it rested on my head.

More quickly, I moved back and forth, sucking and licking him, loving the feel of his fullness in me.

"I can't hold on …" Knowing Jack was closer, I pulled him in further, and harder than I had before just as he thrust his hips into me. He tightened right before his come spurt into my mouth. I kept sucking while Jack moaned and until I had licked every drop from him. It tasted of him; sexy and masculine with a mixture of salt. I couldn't wait to do it again.

Slowly, he pulled out of me and with his hand that was on the back of my head, guided me up so I was standing again; pressed against the door. His hands gently clasped my hips, pulling me toward him before he rested his head right next to my temple.

"That was fucking awesome, Emma." Jack's ragged breath turned me on and I wanted more. "My turn now."

He immediately dropped to his knees. My hands went to his hair when he kissed the inside of both my thighs, slowly blowing a hot breath against my clit as he passed by. With one hand, he moved one leg so my knee rested on his shoulder, opening me further.

"Put the palms of your hands on the wall," he said, looking at me through half-hooded lashes. I couldn't. I needed the grip on his head to keep me standing. I shook my head no. With one hand, he inserted one finger into me, turning it in circles as he pressed in and pulled it out.

One side of his lips twitched up. "Put your hands on the wall, Emma. Or I stop right now." Before I was able to move them, he thrust a second finger into me, causing me to gasp.

He quirked an eyebrow and stilled his fingers, waiting for me to listen.

I did. I didn't want him to stop.

Unfortunately, his phone rang, signaling we had company. I mewled in frustration.

He chuckled softly and kissed my thigh. "Later. I'll take care of you later."

"Jack, please." I begged and I know I sounded whiny, grinding myself against his fingers needing him to finish what he had started. He didn't move and he didn't speak. He did nothing at all as I shamelessly bucked against his fingers, but it wasn't enough. I could see the finish line, my orgasm looming in the distance, growing closer and bubbling more powerfully with every thrust of my hips but still he didn't move his fingers or make any movement to help me.

"I have company downstairs." He smiled wickedly and slowly began to withdraw his fingers. I squeezed them back into me, fighting it.

"Please, Jack. So close …" I was begging and pleading. My face hot with want and my nerves on fire. "… please, finish."

He chuckled once and shook his head. I moved against his fingers again, me watching him, him watching the apex of my thighs and his fingers sliding in and out of me.

I couldn't take it anymore. I took one of my hands off the door and began rubbing my clit. I bucked against his fingers harder right as the tip of my middle finger hit my sweet spot. Jack growled almost instantly.

"It's mine."

I glared at him. "Then finish it." My breath was barely audible, my tongue dry and my throat swollen as I panted for him. Desperately.

His lips twitched into a small smile and his thumb flicked my clit. I moaned, loudly. So close, but so far away. And then my back arched against the wall, as his wet tongue finally … finally began licking me. He sucked and flicked me, while his fingers moved inside me. It was amazing. My entire stomach tightened and my hips moved, and bucked and shifted against his hand and his mouth until I couldn't take it anymore.

I moaned loudly, not caring about the caterers or businessmen downstairs. I didn't care if the entire city of Chicago heard me. Jack pulled his fingers out right as my orgasm hit and grasped both of my thighs, holding me tightly against his mouth as he licked and sucked every drop out of me.

My head dropped against the back of the door and my entire body shook with pleasure.

"Thank you," I sighed.

"For?" He smiled, amused. God, had I really just thanked him for that?

I blushed and then kissed him once he was standing in front of me. "Taking care of me, of course."

His expression grew serious. A slight tightening of the eyes his only tell. "Always."

He nodded once and then reached for his dress shirt. By the time I had my skirt fastened and my sandals back on, Jack was fully dressed and looking more sexy than ever.

How is that possible? When he had his way with me, I looked completely wrecked with swollen lips, flushed skin and matted hair. Jack looked as beautiful as ever.

"I'll go downstairs and let everyone in," I said after I glanced at the clock and saw that it was six o'clock. Time for his dinner party to begin and after I escorted all of his attendees in, I was leaving for a night out with Macy. Although all I wanted to do now was stay in Jack's room and wait for his dinner to be over so he could make good on his promises.

Jack smiled as if he knew what I was thinking. The blush on my cheeks and the lust in my eyes probably gave me away completely.

"Do you have plans for tonight?" he asked me, as he reached for my hand and led me down the hallway.

"Logan's with Penny tonight since I was working late. Macy, Tate and I are going out to see a band we loved in college down in Lincoln Park." It was a gorgeous night out and I loved watching live music. This band, The Nadas, was having a street party. Cheep beer, street dancing, and hotdogs. It sounded like the perfect night when Macy and I made the plans, but now I was so sexually charged I didn't know if I'd be able to enjoy myself.

Jack must have had the same thought because he groaned in frustration and pulled me towards his chest. "I don't want to let you go. I feel like handcuffing you to my bed and not letting you leave until I have my way with you."

My eyes widened in shock and arousal. Please do. Or not.

It creeped me out just thinking about being restrained on his bed … and yet, not. My head spun in a spiral vortex thinking about it. I shook my head to clear my mind. Jack must have thought I was saying no.

Jack chuckled softly. "Maybe another night, then."

I said nothing because I didn't trust myself to speak.

"Go enjoy your night with Macy. We'll just pick up where we left off later. I'll come see you when I'm done here."

I nodded and smiled at the head caterer as we reached the bottom of the stairs. He gave us a knowing smile, as if he knew exactly what Jack was doing with his personal assistant upstairs in his bedroom while they were down there working. I felt my body blush in embarrassment, but Jack simply squeezed my hand in a comforting gesture. In a split second, he squared his shoulders and turned on his professional mask with the grace of a gazelle. God he was sexy.

"Mr. McMillan, a few of your guests arrived while you were busy so I ushered them into your living room and prepared them a drink."

Jack nodded his head in approval. I was thankful the caterer had the wherewithal not to disturb us. "Thank you, Jacob."

Jacob simply nodded his head and returned to the kitchen.

"I'll go make sure everything is okay while you go speak to your guests." I gave him a quick kiss on the cheek, which was outside my rules considering any of his business partners could have seen me, but I couldn't resist.

Jack held me tightly for just a second longer than professionally acceptable before letting me go. I smiled as he walked away, looking as polished as ever.

I took a step towards the kitchen when I heard a knock on the door. Instead of checking on the catering, I turned around to welcome one of Jack's guests.

I opened the door and immediately wished I wouldn't have.

Fuck, me.

Eleven

I felt the color drain immediately from my face.

What in the hell was he doing here? And then I remembered Jack's words from last Friday and I knew. Shit. Marcus was the new attorney.

Of course he was. I never should have brushed the thought so quickly out of my mind. Marcus Whitmore the Third was standing in front of me—his face as pale as the white carpet in Jack's penthouse.

His face showed an equal amount of shock at my presence. I had hoped, every day for the last five and a half years that I would never run into this man again. And here he was, standing at the entrance to Jack's condo.

I covered my arms across my stomach instantly. I wanted to hide my secret from him. The only thing it did was bring attention to the one place I never wanted him to look again. His green eyes dropped immediately to my stomach, almost searing into me. I felt like just by looking at me he knew what I had done.

His hands clenched into fists at his side; full of tension.

We stood there, Marcus still in the doorway, me frozen in the same spot, staring at each other, our silence speaking volumes in and of itself. I don't know how long we stood there, the tension between us flaring so much I thought the space between us might burst into flames.

"You've got to be kidding me." My voice sounded scratchy to my own ears and I felt my fingers ball tightly into fists at my side. There was no way to hide the amount of shock I was experiencing.

"Emma." I wanted to run as soon as my name escaped his lips. I wanted to flee as fast as possible. Pick up Logan and run to some place obscure like Bora Bora and start our lives all over. Unfortunately, my feet became deeply rooted into Jack's perfectly shined wood entryway floor and I couldn't move a single inch. I wasn't even sure I was still breathing.

This couldn't be happening.

He reached for my hand, but I flinched and he stopped himself.

"It's good to see you." His quiet words and recovered look of shock didn't startle me. Marcus was always perfect at playing the role of a smooth player. It's undoubtedly how I got sucked into his vast web of lies to begin with.

"I can't say the same." I eyed him with disgust and pain. His blond hair mirrored Logan's and a small part of me wanted to reach out and mess it up just like I did to his son's. I gasped at my own thought. Marcus was here, looking like a grown-up replica of the boy I gave birth to almost five years ago and he had no idea his son existed.

I watched his eyes flicker back to my abdomen and back to mine.

"You two know each other?" Jack's deeply tense voice finally released my feet from their frozen prison. I jumped and looked to him. Both Marcus and I did. He stood in the entryway, just a few steps behind me, looking every bit the professional CEO he was, but I knew by the tick of his jaw that he was on alert. He felt the tension between us and was clearly confused. And concerned.

I tried to smile when he looked to me, but it was an absolute pathetic attempt at best. I felt like throwing up and knew it showed.

I wanted Jack to comfort me. I needed to feel his arms around me, protecting me from the hell that had just landed in my lap. He must have sensed it because he finally moved closer and wrapped an arm around my waist before turning to Marcus, extending his other hand.

"Come on in." I watched the men shake hands. My self-professed broken man next to me, shaking hands with the man who broke me. I felt bile rise in my throat at the fact that Marcus now worked for Jack and I would be seeing much more of him. I cleared my throat to force the vile taste back down.

Jack's expression was completely professional. Anyone who knew him only on a professional level wouldn't see past the mask of indifference he wore. I saw it. I saw the tension around the outer edges of his eyes and felt it from the hand wrapped firmly around me. His hand pressed tightly into my back. I didn't know how to explain what was happening. Marcus didn't either. But he didn't know the half of it.

Finally, I found my voice. I looked to Marcus and then Jack. "Marcus and I went to school together, Jack."

I tried as hard as I could to look pleasant. To hide the fear and anger that was bubbling just beneath the surface. I was always amazed at how quickly people could shut down their emotions and move on as if nothing bothered them. Jack and Marcus clearly had that gift because they quickly looked to me and then back to each other, looking completely composed and professional.

Marcus looked between us, now inside the condo I spent so much time in and I wanted to kick him out but knew I couldn't.

"Are you two …?" He looked almost sheepish as he started the question, as if his new boss's personal life was any of his business.

Jack's grip tightened around me fractionally. I felt safe instantly. He wouldn't let Marcus hurt me. Then I realized how stupid the thought was. Marcus had the power to hurt me more than anyone in the entire world, he just didn't know it yet.

"She's mine." I finally managed a sincere smile at Jack's possessive tone. Over the last two weeks, it had either driven me to frustration or driven me wild; right now, it was exactly what I needed. It calmed me. Every tightly spun nerve in me began to release and I felt myself leaning into Jack's shoulder, relaxing.

Those few seconds gave me the courage to gather my nerves. I didn't want to screw anything up with Jack and his company. He said that Marcus was important to him, and even though I hated the man in front of me, personally, I knew his connections were invaluable to Jack. I couldn't screw this up.

So I took a deep breath and smiled, pretending that my life wasn't falling apart right in front of me.

"Do you want a drink?" I asked Marcus as politely as possible. At his nod, I moved out of Jack's reach. He scowled at me but I nodded my head towards the kitchen, hoping he'd understand to meet me there.

Marcus followed me to the wet bar where I poured him two fingers of scotch.

"How are you?"

I ignored the question. I refused to look at him afraid I might spit in his face or dump his scotch down the front of him.

Marcus cleared his throat again and I ground my teeth together knowing another question was coming. I could do this. Five minutes and I was out of there and somehow I'd make sure I never came across Marcus again.

"How long have you and Jack been together?"

I snorted and finally looked at Marcus. I resisted the urge to flinch when I saw the left side of lips twitch. It was his one tell that gave away his stress. It was also the exact same thing Logan did when he concentrated on his drawings or building the perfect Lego tower. I hated their similarities. I hated that Logan had anything to do with this man in front of me.

"It's none of your business Marcus." Without giving him the chance to say anything else, I led him into the living room where the other board members congregated. After making sure everyone in the room knew each other, I excused myself.

"Jack will be with you all in just a few minutes."

I turned and left the men without another word and went to the kitchen. Jack was standing hunched over the sink. Even through his suit, I knew that every muscle was tightened as he gripped the counter so hard his knuckles were white. I could practically envision the veins on his forearms sticking out.

"Who is he to you?" He hissed angrily at me. I knew he wasn't angry at me. Most likely he was jealous, but I also knew his lid would flip when I told him.

"He's nothing to me anymore." Except a thorn in my side that was gouging my abdomen and spilling my blood all over the place.

Jack turned to me, inspecting me. He doubted me and I hated it.

I walked toward him until there were only inches between us and placed my hands gently on his biceps. They twitched beneath my hands but slowly relaxed a little bit.

"This is a big night for you and I won't screw it up. Can we please talk about Marcus tomorrow?"

He shook his head adamantly and I knew he was going crazy just imagining my past relationship with Marcus. He hated the very thought of me with another guy before him, and I was about to make him face it head on.

"You need to get out there and have your dinner. Please. I'll tell you tomorrow. It's just …" I turned from him for a second; trying to think of something that could explain it and get us out of this mess and found the right words. The exact words he told me when he refused to talk about his brother. "I don't talk about him. Ever."

He knew what I meant and I hated using it against him, but I was desperate to get out of there. If I told Jack now how I really knew Marcus, I had no doubt he would beat the shit out of him, and that would be the worst thing for both of us. He rubbed the back of his neck and then let out a quiet, frustrated growl before roughly grabbing my hip.

He kissed me roughly, plunging into my mouth without allowing me to catch my breath. Nevertheless, I took it. I threw my arms around him and pulled him closer; taking everything he gave me, letting him mark me as his, even if no one else was watching. He needed the assurance and I gave it willingly.

"You promised me honesty." His eyes flashed in anger and I swallowed slowly, knowing that I did.

"I will Jack. Just not right now." He sighed reluctantly.

"Tomorrow." He growled against my mouth when he finally pulled away, both of us panting desperately.

I nodded. "Tomorrow. And behave tonight."

He walked me to the door, a hand lightly on the small of my back, just as Martin finally arrived.

"Late as always, huh old man?" Martin smiled a wide smile that reached from cheek to cheek as the two men embraced in a typical man-hug; one hand clasped around the other's forearm and two quick pats on the back. I couldn't help but smile at Jack's casual nature around him. It was something rarely seen and I knew he loved the older gentleman in front of us, dressed immaculately in a perfectly tailored suit and a full head of salt and peppered hair.

He smiled down on me adoringly. I loved it. "Hey there, Emma. You staying tonight?"

"No sir, Mr. Crawlson. I'm on my way out right now."

"How many times have I asked you to call me Martin?" He scolded me teasingly.

I smiled cheekily, being around Martin having temporarily erased all the tension. "About as many times as I've called you Mr. Crawlson."

He threw his head back into a full stomach laugh. "Touché." He grinned at Jack. "She's smart, don't let her go."

"I don't plan on it." He smiled at Martin and gestured with his arm for Martin to head into the living room. Leaving the two of us alone for one last minute.

I leaned up and kissed him chastely on the cheek in the doorway. His hands gently cupped my face, holding me stil while he returned the kiss equally soft. He leaned his head against mine and firmly whispered, "Tomorrow."

I simply nodded in understanding. "Good night, Jack."

My legs shook while I walked to the train. Who was I kidding? My entire body was shaking from nerves and shock and anger. I wasn't stupid enough to think I could escape Marcus forever, but that was not how I had ever envisioned seeing him.

I picked up the phone to call Macy and cancel my plans for the night. I just wanted to go home and curl up with Logan in my lap and hold him because I knew, now that Marcus was around, he would want to know what I decided.

"Hey you!" she chirped happily into the phone. The tears I had been holding in suddenly overflowed into one gigantic sob as I waited on the train platform. Thank goodness I lived in a large city full of people used to seeing strange things. No one gave me a second look as I melted down right in front of their eyes. I didn't bother hiding my tears.

"Oh shit. What's wrong?" Macy's happy voice dropped to just above a whisper. I heard her shush Tate in the background. I stood quietly for several minutes while my mind flipped through the images of earlier. Marcus standing in Jack's doorway with a look of shock at seeing me again. His blonde hair and blue eyes made him just as handsome as he had always been, if not slightly better looking now that he had aged some. The immediate tension between him and Jack and Jack's welcome possessiveness of me. The complete and utter shock I felt as I saw him notice me. Shit.

"Marcus." I coughed out his name and finally wiped a tear away. Macy was silent on the other end of the phone and I could picture her face one of confusion. I took a deep breath. "He's a new lawyer at McMillan Holdings. Jack brought him on, one reason being his family connections. He showed up at the dinner tonight." Right after I had Jack's cock deep in my throat. I didn't think Macy needed to know that part. But the very memory sent shivers through me at how happy I had been up until the moment I opened his door.

"Shit."

"Yeah. Pretty much. Listen, I'm going to cancel tonight. I just want to go home and hug Logan and forget this happened and figure out what I'm going to do when I see him again."

"You think you will? See Marcus again?"

I snorted. "You'll probably see him before I do since you work in the building."

Macy sighed heavily. She was my best friend in college. She knew all about Marcus and his dad and the day Marcus Whitmore the Second showed up at my apartment paying me twenty five thousand dollars to 'fix my mistake' as he so eloquently put it. Apparently, it wasn't kosher to be a Senator basing his campaign on conservative family values only to have his son knock up his girlfriend. Offering to get rid of the baby, on the other hand, was totally acceptable. I shuddered at the memory and felt like running to the bathroom to throw up.

"Listen, I'm just not in the mood to party tonight. I'm going to go home and hang out with Logan and try to figure out what in the hell I'm supposed to do now." Like look up plane tickets to Bora Bora.

"Do you want me to ditch Tate and Dean and come hang out? I can bring wine and ice cream."

The wine did sound like a good idea. A case of it. I shook my head and realized she couldn't see me.

"That's okay, Mace. You go out and have fun. I just need to be alone tonight."

I knew she didn't want me to be alone. She had seen me alone after the whole ordeal and watched me struggle to climb out of my insane misery. Fortunately for me, she was a good enough friend to know I meant what I said and she quietly agreed.

I clicked off my phone just as the sound of the 'L' came rushing toward the stop.

Twelve

After sending Penny home early, Logan and I played way too many games of UNO and I let him stay up much later than normal while I simply stared at him. I lost every game of cards and didn't pay a single bit of attention to the movie we watched, or the popcorn and ice cream he ate. Instead, I sat back and drank in every single small detail of my beautiful son. Marcus' son. Their features were undeniably similar with the same curly blond hair and light blue eyes. Even their face shape was similar and even though Logan had never seen his dad, they shared so many similar mannerisms that it sometimes made me catch my breath.

After I read him more books than he requested, I finally put Logan to bed two hours later than normal.

I grabbed a bottle of wine from the fridge and took a swig straight from the bottle—classy girl that I was. I sat alone in my living room, drinking my wine with only one lamp lit for light, and remembered.

I wiped a tear from my eye and nervously held up the test in my hand.

Marcus's eyes widened in shock instantly. "Oh."

"Yeah …" my voice trailed off because I didn't know what to say. I had found out three days before, and waited for the right time to tell Marcus that I was pregnant. We finished our last midterm on Thursday night and I figured now that they were over, and Marcus wasn't stressed from studying this would be a good night. I still felt

incredibly stupid I didn't remember that the antibiotics I had taken for my sinus infection would affect my birth control pills. I was terrified of being twenty-two years old and pregnant. Terrified I would lose the man in front of me who I loved so much. I held my breath waiting for him to answer. I half-expected him to be just as terrified as me and take off running. I wouldn't blame him, I guess. His dad was going to freak out when he found out his son got his girlfriend knocked up. He never thought I was good enough to be involved with a Whitmore … this would be icing on the cake.

I didn't expect a small smile to form on Marcus' lips and then increase until it was so large that it spread from cheek to cheek. He slowly stood up from the table across from me and came around the table, kneeling before me.

"Let's go to Vegas, baby."

My jaw dropped. "We can't go to Vegas, we have school."

"Let's go get married. We'll be a family just like we want, it's just happening sooner than we expected."

I squeezed his hand and laughed nervously. "You can't be serious. We have school … and your dad …"

His smile turned into a serious expression. "Screw my dad, Emma. I'm going to be a dad … and I want to do it right."

I shook my head again, trying to clear the fogginess in front of me. He couldn't be serious. Was he? I closed my eyes tightly. This must be a dream. I was simply dreaming of Marcus being on his knee in front of me telling me he wanted to marry me.

When I opened them, I blinked a few times, shocked Marcus was still on his knees. He looked worried and happy at the same time if that was even possible.

"You can't marry me just because I'm pregnant."

One side of his lips twisted up into a playful smile. "No, but I can marry you because I love you and want to be with you forever, now I just don't have to wait any longer."

I thought of how much I loved Marcus. We had dated for two years already, meeting during our second year of college and instantly became fast friends. That friendship changed at a Halloween party and we began dating after I lost a bet during a game of beer pong and had to go on one date with him. One date changed to two … and soon we were a couple. I loved him. He loved my parents and they loved him. And he loved me. And instead of running, or being angry, he was on his knees in front of me, asking me to rush off to Vegas to get married. It was romantic. I couldn't say no.

Tears pricked the corners of my eyes. I smiled and nodded, not trusting myself to speak.

I threw my arms around him and we fell back to the floor as I fell on Marcus and tipped him off balance.

He moved his hands to my cheeks, holding my face so I was just a few inches from him and smiled at me, happily. "I love you Emma. Marry me."

"Okay, Marcus. I'll marry you."

He pulled me down close to him and my lips touched his. Our kiss was soft and gentle, but soon I felt the familiar stirring in my belly as we moved together on my kitchen floor.

"Damn it!" I shouted and jumped up from my chair. I paced around my small living room feeling like a caged lion, upset at myself for remembering. I didn't want to remember how much I loved Marcus or how wonderful he had been. He left me and allowed his dad to pay me off and I never heard from him again.

I balled my hands into fists as my blood began to boil inside me. Anger was good. I could handle anger; I needed to be angry with him still. I needed to forget.

I jumped at the shrill sound of my cell phone ringing and ran to pick it up. It was Jack. For a second, I thought about ignoring it but I figured he'd probably stalk over here in the middle of the night and show up pounding on my door like he did last week. Best to avoid that again.

"Hey Jack." My words came out slurred and I looked at the wine bottle. It was almost empty. No wonder why I suddenly felt so dizzy.

"Are you drunk, Emma?" He sounded pissed. Just what I needed on top of everything else.

"Probably a little. What do you want, Jack? I said we'd talk tomorrow." I didn't mean to sound bitchy, but I was exhausted and all of a sudden my bed felt like a really good place to be.

"I need to see you. Can I come over?" His voice sounded softer. Maybe he wasn't pissed after all. Maybe, he was just worried about me. It was sweet; him needing me, since I knew Jack needed no one. It made me feel safe and protected. I desperately needed to feel safe.

"Sure …" Before I finished my sentence, I heard a quiet knocking on my door. "Are you at my door?" I didn't bother trying to hide the smile, even though he couldn't see it.

"Answer your door, babe." He hung up, chuckling softly.

Jack looked like shit and I frowned when I saw him. He was wearing jeans and a t-shirt, that fit perfectly, but his eyes were tired and there were lines of stress around his eyes and his forehead that weren't there when I left him several hours ago. His hair was sticking up in all sorts of directions.

Before I could even ask him why, his strong arms picked me up and held me in his arms. I relaxed immediately, wondering how could he make me feel so safe and calm when just a few minutes before I had felt like scratching all the walls like a wild animal. But he did that to me, and I liked it. I needed it.

He buried his head in between my neck and shoulder, kicked the door closed with one foot, and carried me to the couch without saying a word. I just breathed him in because he smelled so good and I needed him as close as possible. Who knew what he would do once he found out my news.

Once he had me curled up like a little doll in his lap with my arms still wrapped tightly around his neck, he slowly brushed my hair out of my face. His eyes were softer, more caring than I had ever seen them.

It suddenly hit me—Jack cared about me. I wasn't just sex or a fling or an employee to him. He really had been telling me the truth that he cared about me and wanted me. I could see it in the depth of his brown eyes as he stared straight into mine. His were filled with worry and fear and I wanted to ease all of his concerns, but I knew that I was just about to add to them.

"Are you okay?" he asked me slowly.

I shook my head. Realizing that Jack truly cared about me was shocking enough on its own accord. I tried to bury my head into his chest to feel safe again because him just asking that question reminded me of all the things I wanted to forget. I didn't want to talk about this now. Actually I didn't want to talk about it ever, but I knew I was going to have to.

The hand that was holding my hair cupped my cheek and pulled me back so I had to look directly at him. "Does Marcus know about Logan?"

My eyes widened in shock. My entire body felt like it was being shocked a thousand lightning bolts and my stomach flip-flopped making me feel nauseous.

"What? How did you know?" I asked breathlessly.

Jack frowned. "It took me awhile. I talked to him over dinner and watched him, trying to figure out why he would upset you so much. The entire time thinking he looked so vaguely familiar. After dinner, Martin said something about you working for me and he did this little twitching thing with his nose. It reminded me exactly of what Logan does when we play video games. He's Logan's dad, isn't he?"

I let out the deepest breath I have ever breathed in my entire life. It wasn't out of relief, either. I removed my arms from around Jack and wiggled out of his arms and off his lap. My body felt all sorts of itchy as I began pacing my room, knowing I was going to have to explain this.

I took another swig from the wine bottle and forcefully set it back down on the table. I wiped my mouth with the back of my hand.

"Fuck … you need to start talking because my mind is spinning in a thousand directions and all I want to do is go kick Marcus's ass right now for putting this look of fear on you."

When I turned to him, he had his elbows resting on his knees but he looked anything but relaxed. His hands were tightened into fists and I could feel the anger rolling off him. I had no doubt he meant every word; consequences be damned.

I ran a shaking hand through my long hair. "Yes, Marcus is Logan's dad. And no—neither of them know."

I felt like I should feel relieved. In all the years I worked for Jack the subject of Logan's dad came up periodically, but all I ever told Jack was that his dad left when I was pregnant. Which was true obviously, but there was so much more to the story and now it was all going to come out. I wanted to feel the weight lifted off my shoulders from hiding something from him, but instead the weight just felt like it was crushing my chest making it hard to breathe.

Jack hissed in a deep breath, his already stressed eyes flashing in anger.

"There's more," I said and sat down on a chair across from Jack, putting as much distant in between us as possible. I rubbed my hands together to make them stop trembling like I had just chugged a pot of coffee but it was no use. I nervously ran my fingers through my hair, before forcing my hands to settle in my lap. Jack's eyes never left mine. He sat there, just watching me—waiting for me to tell him the story.

"Marcus and I dated for two years before I got pregnant. When I finally told him, he asked me to marry him."

Jack's head collapsed into his hands and he rubbed his hair roughly, making it look even more crazy. He muttered an entire string of obscenities so vile it would make a sailor blush. He looked at me, finally, with his lips pursed into a straight white line. "Did you love him?"

I nodded hesitantly.

"Do you still … love him?" He choked out the question as if it brought him physical pain. Hearing the question made me want to throw up all over again.

"God no! Marcus must have told his dad about us, because the night we were supposed to leave for Vegas, Senator Whitmore showed up at my apartment that I shared with Macy at the time. He handed me an envelope filled with cash." I looked away and felt the tears burning the back of my eyes at the memory of the Senator's icy black eyes. He looked at me like I was nothing more than the dirt on the bottom of his shoe and treated me so much worse. "He paid me twenty-five thousand dollars to get an abortion and told me Marcus didn't want to see me anymore."

"Holy fuck. You're kidding me." I thought Jack's head might explode from the news.

I shook my head. "I'm not. I didn't do it obviously … but it wrecked me for a long time, that he just walked away when he promised me so much." I looked at Jack's eyes and wondered what he would think of me for the next part. "I kept the money. For a while I thought of burning it, or returning it. But I was so angry that I decided to say 'screw 'em.' They could afford it and I needed it. I got so sick with morning sickness that I could barely go to school and eventually I dropped out. That was when Macy finally talked to you about me."

"That was a lot of money—you didn't need to come work for me then. Why did you?"

"I put the money in an account and refused to touch it unless it was an emergency. I figured it would at least pay for Logan's school down the road or something, but there wasn't any way in hell I was going to use their money for me."

We sat there quietly for several minutes not saying anything, but my mind was spinning from finally telling Jack about Marcus, and wondering what he thought of me.

Jack finally spoke first. "That explains a lot. Actually."

"What do you mean?"

He shook his head like he was trying to clear it of something. "Marcus isn't close to his dad anymore. He said he has nothing to do with him and hasn't spoken to him in years. It just makes me wonder if it's all connected."

"But you said you wanted his connection to politics—last week, when you told me about the new lawyer you brought on."

He nodded and smiled lightly. "I do … but Marcus has made a name for himself on his own merit. I don't need the connection to the Senator, necessarily. The name on its own is powerful enough." He stared at me with hauntingly dark eyes and I knew he was angry all over again. "And I wouldn't want to be connected to him now after hearing all that shit. Jesus, Emma—he treated you like —"

"I know," I snapped. I didn't want to hear the word whore or trash or whatever vile thing he was going to say. "Will this change anything about Marcus working for you?"

He closed his eyes tightly and when he opened them again, his professional mask of indifference was in place. "You let me worry about Marcus. And let me worry about taking care of you. I won't let them hurt you again … as long as you promise me you don't have feelings for Marcus anymore."

"Can I feel hatred and extreme loathing?"

He chuckled softly. "Sure babe." He stood up slowly and walked towards me. When he reached me, he stuck out his hand. I grabbed it and let him pull me to my feet.

"Let me take you to bed." He looked at me through hooded lashes and suddenly I saw the desire and want he had for me. I wanted him too and it made my head spin. How could I go through so many emotions in one night and then want him so fiercely with one simple look?

We walked to my bedroom and got undressed in complete silence. This wasn't the quiet of Jack needing control, though. He crawled into my bed and I frowned when I noticed he was wearing his boxers.

He laughed at me and pulled me to him, wrapping an arm around me in an intimate gesture. It was comforting and felt strange. I wanted to be held and comforted, but Jack wasn't the comforting kind of guy. I was used to controlling and wanting and predator Jack. This soft side threw me for a loop.

"I need you," I whispered into his ear right before I gently began sucking on his earlobe. I moved down his neck, and smiled against him as I felt his excitement begin to grow and a deep groan escape his throat.

His arm tightened around my waist, but he slowly pulled away.

He rejected me.

"I'm not screwing you tonight. You've had too much to deal with and you drank almost an entire bottle of wine."

I nuzzled my nose against his chest. I needed to forget. I just wanted Jack to make me forget. I moved down just a bit and licked around his nipple, smiling as his body responded to me even if he wouldn't. He might be able to push me away, but he wanted me.

He growled and threw me back down on the bed. I smiled in victory but it was short lived when he stared down at me.

"I'm not fucking you tonight, Emma." He roughly pressed his mouth against me and ground his erection into my crotch. "Now go to bed … we have more shit to talk about tomorrow with all of this and I need to get out of here before Logan wakes up."

I frowned at the thought of him leaving. "I don't want you to leave," I whispered, hoping he wouldn't verbally reject me again.

An eyebrow arched and his sexy smirk appeared. "You're breaking your last rule for me?"

Screw my rules.

I smiled and he rewarded me with another scorching kiss that I felt down to the tips of my toes and moaned as he moved against me one more time. Before I could push back and encourage him further, he rolled off me and pulled my back to his chest. I smiled when I could still feel his erection pressed into the back of me.

"Tease," I muttered.

He brushed his nose against my hair and breathed in lightly. "I'll be here when you wake up."

I woke up feeling all hot and bothered. It took me a minute as my body moved on its own accord to realize why, but then I felt the familiar warmth of Jack's breath against my thighs. I moaned and lifted my head a little bit so I could see him.

"Good morning," he muttered, his lips pressed against me and then flicked his tongue out once, and then again right where I needed him to be.

I tried to smile, but instead I threw my head back and moaned because it felt so good. My body began writhing as I pushed my hips up, closer to Jack's mouth, needing more of him.

"Jack ..." I called out softly, trying to be mindful of Logan in the other room and not wanting to be disturbed from the best wakeup call in all history. "I need you."

Ignoring me, he continued licking and sucking my clit, and I felt my orgasm began to build; that fire quickly turned into a blazing inferno as he thrust two fingers in. He moved so quickly and roughly inside me that it took no time at all until I cried out in ecstasy and felt my inner walls clamp down on him. He slowly crept up my body, keeping his fingers inside me, slowly pulling out every wave of my orgasm.

I pulled him to my mouth and kissed him roughly. Begging him to take me again. I was so satisfied, but still needed more of him. I was terrified last night that he would flip out and end things when I told him about Marcus but instead he stayed, and cared for me and comforted me and I needed to show him how much I appreciated it. How much that simple act meant to me.

I moved my hips against him as he ground into me, now completely naked.

"I need you," I repeated against his mouth, both of us breathless as he pulled away. He moved to get off the bed but I pulled him back to me.

"I'm on birth control, Jack. I don't want you to wear anything." I didn't want any more barriers between the two of us. I wanted to feel him against me and have him feel me, completely, and this was the only way I could think of to show him how much I trusted him.

He groaned ... it sounded like frustration ... and placed his forehead against mine. A light sheen of sweat covered his forehead and I smiled to myself thinking that I in part caused it. "I don't …"

"I know." I moved his hand from my hip to my inner arm and pressed his fingers against my arm firmly so he could feel the tiny little bump. "I got it a year ago and it's good for three. I just want to feel you, Jack. Feel everything."

His mouth came back to mine and I gasped in pleasure immediately.

"You taste so good, Emma. I want you."

His mouth licked against my lips and moved to my jaw, and then my throat. He tasted every single inch of me body as I moved against him, moaning and wanting more.

"You're killing me," I breathed out and arched into him as he slowly licked one of my nipples, his hand playing with the other one until they were both pulled and teased and sucked and licked into bright pink little buds. Every touch shot a blast of pleasure right through me.

He looked up with a wry grin. "But what a way to go."

Then he went back to work, our hands moving quickly all over one another. His hips moved back and he looked at me, questioning whether or not I was sure. But I was; and even if I had lost my nerve, I was so closing to coming that I wouldn't have taken the time to tell him no anyway.

I moaned and moved against him as I felt his bare tip at my entrance.

"Now, Jack," I pleaded.

I moved my hands to his hips and pulled him against me, but he remained still … too strong for me to make him do anything.

He arched an eyebrow and smiled. "Fast or slow?"

"Hard. And now." I panted while glaring at him and still trying to arch into him.

He tsked at me twice, smirking. "I control this Emma."

I fell back against the pillow, exasperated, and oh so close to heaven. He chuckled softly and reached around to the back of my neck with one hand forcing me to look at him. His eyes were almost blacked out and his jaw clenched. He was having a hard time maintaining that control he so desperately claimed he had. I smiled and wiggled against him again, teasing him, and pleading with him at the same time.

He thrust into me, hard, just like I wanted it, hitting the back of me in one smooth move. He groaned and my eyes rolled to the back of my head it felt so good. I bit my lip to keep from crying out, lost between the perfect mix of pleasure and pain. God I loved the way he made me feel.

He lowered his mouth to my ear and pulled out slowly, and thrust himself back in just as hard as he had done before. "Is that hard enough for you?"

I could only groan in response and already felt my walls clenching around him.

He stilled for a moment, and kissed my ear. "Damn this feels so good …" he whispered and began to move again, slowly. It felt tender and calm, like we had all day to spend in bed doing nothing except exploring each other.

Jack pulled back, rested his elbows next to me and cupped my face with his hands. I couldn't have looked away if I wanted to. And I saw it in his eyes, as he slowly moved against me, feeling every ridge of his thick cock pulse inside of me. This wasn't fucking to him; or screwing me … this was making love. The knowledge, coupled with the amazing sensations inside me, threw me over the edge. I looked straight at him, keeping my eyes on him the entire time as I let out my cries of ecstasy while my body squeezed him further inside and my hips bucked against him.

His mouth dropped and he thrust into me one last time, following me over the edge.

It was the best sex of my entire life.

He slowly rolled off me and brushed a few loose strands away from my face as I smiled lazily at him. I felt completely sated.

I felt happy. Fulfilled. Complete.

"That was amazing," he said softly against my cheek, his lips just barely touching mine.

I turned so I was facing him, my free hand softly outlining the muscles on his arms and chest. I ran it up his body until I was rubbing my hand along the light covering of prickly hair on his cheeks. "You are amazing."

"So, not to totally kill the mood here, but what do you think you're going to do about Marcus?" He arched any eyebrow. "Now that you've seen him, are you going to tell him about Logan?"

It totally killed the mood.

Thirteen

His question was like a glass of cold water—a very large glass—or a pitcher filled with ice cubes, dumped all over me leaving me a shivering pile of mess on the floor. I heaved a deep breath in frustration that not only was my perfect after-sex moment ruined; it was a question I absolutely didn't want to answer. Mostly because I had no idea *how* to answer it.

I swung my legs over the side of the bed and sat up, throwing my face into my hands. I rubbed my face against the palm of my hands when I felt Jack move and his body come and sit next to me.

"I don't know, Jack. I think in some naïve little world I live in, I was expecting him to just disappear completely."

I stood abruptly and looked at him. "I need coffee if we're going to talk about this. Do you want some too?"

"I'm going to take a shower first if that's all right. But Emma, I want you to think about something." At my raised eyebrows, he continued. "I know what it's like to be without a dad. Even if the dad sucks, I wouldn't wish that on anyone; especially Logan."

He grabbed his clothes and walked into the bathroom, shutting the door quietly. I stood there for several minutes staring at the door he walked through with my jaw hanging wide open. Well … what in the hell was I supposed to say to that?

Ten minutes later, Jack came out of the bedroom looking positively perfect. He poured himself a cup of coffee, grabbed a bagel off my counter and took a huge bite once he joined me at the table.

I cupped my coffee mug and blew gently. It was all for show. I'd been staring at the full cup ever since I took my first sip ten minutes ago.

"I think you're right," I said regretfully.

Jack nodded as if he knew I would say that all along. "It's a habit."

"Shut up. This isn't funny."

He winked at me and took another huge bite of the bagel, his voice sounding muffled when he spoke. "It's a little funny."

"Well at least one of us can have some fun today," I muttered and then took another sip of my coffee.

"Here's what you need to understand." Jack's eyes changed to a dark brown and his lips pulled into a tight smile. I watched as he set his coffee down and gingerly clasped his hands together on the table. I imagined this was very much the same posture he took when he was about to enter into a hostile takeover of some corporation. He was all business again, but his expression was fierce as he steeled his gaze at me.

"You're mine. And I protect what's mine. I'm going to handle Marcus working for me, and together—you and me are going to handle the shit about him being Logan's dad. But I promise you this; I will take care of you, and I will keep you safe. And if he steps off the very thin line we're going to give him to prove that he's not the douchebag dumbass he used to be, then his ass is mine." He quirked an eyebrow at me. "You got me?"

Yeah … wow … I got him … there were just so many things wrong with that statement. And yet, it all sounded so good. I was his to protect and keep safe and take care.

Not a problem.

It was the best thing I had heard in weeks … possibly years … and I instantly wanted to cling to the small amount of hope he gave me, that everything was going to be just fine.

I didn't want to waste the time arguing about the wrongness of his possessiveness because the rest of it felt so perfect, so I nodded and smiled sheepishly.

His.

He was right. I absolutely, positively belonged to him.

When Jack was done with his coffee, he stood up and scribbled something down on his business card. I cringed when he handed it to me.

"That's his number. Call him when you're ready; but if it's okay, I'd like to be there with you."

I stood up and gave him a quick kiss. "For someone who was sure they'd fuck up a relationship, you're pretty good at it."

He rewarded me with a kiss much less quick than the one I dished out, and a smile that showed his perfectly white teeth.

"Only for you." He ran his hand through my hair gently and smiled down at me. "I've got some things to take care of this morning. Talk to you later?"

I walked him out and once the door shut behind me, I sat down on the table and stared at the card. My pulse raced just thinking about calling Marcus and telling him about Logan. Would he even want anything to do with Logan? He was so quick to walk away years ago, maybe he wouldn't claim him. I wondered what hurt more—the fear of Marcus wanting to know Logan, or the fear he wouldn't?

Since Jack's business card wasn't going to give me any answers, I threw it on the counter and went to take a shower to get ready before Logan crawled out of bed.

Almost two weeks went by and neither Jack nor I broached the subject of Marcus. He had mentioned his name, regrettably, in passing a few times when it involved work, but Jack stayed true to his word and didn't say anything about me telling him about Logan.

I appreciated the space. I needed it.

The truth was, as soon as Jack told me he thought Logan deserved to know his dad, I agreed to tell Marcus. I was just doing a really good job at avoiding the 'when' of the whole thing.

I had other things on my mind.

Like the fact that I was in a limo, on my way to the Children's Charity Ball with Jack and it was officially our third date.

I knew I shouldn't have cared.

I was falling in love with Jack, avoiding dealing with Marcus out of fear of rejection—again, and still a bit afraid that Jack was still going to leave me. The last one wasn't a big deal until tonight when I stepped into the limo and then the seriousness of the night and the fact that I knew I was going to be seeing Marcus at the ball came crashing down on me.

I was about to see the first man who tore my heart out of my chest. It took years to recover from the betrayal. I wanted to wrap myself in bubble wrap and steel to prevent my heart from being broken because after knowing Jack for so many years, and being 'with' him for the last month, he sat poised to be able to do the exact same thing to me all over again.

I hated not being able to trust him fully. Would I even be thinking these things right now if Marcus hadn't walked back into my life?

It was a question I couldn't answer.

What I did realize earlier today was that Logan's birthday was coming up in two weeks. What better present could I give him than his dad? I thought of wrapping Marcus up in a large air-tight box with a big red bow and snorted.

"Where are you?"

I looked away from my window and down at Jack's hand resting firmly just above my knee, one eyebrow raised in question at the blank look on my face. I immediately felt the warmth from his hand spread to my legs, and then everywhere else on my body. I still couldn't believe how a simple touch from him could instantly turn me on. I felt the heat rise to my cheeks and I looked at him and smiled.

"Are you going to tell me what's wrong?" he asked me cautiously.

A breath left my mouth in an unattractive manner. What's wrong? Only everything. And yet, Jack's simple touch had the ability to calm me. Should I even be concerned about it being our third date? He was probably going to tell me to tap my shit down, or screw me senseless.

Which really—sounded okay to me. Maybe I could use the stress relief.

"You've been quieter than normal all night. Tell me."

I looked out the window, needing to take my eyes off him in order to gain a semblance of control. My bottom lip started quivering, betraying me instantly and I knew he saw it when his hand left my thigh and gently cupped my chin between his thumb and index finger. He turned my chin to him slowly, until I had no other choice but to stare directly into his brown eyes.

"Tell me." His voice was rougher than before.

"It's our third date tonight."

"And?" A slight twinkle of amusement flashed in his eyes before he shuttered it. I was instantly embarrassed. He looked like he had no clue what I was trying to say.

I sighed. My chest heaved out and in quickly, just once. I rubbed my fingers together trying to stop them from shaking in my lap.

"You always end things after the third date." My words came out just above a whisper. His hand left mine immediately and fell to his lap, like I had shocked him.

I looked away from him, terrified of what he was going to say. I wondered if he would stop the limo and just have me leave right then.

"Look at me."

I listened immediately because when he spoke to me in the dark and sexy voice that he usually reserved for the bedroom I had no other choice but to obey. I was just shocked that he was using it now when I was clearly so upset.

"You think that's what is happening here?"

"I've known you for five years …"

"And I've wanted you for five years."

His admission startled me. I mean, he had told me this before, but somehow in this moment, it sounded … heavier. More important, maybe.

"What?" I asked, just barely breathing.

He smiled widely at my bemused expression.

"Would it help if I told you I was falling madly in love with you?" Holy shit. Jack looked nervous. I couldn't tell if he was messing with me to get me to smile—which worked, by the way—or totally serious. Jack didn't let anyone close enough to love them; or care about, really. But yet, he had gotten close to me. He had broken all his dating rules for me and Logan and I instantly felt like a shmuck for bringing this up now.

"Are you?"

His lips twitched a bit into a smile but then he frowned- like maybe he wasn't so sure himself what he was feeling.

"I don't love anyone, Emma," he said and my heart dropped to my stomach. Without another word, he grabbed my hips and flipped me around so I was no longer sitting next to him, but straddling him. Thankfully, my floor length black silk gown had two slits cut up to the mid-thigh or the outrageously expensive thing would have ripped. The movement was so quick it caught me off guard and a gasp left my lips. Jack's eyes darkened as he looked at my slightly opened mouth.

I blushed as I thought of all the things I'd like to do with my open mouth.

He made a face and then closed his eyes shut. When he opened them again, his expression was softer and my body warmed all over. "I think I could make an exception for you. And Logan."

I think that was the closest expression to being in love with me I was going to get. But I had to make sure.

"What are you saying, Jack?"

He sighed heavily before grabbing my hips and pulling me toward him. I went willingly with a small little smile on my lips.

"I think that what I feel for you scares the shit out of me, and if it's love, then I have no fucking idea why people choose to do it willingly."

I could have been offended, but I saw a teasing smirk on his lips. This was Jack. The Jack who claimed I caused him to be out of control and all sorts of crazy. If that was his idea for love—I was all for it, because I often felt the same about him.

Before I could give him any shit, or change the subject, he continued. "For the first time in my life I find myself wanting to leave work early just to see you. I walk by stores and want to pick out crap for you and Logan." I rolled my eyes at crap, but wisely shut my mouth. "When you're not around, you're all I think about. When you're in my home—I never want you to go. This shit is all new to me and it's confusing as hell most of the time, but the rest of the time I just fucking love it."

Well hell. What's a girl supposed to say to that?

Easy. Nothing. I answered Jack in the only way I knew he'd understand completely.

I slowly began hiking up the bottom of my gown that kept me separated from him and leaned back. I quickly pulled his dress shirt out of his pants and unbuckled his belt. He lifted his hips—and me at the same time, while my shaking fingers nervously undid the button and zipper on his pants so I could pull them down.

I pulled away from the kiss and stared down at his enormous erection, standing straight up, waiting for me. I licked my lips in anticipation.

And then noticed he wasn't wearing any underwear.

I smiled. "Commando?"

I watched his breathing become shallow as he looked down at his own erection standing at attention between us. Without speaking, his hand went under my dress and slowly dragged up my thigh. I shivered in anticipation. All my nerves immediately left as his hand travelled further up my thigh.

He grinned victoriously and immediately plunged two fingers deep inside me.

"Ah!" I cried out loudly and sank into him. I shifted against him, trying to move against his fingers but his other hand grasped my hip, restraining any movement. I peeled back from his chest slowly and looked down on him through half-opened eyes.

"I'm sorry for doubting you," I whispered as I laid my head against his temple.

He shook his head at the same time he moved his hand against my clit. I moaned and tried to shift against him but his hand on my hip prevented me reaching the spot where I knew I would find the most pleasure. I groaned in frustration as his eyes darkened in front of me. His lips pursed.

"I'm going to bury myself in you until you forget that you ever doubted for a single second that I don't want you for more than three fucking meaningless dates."

I didn't have any time to consider what he said because his mouth was on mine, moving ferociously against mine. I opened immediately, allowing him to plunder me with this tongue. His plan was working. He made me forget my doubts, my fears … my name. His hand ground against my sweet spot roughly and his fingers moved inside me roughly I was almost ready to come. Never in my life could anyone turn me on so quickly

"You want it, don't you?" He asked me roughly and I saw the desire in his eyes. I couldn't take my eyes off his gorgeous cock. I wrapped one hand around the base firmly and pulled up slowly, putting the exact amount of pressure on the underside that I knew drove him wild. I rubbed the drop of pre-cum gently over the tip and smiled as I watched his perfect abdomen muscles tighten.

He bit into my neck causing the perfect amount of pain and pleasure while he licked me to soothe the pain away. His fingers pressed into my pussy again. I felt my insides pulsating around his fingers and knew I was just a few more shifts away from exploding all over him.

I moaned when his hand moved against me again and my stomach clenched. I wanted that release. I needed it. He leaned in and kissed me roughly, taking away my every breath and worry before quickly moving away and resting his head against the back of the headrest. An evil grin spread across his lips and I cried out in sorrow when his fingers abruptly pulled from me. I bit my tongue as I watched him lick my cream off them.

"Yes. I want you."

"I want you, too. I've wanted you for a really long time." He grabbed both hips firmly and thrust me right down over his erection. I gasped loudly as he filled me completely.

"You're so tight," he moaned into me and shifted his hips up. I braced myself with both hands on each side of the back of his chair next to his head. I couldn't move my hips. I couldn't do anything except take everything he gave me and I wanted it. I wanted him like I had never wanted anything more in my life.

He thrust into me harder and I smiled.

"You're mine," he growled against my lips. "I promise you. I will protect and care for you and Logan as long as you let me."

Sounded fan-fucking-tastic to me. He moved against me and as my orgasm grew closer, all worry about Jack and Marcus left me. All I could think about was the amazing man in front of me who wanted my son and me.

I cried out and collapsed against his chest. I came so quick and hard I thought my heart was going to explode but Jack kept pounding into me, over and over again and another orgasm quickly began to bloom in me.

One of his hands cupped my cheek. He lifted my face so I was inches from his and the lighter grip on my hip allowed me to move against him.

"I fucking love you Emma. I know it's fast and crazy and there's a whole load of shit we have to deal with, but you need to know that."

I couldn't have taken my eyes off of him if I tried. The way he stared at me, while I moved against him left me feeling lightheaded and dizzy.

With one more fierce lift of his hips, I found my release in him as Jack clenched his jaw and pulled me down hard on top him. My clit hit the perfect spot on his groin and we released together, our eyes locked on one another.

Fourteen

"Wha … what did you say to me?"

"You heard me," Jack said and brought his lips to mine, gently. They felt like a soothing feather against my swollen lips. "I love you."

Holy shit. He did say it. I wasn't imagining it.

"That's not exactly what you said." My lips twitched in humor. I wanted to throw my arms around him and make him take the limo back home and I wanted to laugh. And then I wanted to throw up. Jack McMillan, the man who doesn't get close to anyone, loved me.

Holy shit. Again.

He scowled. "I said I fucking love you. And you're starting to piss me off with that look full of all sorts of crazy you're giving me right now."

"Well, that sounds more like you," I said and leaned in to kiss him again, both of us wearing small smiles.

"You drive me crazy, you know this right?"

I hmmed against his lips and kissed him again. "I'm in shock. I don't know if I know what to say right now."

"How about you love me too?"

I pulled my eyes to him and saw him in a way I never had before. This man—the financial genius—looked more innocent and like a needy little boy than I had ever seen anyone in my life look before. He was vulnerable before me. Baring his heart and soul in a way he had probably never done before. He could be an arrogant asshole. He could command me to do things my body instantly did without any thought. And he promised to protect me and Logan. We were his.

And he was mine.

I lusted after him for two years. I knew him better than almost anyone, probably. And there wasn't a single thing I didn't love about this man in front of me.

I cupped his cheeks softly with my small hands and rubbed them against his soft stubble. I leaned in a kissed both of his cheeks and then his jaw, before moving to his mouth.

He sat still, letting me move against him and kiss him tenderly. He seemed frozen in time as if the intimacy and tenderness of a woman to him was unexperienced.

"I love you," I whispered into his ear as I leaned forward. "There isn't a single thing about you I don't love."

It wasn't the most romantic setting; straddling him in the back of a limo while we professed our love to one another. But the instant his lips touched mine, I knew it was perfect. It was how Jack did everything with me. I pictured him setting up spreadsheets and graphs and commanding a boardroom and creating a pro and con list of reasons why and why not to love me. And then I pictured him seeing me in a doorway and throwing all of it on the floor in a mad second of craziness, like he always said he felt around me.

It was us. Messy and wild and I wouldn't have it any other way.

Slowly, the car pulled to a stop and Jack pressed the intercom button next to him. "Give us a minute before opening the door," he told his driver, Shane.

I blushed a thousand shades of pink as I looked down between us.

Slowly, I climbed off him and adjusted my dress while he tucked everything back into his tuxedo pants.

He took my hand firmly and steeled his dark brown eyes on me. "I want you to know before we go in there that I mean every word. I didn't say this because of Marcus or whatever bullshit we may face tonight." I took a deep breath before he continued. "You and Logan are my world and I love you both. I will do anything to protect you and keep you both safe. You get me?"

I got him. I wiped away a tear and gently pressed a finger underneath my eyes to prevent my mascara from running.

He not only loved me, but he loved Logan. That alone was more powerful and emotional than anything he could have just said to me.

I couldn't speak for fear of more tears so I simply nodded and took in Jack's eyes as he smiled at me. His dimple appeared on his left cheek. I leaned forward and licked it.

"I've always wanted to do that," I said with a smile.

Jack threw his head back, laughing. "Get out of the car, Emma."

I had never attended a charity ball before in my life. And as I walked into the ballroom at the Omni Hotel, I hoped I never had to attend one again. This wasn't my life. This was Macy or Tate's, and obviously Jack's. I knew for a fact Macy had her cotillion in a hotel just like this when she was a teenager and introduced to Chicago's elite society.

The thought made me snicker as we crossed the threshold into the hotel and the most extravagant setting I'd ever seen. Crystal chandeliers dripped everywhere. Lights sparkled all over the place as if we'd stepped out of the city and into heaven with streets paved with gold. I was walking on clouds and living in the stars at that exact moment. Women drenched in diamonds and emeralds and jewels I couldn't place walked by us with the dignity of royalty and their men looked just as regal.

I had never felt so homely. Odd considering Macy picked out my dress and on the outside, I probably looked like I fit right in. Inside I was a quivering pool of insecurity.

Jack gripped my elbow tighter and pulled me to him. "You are the most beautiful woman in the room tonight."

I looked up at him and smiled as he looked down on me. I wondered if anyone could see our swollen lips or our mussed up hair. Hopefully not.

"I'm good," I whispered back and smiled even though I felt my lips tremble slightly and my knees felt like they could give out at any second.

Jack nodded and removed his arm from my elbow and wrapped it around my waist, securing me to him. "Let's go find Martin and Marissa and get you a drink."

Best plan I had heard all night. I followed Jack as he led me through the room. I didn't miss the looks from the women with one eyebrow raised and pursed lips as they perused me on his arm or the way they flicked their hair and their mouths dropped slightly as they looked at him. They were all wondering what in the hell I was doing with Jack McMillan.

It was, ironically, the first time I had wondered the same thing.

By the time we reached Martin's table, Jack's arm around my waist was tighter and my entire body was humming with nervous energy. I expected any minute for Jack to furrow his brows at me and tell me to tap my shit down. But he didn't, and I was oddly disappointed. Strange that that one sentence from him could be so calming.

"There's my favorite girl." Martin affectionately leaned in and gave me a kiss on the cheek.

"Good evening, Mr. Crawlson," I said softly and turned to his wife when he let me go. "Mrs. Crawlson."

"Emma," Martin scolded me and I wrinkled my nose.

"Fine. Martin and Marissa, it's lovely to see you both."

"Finally!" Martin exclaimed with an energetic clap of his hands, "Five years and you've finally called us by our names." Jack chuckled softly and Marissa lovingly held her husband's elbow.

"It won't become a habit," I assured him with a large genuine smile. I took the champagne that Jack offered from a nearby waiter and soaked in the room.

We spoke with the Crawlson's and a few of Jack's business associates and competitors until it was time for our sit down dinner. I felt more comfortable in the company at the table while I listened mostly to the men discuss business and the women discuss designers and fashion. I wasn't completely ignorant when it came to fashion. Macy had been my best friend long enough that I was able to hold my conversation, but I spent most of the night distracted—looking for Marcus, who I knew was there somewhere.

I was waiting for the other shoe to drop, for my moment to tell him about Logan and potentially, when my life would change.

I must have tensed up because Jack pulled me closer and stopped his discussion with his CFO and turned to me, concern marring his features.

"You okay?" he asked me as he leaned down and brushed his lips against my ear. To anyone else, it seemed like a typical whispered conversation, but that one simple touch—of his breath so close to me - sent chills down my spine. Jack laughed softly and flicked his tongue out barely grazing my earlobe. "Later, babe. I promise. Now tell me what's wrong."

I shook my head to clear my thoughts, and then tensed completely when I saw him. Marcus looked just as handsome as he did when we were younger as he approached us with his perfectly fitted tuxedo. He was dateless, and stopped to shake a few hands. I grimaced when I saw him smile. His dad, the effervescent politician, used the same manufactured smile.

I hated it.

Anger and disappointment rose in me and I tightened my shoulders. I felt the pain in the palm of my hands and looked down to realize I was clenching my fists tightly together. I had never wanted to hit anyone in my entire life; but at that moment, when I saw that slick smile, I wanted to push it off his face and scream all sorts of obscenities at him. I wanted to embarrass Marcus like he had embarrassed me.

I wanted him to feel the pain I felt when I opened the door the night we were supposed to elope only to see his father standing in front of me with that same damn smile, his eyes filled with malice, and his hands filled with a large padded envelope.

I took a deep breath and looked to Jack. His jaw was tense and I noticed his hand on my hip was holding me so tightly he might actually bruise me.

"I don't know if I can do this, Jack." I looked at him with frightened eyes but rolled my shoulders back, standing as straight as I could trying to mask my fear. I refused to let Marcus see how much he affected me. I had to get control of myself before my fantasies of pain and revenge played out in a room full of some of the most prominent members of Chicago's society.

Jack turned me to him so my back was to Marcus and placed his hands firmly on my shoulders. He slowly brought his eyes from Marcus down to me and smiled. It took a minute for the tension to leave, but slowly I watched the affection he felt for me fill his eyes.

It helped immensely. I needed the reminder I wasn't alone and that Jack was here to support me with this.

"We'll tell him after dinner so we can leave immediately if you need to."

My bottom lip trembled and tears filled my eyes. "I can't, Jack."

He softly brought his hands up to my neck and laced them together behind me. His thumbs came up and brushed just under my chin. I loved when he held me like this. His hands were large and strong and I loved how the roughness of his hands rubbed against my soft skin.

"I won't let him hurt you," he said softly and leaned in to kiss my escaped tear away from my left cheek.

I knew I needed to do this. Jack was right—and had been for weeks. Marcus deserved to know the truth and even if I didn't want anything to do with him, Logan had the right to know his father. And I had Jack standing in front of me, keeping me safe. He would do whatever he could to keep me from being ruined by this.

I nodded and noticed that it was time to sit down to eat.

"I just need a few minutes. I'm going to go to the bathroom to freshen up a little bit, okay?"

Jack released his hands but kept his gaze on me. "Want me to come with you?"

With one hand resting on his elbow I nodded towards our table. "It's fine. I'll be back in a little bit and then we can enjoy our food."

I'm pretty sure I wouldn't eat a single thing of the delicious food that we'd be served but it seemed to comfort Jack, and that was all I needed to do.

As I walked away to the restroom, I saw Marcus follow me out of the corner of my eye. I focused on the artwork in front of me, some portrait of a woman with a tortured expression and refused to look at him; too afraid that if I did my expression would mirror the artwork.

After taking a few minutes to rub cold water on the insides of my wrists and dot my neck with paper towels, I was finally able to take a deep breath and relax. I walked through the door of the women's restroom, only to gasp in fear when an icy cold hand gripped my arm.

Before I knew what was happening, my back hit a wall, and my attacker's forearm pushed against my chest, keeping me pinned in place. I gasped loudly, and waved my head around, trying to see if anyone saw what just happened to me. It was then I recognized the evil, slimy looking pair of steel-blue eyes. They haunted my dreams for months, years even after Marcus left. There were a few more lines around the eyes now, and my attacker's hair had more silver in it; but other than that, he looked the same. I resisted the urge to spit in his face.

"Senator," I spit out. I would not allow this man to scare me again. Even though every nerve ending in my body was sparking with fear.

He leaned in to my ear making me cringe in disgust. He smelled like scotch, just like always. "I see you've moved on to whoring around with even more successful men now. I should applaud your good taste."

"You don't know shit."

He tsked at me twice. "That's not how a lady speaks. Although I suppose with how easy you spread your legs for the rich, you're not much of a lady are you."

"Get off me, Senator, before you regret it."

He pushed his arm into me and then took one step back. We were still standing much too close for a casual conversation if anyone should walk down the hall and see us, but at least I was able to breathe again.

"What do you want?" I asked with ragged breaths. I still felt the pressure of his arm against me and rubbed it tenderly, hoping it wouldn't bruise.

"You will let Marcus see his son. And me." I paled instantly.

"You … you know?" I asked as I felt all the blood rush from my head and straight down to my toes. It may have even seeped directly into the plush carpeting beneath my feet. Marcus's dad knew I had a son.

He scoffed. "You didn't think I was going to give you that money and then just trust you'd do the right thing, did you? I've watched you and Logan occasionally for years, in order to anticipate you reaching out to Marcus. It's impressive, really, that you never caved. I appreciate your tenacity."

He knew Logan's name. He fucking new my kid's name. I wanted to throw up. I wanted to bash his skull in and run away to Bora Bora like I did the night Marcus showed up at Jack's penthouse. But this … Senator Whitmore knowing the details and knowing he'd actually *watched* us made my skin scrawl. I felt like I had a colony of ants crawling up my entire body, itching me and fighting for entrance into every pore of my body. I fought the urge to scratch my arms and legs and faced him bravely.

Five years ago, he had walked into my apartment and demanded I follow his rules.

I wouldn't bow to this asshole ever again.

"You're incredible. You try to pay me off to get rid of, what did you call it, a 'mistake?' And now you think you can demand to see him? Get over yourself. You'll never lay a single finger on my son."

I turned to walk away from him, but his voice stopped me.

"Do you really think Jack McMillan is still going to want you when your picture is splayed all over the paper as a whore, someone willing to spread her legs for her employer? He'll be ruined. And it will be your fault."

He took a deep breath, brushed his hands roughly down the front of his suit and continued, completely composed, ever the politician. His smug grin was evil.

"I should have followed up before and made sure you got rid of it. That was my mistake, letting it get this far, but this time I'll make sure you do what you're told. That boy of yours is a Whitmore and I'll make sure he's raised like one even if his mom's a whore." His venomous words were spat so harshly I recoiled, wanting to get as far away from him as possible, but what he said next—with a look of evil joy—was so much worse.

"Do you realize that I can find a judge to give me grandparental rights? They exist, you know … and no one in Chicago, or Illinois for that matter, would deny me the right to see my grandson."

My stomach rolled and I turned to the bathroom.

"Get away from her," a familiar voice snapped from the other end of the hall.

Fifteen

I had never been so relieved to hear Marcus' voice. In the recent weeks just hearing his name made me cringe, but tonight those four words washed away all the prickly feelings on my skin.

I hated it. But I was glad to see him, walking down the hall with his hands tightened into fists at his sides.

I looked to him and his dad, feeling the thick tension between the two of them. When Marcus reached us, they squared off, facing each other like two men in a boxing ring. I instantly wanted to know why they seemed to hate each other so much. Marcus was always the perfect son, wanting to please his father, hesitant to do anything to risk sullying the family name. Even at the time, I knew that was why Marcus never contacted me again. He walked away from me because his dad told him too. I wondered now, briefly, if he regretted it.

But here he stood, ready to battle his dad on my behalf, five and a half years too late.

Marcus didn't buy his dad's perfectly groomed, and completely false smile. "Hello son."

I watched Marcus cringe at the word and again my curiosity peaked, but now was clearly not the time to interrupt.

"Stay away from her," he spit out again, his hands tightening even further at his sides.

His father looked from him to me, completely ignoring his son's comment. "You'll make the right call. I know you will."

"She won't do anything you tell her to do. And you'll leave her alone."

The Senator walked away without another word, leaving Marcus breathing heavily, his hands stretching out as if to relax. I stood there stunned, wondering what in the hell just happened between the two of them.

Without warning, he turned to me as if he just remembered I was there. "Come on, I'll take you to Jack."

His voice was kind and gentle. I was wary, but too shaken by the entire experience to deny him when he lightly held onto my elbow and began walking back towards the ballroom.

"I'm not the same guy you knew, Emma." His eyes stayed focused straight ahead, but his words were softly spoken.

"You seem to hate your dad."

He nodded once. "I haven't spoken to him in years. At least, not unless I've absolutely had to."

He turned to me, and dropped his hand from my elbow when we reached the large room. His hands went to his pockets and he shifted uncomfortably. "I have a lot to explain to you, a lot to make amends for."

He rubbed his hand through his hair and frowned.

"I know all about the money my dad gave you," he spoke so quietly I was almost afraid I misheard him, but at the same time, I felt the ants begin to crawl all over again. I couldn't talk about this here with him, not without Jack. I turned my head to the right to find my table. As if he knew I was looking for him, Jack's eyes locked with mine immediately and I saw panic fill his eyes when he saw me standing next to Marcus.

I breathed deeply and relaxed as Jack excused himself from the table and began heading our way.

I lightly put my hand on Marcus's elbow and pulled him back into the hallway and away from any eyes in the ballroom.

Marcus continued, "I want you to know that I found out the truth of what he said and did to you just over a year ago. I thought you left me. The night I was getting ready to pick you up, my dad showed up and told me you had called him and asked him for money."

"What?" I asked, shocked. Although I shouldn't be. "He told me you decided you didn't want the baby."

Marcus nodded and I instantly felt Jack's presence next to me.

I didn't need to turn to him to be comforted. He knew what I wanted as he wrapped an arm around me. Marcus looked to Jack, nodded once and then looked back to me.

"I know. We got into a bad argument over a year ago when my mom … when she died. He was drunk and admitted everything he did to us all those years ago. I wanted to call you and apologize then, but I just couldn't."

He sighed heavily and turned away from me. I remember hearing about his mom's death in the news. At the time, I didn't want to care about her death at all. Unfortunately, she had been fairly decent to me in the years Marcus and I were together and I was saddened to hear about her dying of cancer. I noticed he struggled with the last word and my interest peaked at what happened to his mom. Whatever it was; it was not pretty.

He turned away from me slightly. It was that moment, where I was overcome with how completely similar Logan looked like him. His nose twitched slightly and I almost gasped out loud. It simply reminded me that he hadn't spent a single day around his son and yet they shared the same mannerisms.

"I was sorry to hear about your mom. She was a nice woman," I said softly, offering whatever pathetic condolences I could give. I wasn't shocked at all about what he said about his dad. Based on all the information I had just found out, I realized Marcus's dad could do anything he wanted and probably get away with it.

Marcus scoffed and turned to me, his eyes a steely, angry blue. Jack's hand tightened on my waist and he pulled me back from Marcus. I apparently wasn't the only one who saw his sudden change to anger. "My mom didn't die of cancer, Emma. She killed herself when she finally realized how many times my dad had cheated on her."

I gasped. Behind me, I heard Jack inhale a breath in between his teeth.

"Regardless of the shit with my mom and dad, I want you to know I'm sorry." That got me. Marcus never apologized for anything. Ever. In his father's mind an apology was a sign of weakness.

I arched an eyebrow saying nothing, but leaned back into Jack for help to keep me standing.

"I have a lot to apologize to you for. I've wanted to call you and explain … and then my mom …" he paused, pinched his eyes shut and rubbed a closed fist across his forehead. When he opened his eyes again, his hands fell to his sides. "I was an asshole. I was immature and unable to stand up for what I wanted and what I thought was right, and I'm so incredibly sorry for running and trusting my dad at all."

"This apology is about five and a half years too late."

"I know. I know it is." He lowered his eyes briefly before looking back to me. When he did, he looked so much like the young twenty-year old boy I knew years ago during my second year of college. His hair was a little shorter now, shaggy but still professional enough, and his five o'clock shadow was slightly scruffier than it was when he was younger. His eyes held a weight in them, a pain that wasn't there when I knew him before, but he was still just as handsome, if not more.

Marcus Whitmore drew attention from every female he passed when we were at DePaul. I had a feeling that hadn't changed at all as his eyes pierced mine, pleading with me silently.

I saw a man standing in front of me and not the rich, albeit completely beautiful and gorgeous, boy I used to know.

Marcus had grown up. I just didn't know if I could trust him.

But it wasn't up to me. Logan wanted to know his dad, regardless of whom he was or where he came from. A tear escaped my eye and I brushed it away quickly, thinking of how Logan had asked me at the start of the pre-school year last year why he didn't have a daddy like the other kids when they had to draw family pictures. It made my heart crumble at the time, not knowing what to say, but knowing that my explanation of how he didn't have a dad but Uncle Tate was pretty special didn't appease him nearly enough.

As if reading my mind and knowing I was debating something important, Marcus reached out and took my hand. "I'm not the kid you knew Emma."

I turned my head to Jack and wiped away another tear. He looked down at me, and for a moment, I forgot Marcus was standing behind me. Jack simply pulled his lips into a tight, but understanding smile.

He put one hand on my cheek. "You can do this, Emma."

I nodded and turned back to Marcus. His eyes were furrowed in confusion and I almost lost it then, looking at my son's father who had no idea I was about to rock his world.

"What's going on?" He flipped his eyes between Jack and me before flexing his fingers nervously at his sides.

I did the one thing I never thought I would do. Reaching in to my wallet, I withdrew a small school photo and handed it over to him. His fingers grasped it gingerly, and I saw his hands shake just slightly.

"This is your son, Logan. He'll be five in two weeks. I didn't use your dad's money and I didn't do what he told me to do."

I watched his face distort in front of me as he flickered through way too many emotions for me to place. His thumb softly swept across the edges of the photo while he took in every feature on Logan's face and my heart softened towards him against my own will.

I never knew what new mothers meant when they said they watched their husbands fall in love when they held their child for the first time, but watching Marcus now, I totally understood. His love for Logan was instantly tangible and several minutes later when he finally pulled his gaze from the photo to mine; so was his regret.

I didn't know what to say, so I stayed silent while Marcus' eyes flitted back and forth between the photo and me letting him have this time to process everything he needed to. Five and a half years ago, when I told him I was pregnant, my heart had burst with joy when he offered to elope immediately and get married and start our life together just as we had dreamed. But within forty-eight hours all that joy was crushed to pieces.

As I watched him reverently holding the photo of his son, I realized for the last five years, regardless of who had been in my life to help and support me; the one person I always wanted there, the one person who should have been there, was standing right in front of me. My heart broke all over again realizing what Logan and I had missed out on—a real family.

"He's beautiful," Marcus whispered. Had I been standing mere inches further away, I would have had to strain to hear him.

There was a softness, a longing in Marcus's eyes I couldn't deny or turn away from as he looked at me. It caught me so off guard it took me a few seconds to remember that he had actually spoken.

I simply nodded in agreement, a slight smile spreading on my lips. "He is. And smart, too."

"Just like his mom."

I should have been flattered by the comment, but instead I was scared. What did it mean for me now that Marcus was back in my life and knows about Logan? How would things change? Would this affect my relationship with Jack?

I looked up at Jack again and saw him eyeing Marcus's reaction. There was a sadness in them, and I wished I could ask him what he was thinking. I didn't want this to change anything, but I was terrified it was going to change everything.

"Can I meet him?"

I eyed him for just a second before I saw the innocent desire in his eyes.

I rubbed the back of my hand across my forehead. "I need to talk to

Logan. Can you give me some time?"

Marcus nodded and looked to Jack. "You knew about Logan?"

Jack nodded and released his hands from my waist only to put them in his pockets. He straightened his entire body and glared at Marcus fiercely. "I've known Logan since before he was born, Marcus. I hired Emma when she was still sick from pregnancy and heartbroken over the guy who left her."

My eyes widened. I wasn't sure that last part was necessary, but then I realized this was Jack's way of protecting me. In so many words, he was letting Marcus know that Logan and I were both his—and that he'd been the man taking care of us. It cut Marcus deep, I could tell from the sadness and regret in his eyes, but he simply nodded and pursed his lips before turning back to me.

"I'm sorry I wasn't the man you needed me to be." He flipped the picture around so I could see Logan's face. "But I'd like to get to know him. More than anything, I want to know my son."

I nodded slowly. "I'll call you soon."

He went to hand me back the photo of Logan but I waved him off. "You keep it," I said softly and reached for Jack's hand.

Marcus gently placed the photo in his wallet and smiled slightly. "Thank you," he said and walked back to the ballroom leaving Jack and I standing there in completely silence.

"Let me take you home," Jack whispered softly in my ear. My eyes were glued to Marcus as he walked away and took his seat at his table.

I nodded and let Jack quietly lead me down the hallway and out the door of the hotel to Shane and the waiting limo.

The ride back to my apartment felt like it took forever. Jack and I said nothing to one another as we entered my building.

I shrieked when I opened the door to the apartment and saw Tate and Macy making out on my couch like teenagers.

"Shit, guys!" I yelled as Jack muffled a laugh behind me.

Macy was shirtless and straddling Tate on my couch. As soon as I yelled, her face fell into Tate's shoulder and he wrapped his arms around her, covering her back. He peeked his head around her shoulder and for the first time since I'd known him, he blushed a furious shade of hot pink.

"Sorry … we didn't think you'd be back so soon," Tate said with a look on his face that he really wasn't sorry at all.

I tossed my clutch bag and my keys on the entry table and walked into the kitchen so I didn't have to look at my two half-naked friends sprawled out on my couch.

"Hey, man—it happens." Jack laughed and followed me.

"That's not helping. I'm going to have that image burned in my brain whenever I look at my couch now," I scolded him as I reached for the wine bottle.

"You could have at least used my room!" I shouted to Macy while my back was turned away from them. I heard them rustling around in the living room—hopefully getting dressed.

"Do you mind if we go finish up in there then?" Tate asked while laughing.

"No!" Jack shouted. I looked at him with my mouth hanging open. "That's our room and we'll need it later."

I laughed and took my first drink. "You think so?"

It sounded really good at the moment, and at least the images of Macy and Tate practically screwing on my couch relieved my stress and worry from my interactions with Marcus and his dad.

Jack was smiling a boyish grin while he poured himself a glass of wine. I didn't see that look nearly enough and I didn't want him to stop looking so happy, so I didn't bring up what Marcus's dad said. My lips lifted a bit when he winked at me. "I think you might need a stress reliever later."

I agreed, and I knew he would too once I told him the rest of what happened.

Thankfully, Macy and Tate sauntered into the kitchen with sheepish smiles on their faces and I knew I could put it off a little bit longer.

"So why are you back so soon?" Macy asked when she reached for a glass too. Apparently, it was going to be a drinking kind of night. I needed it, and wasn't in any big hurry for them to leave either - being surrounded by my best friends sounded awesome.

I sighed and sat down at the kitchen table. "We ran into Marcus at the dinner tonight and I finally told him about Logan."

"You what?" She asked with eyebrows raised, her wine glass frozen in front of her lips.

I closed my eyes and shook my head. "I couldn't avoid it any longer. Logan's been asking about his dad, and after Marcus defended me in front of his dad …"

"What?" Jack hissed and I instantly realized my mistake. Shit. "You didn't tell me that he was there. What happened?"

Jack's anger was palpable as Macy and Tate joined me at the table. Jack on the other hand, firmly planted his hands on his hips and puffed out his chest.

I rolled my tongue in my mouth and then across the front of my teeth trying to find the words. I didn't want to share everything in front of Macy, but she knew the whole story anyway.

"He pushed me up against the wall when I came out of the bathroom …"

"He put his fucking hands on you?!" Jack shouted and I winced.

"Can I finish?" I asked gently and then took a large swallow of my wine, finishing it in one large gulp. I pinched my eyes and swallowed slowly to ease the burning in my throat. "He knew about Logan, Jack. He said that he's kept an eye on us over the years in case we approached Marcus. And then, he called me a …"

My voice trailed off, not wanting to finish. Macy put her hand on mine and looked at me with wide eyes.

"He called me a whore," I whispered and then closed my eyes expecting another outrage from Jack. Instead, I heard the sound of glass shattering on my wall. My eyes flew open and I saw Jack roughly rubbing his hands through his hair and large mess of red wine falling gently down the back wall of my galley kitchen.

"Fuck!" Jack turned to me, looking completely manic, and took a deep breath when he saw my widened eyes. He turned back to his mess and then back to me slowly. "I'm sorry … I'm just pissed that you didn't tell me while we were there so I could take care of it."

I scoffed. "And what would you have done? Kicked his ass in front of hundreds of people, Jack?"

His nose wrinkled a little bit. "Maybe."

"Right," I said with a faint hint of laughter. I didn't doubt he would have done something.

Jack moved quickly and knelt down in front of me. "This all happened right after I told you I'd protect you and keep you safe; and then I didn't. Why didn't you tell me there?"

"Because Marcus interrupted him and made him leave and then he started apologizing for everything that happened, and then you showed up." I placed my hand on his cheek, but then looked at Macy and Tate. They seemed to understand the look I gave them that said get the hell out of here, and took their cues silently.

I didn't say anything else until Macy was at the doorway, Tate holding the door open for her. "Call me tomorrow, okay?"

I nodded. "I will. Thanks for watching Logan for me, tonight."

Tate gave us a fake salute as they walked out the door, "Thanks for your couch."

The door shut and I heard muffled laughter from behind it. "Asshole," I muttered and turned back to Jack.

He looked tortured.

"He said if I don't let him have a relationship with Logan, that he's going to spill our affair all over the papers and then he'd go to a judge to get rights as the grandparent."

Jack closed his eyes and pursed his lips. When he opened them again and looked at me, he was calmer. "I won't let that happen. Let me deal with this shit okay?"

"Jack …"

"No, you need to listen to me. I'm not letting that asshole use his power to manipulate you ever again. You have enough to worry about with introducing Logan and Marcus, and I'll take care of his dad. The man will never have anything to do with Logan unless you agree to it, you get me?"

He looked so fiercely serious, I couldn't argue with him. "I get you."

"Now … let's go relieve some of that stress."

I looked at the wall behind him that was still dripping wine. "I need to clean up your mess."

He looked at the wall and then back to me with a roguish grin, "I'll do it tomorrow. There's more important things to take care of right now."

I snorted. "You know how to clean?"

"I can be domesticated," he stated. It reminded of the very first night he ran into me on my blind date and I couldn't stop myself from smiling at the memory.

"You're anything but domesticated, Jack." He picked me up like a rag doll in his arms and nuzzled his chin into my neck.

"Then let me show you how naughty I can be."

Sixteen

"Will my dad like me?"

We were sitting on a park bench at a playground near our house waiting for Marcus while I held Logan in my lap and softly ran my hands through his hair. It wasn't the first time he'd asked the question in the last few days since I told him he had a dad and that Marcus wanted to meet him. My heart broke a little bit each time he asked though, especially when he looked at me with wide, nervous eyes. I hated this.

"Of course he'll like you, Logan," I said softly and pulled him to my chest, hoping he couldn't hear the frantic beat of my heart. I knew Marcus would love him. I wasn't worried about that, his face when he saw the picture told me all I needed to know. What worried me—terrified me—was his dad making good on his threats.

I pressed my teeth together and with closed eyes, sighed heavily. How do you explain to a four-year-old why his dad hasn't been around? Or why he wanted to know him now? I'd been through days of questioning, and lots of tears—mine and Logan's—as we talked about Marcus being gone for work and just now back in Chicago. I couldn't bear to tell him the truth, and I didn't think he needed to know it anyway. He was too young to understand. Hell, I still didn't understand.

My phone rang with Jack's ringtone and I cringed. He wasn't happy about me meeting Marcus alone, although after hours of arguing the night before I knew this would be easier for everyone. He had called me every thirty minutes all morning since he left my apartment this morning checking up on me and trying to get me to change my mind.

"Hey, Jack," I said softly and watched Logan's eyes light up with a large smile. He was growing to love Jack. I wondered if it would change how he interacted with Marcus.

"Is he there yet?" His voice was impatient and I sighed.

"Not yet." I looked at the time on my watch. It was still five minutes before we agreed to meet. "He should be here any minute. And I promise, again, to call you as soon as we're done here."

"Don't bother," he said gruffly. "I had a meeting come up this afternoon and I might be tied up for the rest of the day."

He sounded annoyed, and slightly pissed off. I didn't know if it was me meeting Marcus or this new appointment. Regardless, I didn't want to argue with him about it. We'd fought enough over the last couple of days.

"Okay …" I said reluctantly. "Will I see you later?"

"Maybe. I need to go, but I'll call you when I can."

I ran my hands through Logan's hair again and shooed him off towards the playground.

"Is everything okay?" I asked once Logan was climbing up the slides.

"Nothing I can't handle. Be safe, and called Shane if you need anything."

He hung up without giving me a chance to say good-bye and I sat there staring at my phone, looking at Jack's name flashing on my disconnected signal. Something wasn't right and something else told me it didn't have to do with me meeting Marcus.

"Hey Emma." I closed my eyes and took a deep breath when I heard Marcus' familiar voice. It was deeper than it used to be, but sounded so similar to the loving way he used to talk to me that my spine tingled.

I looked at him, standing next to the park bench and waved for him to sit down next to me. He took his seat and clasped his hands together, his right foot bouncing.

"Nervous?" I asked with a slight grin as I looked at his legs.

He stared out at the dozens of screaming and smiling kids on the playground and said nothing for several minutes while his heel kept bouncing away.

"I don't even know which one he is …" his voice trailed off and finally he took his eyes off the strangers on the playground and turned to me. "I'm a father, Emma. And I have no idea who my son is. You have no idea how that feels."

I grasped my phone tightly in my hands, suddenly scared he was going to lash out at me for keeping Logan a secret for so long. I looked away from him, afraid he would see the fear in my own eyes, but he kept talking.

"I don't blame you, you know. I'm just pissed and angry at myself for not realizing sooner what an asshole my dad is." He ran his hands roughly through his hair and cursed. "All I've been able to think about since you told me about Logan is all the plans I had for us. I wanted to marry you and make a life with our child, and now it's all so fucked up that I can't even look at these kids out here and recognize my own son. Do you have any idea how shitty that makes me feel?"

I turned my head away from him and swallowed down the tears that threatened to spill over.

"I'm sorry," I whispered.

Marcus snapped at me. "You don't have shit to be sorry for. I told you, I'm not mad at you. I've held on to so much anger for the last few years with my dad that I'm pissed I ever trusted him over the only woman I've ever loved …"

"Marcus," I gasped, startled at his admission to me. Why was he even bringing all of this up now? I didn't agree to meet him to discuss our relationship, I just wanted him to meet his son and suddenly I felt too overwhelmed by everything to say anything at all.

He raised a hand and cut me off. "Just let me say this, okay?" At my nod, he continued. "You have no idea how much it broke my heart when my dad came to me and told me you asked for money to get rid of our baby. I was too angry and too upset to think rationally. If I would have taken even a second, I would have known you'd never do that. I just … I never thought my dad would lie like that. When he admitted the truth, I wanted to find you, but then I was too scared and too ashamed to admit everything to you. I failed you when you needed me most, and for that—I will always be sorry."

I wiped away the tears that I couldn't fight down any longer. It was too much. Too overwhelming and in the open park, I felt walls crushing down on my chest. What would have happened had he come to me years ago?

"And now you're with Jack," he spit it out like he was pissed. Or maybe jealous, given his confession. Perhaps he was still disappointed in himself. I didn't know, but I turned to face him and saw anger in his eyes.

"I am."

"Do you love him?" Marcus' voice sounded so pained, I couldn't say anything at all. Why did I feel bad about this?

I let my silence speak for itself and turned to the playground. Logan stood on a walkway between two slides, his hands gripping the rails and his eyes wide, watching us. I waved to him in a gesture for him to come over and I saw the fear and nerves flash in his tiny little innocent face.

"He's not good enough for you," Marcus stated and my jaw tightened in annoyance.

"We didn't come here to talk about Jack, and I won't discuss my relationship with him, with you of all people." I turned to see Logan slowly walking towards us. "Your son wants to meet you and he's nervous as hell that you won't like him. Don't mess this up."

"Sorry," he whispered and then wipes his palms nervously on his thighs. "What do I say to him?"

I laughed softly. "Say hello, and then play with him. It's all he wants, Marcus."

Logan walked over to me and molded himself to the side of my body.

He looked at Marcus with scared little eyes as he tried to hide himself from him. I pulled him onto my lap so he was cradled against my body and held his head against my chest, his face staring directly at his father.

"Logan …" I choked out, tears threatening to spill over again, but I swallowed them down. "This is your dad, Marcus."

I felt Logan stiffen in my arms and looked to Marcus. With my eyes, I pleaded for him to show Logan some love. Slowly, Marcus reached out his right hand.

"It's wonderful to finally meet you Logan," he said softly but with tears spilling over his own eyes. I could see Marcus' own fear in his eyes and I wondered if he was just as terrified as Logan.

Logan stared at the large hand offered to him and then slowly looked up at me. He pursed his lips and frowned when he saw my tears, but I nodded and with a smile, encouraged him to say hello.

His little hand disappeared into Marcus's when he finally reached out to hold it. Marcus breathed out a loud exhale and with his free hand, he wiped away his own tears.

"Hi." Logan's soft and timid voice brought more tears to my eyes and Marcus's. I shut my eyes tightly until I felt more in control. Silence surrounded the three of us. I knew kids were shouting and cars were driving by. I'm sure in the distance a car alarm was going off, and adults were chatting on cell phones, but in that moment, there was nothing else in the world besides the three of us.

Finally, Marcus smiled and covered Logan's small hand with his other one, holding it softly between them. "I'm so sorry I wasn't here earlier for you."

Logan smiled. "My mom said you were gone for work and just came back. She said you had to travel a lot but didn't have to do it anymore."

I wrinkled my nose at the little—okay, enormous—white lie I told Logan. I pleaded with Marcus silently for understanding and he sent me his silent thanks.

Marcus nodded. "I did."

A tear fell down Logan's own cheek and my own throat burned from the emotions splayed all over his pudgy little cheeks and innocent face. God I hated this.

"Are you going to travel anymore?" he asked so softly I was afraid Marcus didn't hear him.

But he did, and he moved to wipe a tear off Logan's cheek and then his own with the back of his hand.

"I will never leave you again," he said seriously and then turned to me. "I promise."

Logan took a deep breath and then smiled the largest smile I had ever seen on his little face. "I turn five in … .how many days, mommy?"

I chuckled through my tears. "Two weeks, baby."

He scrunched up his nose. "I'm not a baby," And then looked at his … dad. "Two weeks. Will you come to my birthday party? Mommy's taking me to a place with lots of things to jump on. I forget what they're called."

"Trampolines?" Marcus supplied with a smile that practically mirrored his son's. They were practically mirror images of each other and something in that moment, felt like they had always known each other.

Logan nodded enthusiastically and hopped off my lap. "Yeah, those things. Can you come?"

Marcus nodded. "I wouldn't miss it for the world."

"Do you want to play with me?" Logan asked and then looked at the sand pile to our right filled with empty buckets.

I looked at Marcus, still dressed in his fancy and well-tailored black suit. He had come to meet us directly from work. The idea of him sitting in the sand made me laugh.

Marcus shot me a look full of mischief and amazement. Before I knew it, he had thrown his suit jacket over the back of the bench, and was removing his socks and shoes.

He held out his hand for Logan who, this time, took it without any hesitation. "I love to play in the sand."

I watched the two of them walk away to the sand pit, content to sit back and watch Logan playing with his dad for the very first time ever. It was absolutely perfect. I pushed back the sadness and the guilt, and for the first time in almost five years, watched with my own eyes—a scene I had envisioned from the moment I found out I was pregnant.

Hours later, after ice cream and Marcus asking Logan a gazillion questions about himself—to which Logan enthusiastically responded to - Marcus walked us back to our apartment. I was starting to worry since I hadn't yet heard from Jack, even though I had sent him a text at the park letting him know we were still there. He never responded which was odd. No matter what he was doing, Jack had always responded to my texts since the very first date we had. He even sent me dirty messages in the middle of board meetings. To not get a reply from him at all worried me.

"Do you want to see my Legos?" Logan asked Marcus when we reached our building. Marcus smiled, but looked to me.

This was more than I had planned on. I figured after a few hours of playing at the park, and walking and having ice cream, Marcus would be eager to get home. Logan may be his son, but kids were exhausting when you weren't used to them.

I looked at Logan, who was eagerly awaiting my answer. I couldn't say no. Not when his hand had been firmly clasped in Marcus's for the last two hours. He wasn't ready to say good-bye to his dad yet and I didn't blame him.

"Sure," I said with a smile and looked at Marcus—relief flooding every feature on his face. "I'll cook dinner while you guys play. You can stay if you want."

"I want. Thank you."

I led us into the apartment and shooed Logan in the direction of his room after instructing him for the five thousandth time to put away his shoes and hang up his jacket. Marcus watched him skip down the hall before turning to me.

"I'm not sure how to thank you enough for today."

I brushed him off, although I was in awe how easy the day had gone. After the first few uncomfortable moments between the two of them, they had found their rhythm and by the time we left the park to get lunch, Logan and Marcus smiled and talked as if they'd known each other their entire lives. It was surreal and comfortable at the same time.

"It was the least I could do."

He took a few steps towards me and I flinched when his hand came out and cupped my cheeks. I turned my eyes away from him, afraid of what I would see if I looked at him. Marcus sighed, but didn't remove his hand.

"You didn't have to do anything. And I don't think I could blame you one bit if you never told me about him. But you did, and you have no idea how thankful I am right now."

He shoved his hands into his pockets and took a few steps back.

"I feel like we were the family today that I always wanted."

I inhaled a quick breath and turned from him. For years, I kept hoping Marcus would someday walk back into our lives and all would be forgotten. A stupid naïve dream from a heartbroken young girl, but I wasn't that young girl anymore, and it was happening before my own eyes. Except now I loved Jack, and I didn't fully trust Marcus.

"Dad!" Logan yelled from down the hallway, growing impatient with Marcus's delay in getting to the bedroom.

I smiled faintly. "You better go—your son wants you."

"God that sounds so awesome." He shook his head as he walked down the hallway. He turned back to me when he reached Logan's room. "I meant what I said. This is what I've always wanted."

I turned away without a word and stared lamely at my freezer, trying to find something I could defrost or cook for dinner. Except my mind wasn't working properly. Instead it was flooded by memories of the day, the comments from Marcus about this being what he wanted, and my concerns for Jack.

I slammed the door shut, grabbed a beer from the fridge, and called for pizza.

After I ordered the pizzas, I sent another text to Jack letting him know I was back home with Logan and everything went well.

Not that it mattered, he never texted me back.

What in the hell was going on?

Seventeen

I nervously entered Jack's penthouse apartment the next morning. It had been a tough morning with Logan, me explaining to him why he couldn't see Marcus again, and reassuring him several times that we could call him after work.

Then I received a text message from Marcus, thanking me again, for telling him about Logan. I flip-flopped between feeling happy that Logan finally got to meet his dad, and frustrated that Jack never called or replied to my messages from the day before.

"Jack?" I called out quietly as I shut his front door.

I was met with complete silence. I walked around his penthouse, looking for any sign that he was still at home, but found nothing. I frowned when I entered his bedroom and my heart started beating faster.

His bed was completely made. Jack never made his own bed, and if his bed was made, that meant that he didn't come home the night before.

Worry filled me instantly. Something had to have kept him from calling me back, and something—or someone—kept him out all night long. I hated doubting him, especially after the prior weekend when he told me he loved me. Maybe it was too much for him? Maybe he realized that loving me was too dangerous or risky for him. Maybe he realized that feeling out of control around me wasn't worth it anymore and he found someone else.

I sighed and closed the door to his bedroom. I would deal with my feelings about the cleanly made bed later, but I had to figure out where he was.

I chewed nervously on the outer corner of my thumbnail when I entered his office and sat down at his desk. I had bills to pay, but first I wanted to call Macy. Surely, she had heard from him.

I dialed her number from Jack's office phone. She answered on the first ring, her voice breathless.

"Jack, thank god you're finally calling. The phones have been ringing …"

"It's me, Macy."

"Emma? Have you talked to Jack today?" She sounded shocked and worried, and I immediately put all my doubts of Jack on hold.

"No. And I didn't hear from him last night either."

She gasped. "He didn't check in with you after Marcus left? I would have thought he'd be babysitting your door waiting for him to leave."

I shook my head and cringed when I chewed right through my thumbnail.

"Yeah, I know. When was the last time you talked to him?" I asked, although I had a fairly good idea, based on when I talked to him yesterday.

"He left work early yesterday, saying he had something come up, and I haven't heard from him since. We have a board meeting in a few minutes and I needed him here like twenty minutes ago."

I played with my hair and wrinkled my nose, trying to think of where he could possibly be. Who would he have met with yesterday, and who could it have been that he wouldn't have told me or Macy about? And who could have kept him out all night? Instantly, I knew.

"Is Martin in?" I asked, light suddenly dawning on me.

Macy sighed. I could hear her frantically tapping her pencil against her desk through the phone line. "No, he's not in either."

"It's okay. I think I know what they're doing—can you transfer me to Martin's private line?" If Jack wouldn't answer me, maybe Martin would.

At least now I had a pretty good idea of who they were helping.

Martin's voicemail picked up immediately.

"Hey Mr. Crawlson. Macy and I haven't heard from Jack since yesterday. I was just calling to make sure he's okay and I have a pretty good idea that this has to deal with … B. Can you send me a text when you get a minute just so us girls stop worrying? Thanks."

I didn't know if Jack told Martin that I knew about his brother, but hopefully me using the nickname I remembered Jack using before when he called would be enough for Martin to understand.

I put my head in my hands and rested my elbows against Jack's desk, sighing deeply. This wasn't like him. There's no way he would just skip work without letting anyone know. I don't know if I had ever heard of him missing a day of work. And if something was going on with Brian, based on what Jack had told me about him before, then something could be really wrong.

Regardless, I still had work to do. I took a deep breath and began sorting through the pile of bills on Jack's desk that needed to be paid. When I was done, I filed them away and tossed the envelopes into his garbage can.

I bent over to pick up a piece of crumpled paper and frowned. It wasn't here yesterday when I vacuumed, so at some point Jack had come home. Slowly, I crumpled it and then gasped in surprise. It was a paper, bank withdrawal slip from the bank maintaining Jack's personal account. Yesterday at four-thirty, based on the slip, he withdrew fifty thousand dollars. Cash.

I jumped when my cell phone went off and then felt defeated knowing it wasn't Jack's ringtone.

Reluctantly, I left Jack's office with my phone in hand and headed to the kitchen.

Jack's fine. Said he'd be home later. Surprised—happily—he told you about B. Martin

I wrinkled my nose but felt my shoulders relax. At least Martin knew where he was. It still didn't explain why Jack hadn't contacted me though.

I stared at the message when my phone starting ringing again and Macy's name flashed on the screen.

"Yes?" I asked.

"I just wanted you to know Jack just got in, but he's really pissed off and said he wasn't staying long." I cringed at Macy's concerned voice that came out just above a whisper.

I exhaled heavily. "Thanks for letting me know. Talk to you later."

By the time the afternoon hit, I was done worrying about Jack. Instead, I was just pissed off. He had to have known I was worried about him. He had to have also known that Macy and Martin told him I was looking for him, and I still hadn't heard from him. Not even a single message saying when he'd be home from work, what he needed me to do, or if he even needed me for dinner.

I was packing up my bag for the day—early, because screw him—when he finally walked in the door. He looked perfectly polished in his tailored suit, but I could see tension in his face and dark circles under his eyes. Wherever he had been the night before, left him looking like crap.

"Enjoy your night?" I asked sarcastically and resisted the urge to shrink back from him when he scowled at me.

Jack was pissed. Tense all over, and clearly not in the mood for my sarcasm.

I crossed my arms in a defensive gesture. I was pissed and I wanted answers.

Seeing that I wasn't going to get any, since Jack didn't bother answering me, I turned and picked up my purse.

"I'll see you tomorrow," I said and held my breath as I walked past him.

His hand reached out and firmly grabbed my elbow. "Where are you going?"

I spun around and shot him a look. "Excuse me?"

"I need you." I recoiled at his voice. Jack always sounded confident and borderline arrogant, but lately, with me at least, he had been softer. This tone was nothing like anything I had heard from him before. He sounded cold and distant from me.

I hated it. I also hated that my body responded regardless of what my brain was thinking. I felt a warmth pool between my legs when I saw his arousal through his suit pants.

"Where were you?" I asked, trying to fight my attraction to him. I had a feeling I would lose, but it was still worth a shot.

Jack shook his head and closed his eyes. When he opened them, he looked less angry, but still just as distant. He said nothing, which gave me my answer. He wasn't going to tell me anything.

"I saw the bank receipt from yesterday."

His eyes flashed to black. Apparently, that was the wrong thing to say. "Were you snooping in my office?"

I snorted. "I paid your bills and it was on the floor. Sue me for cleaning up after your lazy ass."

I tried to rip my arm away from him but he just held me tighter, and pulled me flushed to his body. I fought the urge to rock into him.

"I can't tell you." His voice left me certain that I wouldn't get any answers. I didn't actually need them, but an apology would at least have been nice. Based on the firm line on his lips, I doubt I'd get that either.

I exhaled heavily. "Fine," I said and tried to relax into him just enough for him to let me go. He didn't. As soon as I relaxed, he pulled me closer to him with his other hand and held me tightly.

He lowered his head against the top of mine and the muscles in his back relaxed. It wasn't a lot, but enough to let me know he wasn't going to explode in anger.

"I need you," he roughly said against my ear. My entire body trembled under his touch as his hands moved to my hips.

He sounded angry, but vulnerable. I wanted to let him do what he did best and make love to me. I also wanted to knee him in the balls for being suck a prick.

I shook my head, determined to fight the intense attraction. "I'm not your sex toy when you're pissed off at the world, Jack. Let me go."

He didn't relent. His nose tickled the soft skin on my jaw, down my neck to my collarbone, where he licked it softly. I moaned, but my head still tried to fight against what my body clearly wanted. He laughed softly.

"You know you want this. Let me give you this."

My entire body involuntarily trembled. He had me and he knew it. And even as I leaned into his kiss, to his hand that was warm, but still didn't feel quite right against my skin in that moment, I knew it was going to be a big mistake.

In what felt like a mere second, Jack had me picked up and was putting me back down at the back of his couch. He turned me away from him and placed my hands on the back of his couch.

He pulled my pants down and I stepped out of them. "Let your juices fall, Emma. Show me how much you fucking want me."

I shivered at his words. I couldn't deny it turned me on, but there was still something about Jack that was off. He wasn't talking to me, or acting like he actually gave a crap about me and I felt too exposed with my bare ass pointing up in the air for him to see.

I heard his zipper go down and resisted the urge to tighten up again when his large, firm hands grabbed my hips. Without another warning, he thrust roughly into me.

I cried out from the harshness, but Jack made no move to apologize. My knuckles turned white as I grabbed onto the back of the couch. My feet rose up onto my toes with every thrust into me. He pushed so hard into me that I knew it would leave bruises, on the inside, and on my hips where he held me tightly.

"Jack!" I shouted. It hurt, and it felt so damn good at the same time. I wanted to be pissed, but the more he rocked into me, playing with my clit with his fingers, my body submitted while my brain was still three steps behind, still trying to figure out what was wrong with him.

"Come for me," he demanded into my ears. He laid his entire chest over me and removed his hands from my body, placing them over my hands. I couldn't move an inch to get him off of me. All I could do was take it.

I came, screaming in bliss and frustration, but if Jack noticed he didn't care.

He pounded away, moaning, his chest sweating all over my back. He didn't care about the tears that started to fall from my eyes and dripped onto his arms and hands. Wherever he was, he wasn't with me. It scared me. Not because he hurt me, but because this wasn't my Jack. Jack was powerful and bossy in bed, but he wasn't this big of a prick, ever.

I wanted him to tell me what was wrong, not maul me to relieve stress and his anger.

Jack leaned off me, still pounding into me fiercely, and groaning in pleasure. He wrapped my hair around his hand and pulled me up a little bit, his other hand moving towards the front of me. He rubbed my clit fiercely with his free hand and my body responded again.

I felt another orgasm stir as Jack moved his hips in a circle.

"That's it baby," he murmured into my ear.

He sounded evil, and I hated it. I hit another orgasm, and Jack thrust one more time into me, he moaned his released and dropped us against the back of the couch.

He didn't even give me time to come down from the most anger-filled orgasm I ever had before he pulled out and zipped up his pants. With my legs still shaking, I embarrassingly, bent down and pulled up my pants, noticing he had destroyed my thong underwear in his haste to remove them.

I glowered at them in disgust before I stood up.

Jack was staring at me; his eyes void of every emotion. God, I wished I had the ability, but I didn't.

I had never felt so furiously angry with anyone in my entire life. In that moment, I think I hated Jack more than I hated Senator Whitmore. He didn't even blink as I wiped away the tears running down my cheeks. He put his hands in his pockets and just looked at me, expressionless.

Why? I didn't do anything to him, and if he was busy with Brian, I had absolutely nothing to do with it.

Why did I even fucking care?

He opened his mouth to say something, but then closed it.

"What?" I asked, my voice shaky.

We stared at each other for who knows how long and Jack's expressionless face changed to sadness, just for a second before he closed off his emotions again. His hand ran roughly down the front of his face as if he was trying to wipe them away.

When he spoke again, he shattered me.

"You're fired, Emma. Effective immediately."

Before I knew what I was doing, the palm of my hand connected with Jack's cheekbone. His head snapped to the left making a cracking sound and my palm instantly burned.

He rubbed his tongue across the inside of his cheek that I had just smacked, and still—he said nothing.

Asshole.

"You're an asshole, Jack."

As I turned to leave, I saw, what I thought was a flash of fear, or panic flicker through his eyes.

"Emma," he said, his voice hoarse.

I paused, hoping he'd stop me from leaving. That he'd tell me he was being a jerk and that he was sorry. Then we'd sit down and calmly talk about what was going on, what was bothering him so severely.

The flicker in his eyes disappeared as he took a deep breath, rolling back his shoulders and standing straight and tall. He shook his head, and said nothing.

I was a naïve, foolish girl.

I pursed my lips and swallowed my tears. I wouldn't let him see how much this affected me. He had given me a job, my lifeline when I needed it the most, and then made me fall in love with him.

Only to rip it away when the first sign of trouble appeared.

A bone-chilling silence filled his apartment as I picked up my bags and purse for the last time. He said nothing, gave no showing of an emotion as I walked away from him.

Tears erupted once I was finally enclosed in the safety of his elevator doors.

I was just walking into my apartment with Logan and Penny when my cell phone went off. I ignored it, knowing it wasn't Jack. Not that I was expecting him to call, or text, or fucking apologize for the way he manhandled me.

The only people who texted me were Macy and my parents, and I didn't want to talk to either of them for fear I might lose any hold I was maintaining on my emotions; however small it was at the moment.

I paid Penny and began running Logan's bathwater, thinking about dinner and trying as hard as I possibly could to forget my nightmare afternoon with Jack. More tears would come, I was sure after Logan went to bed, but I didn't want him to see me upset.

"Come on in the bath now, buddy," I called to Logan once the tub was filled. He happily jumped in and once he began playing with the water toys, I braved my phone.

It was from Marcus. I smiled reading his text.

Can't stop thinking about Logan. Can I see him tonight? I can bring dinner.

I wasn't in the mood for company. Especially Marcus. I also hated the idea of telling him no. He had so much fun with Logan the day before.

I checked my watch and realized that I was starving and hadn't eaten anything all day. I also didn't feel like cooking. I also really didn't feel like company and the thought of having to put on a fake smile for Marcus tonight was totally unappealing when I felt like throwing up. On the other hand, if he was there, he could take care of Logan while I wallowed in my self-pity and anger.

"Hey, it's Emma," I said when he answered. I smiled at Logan as he splashed in the bubbles and played with his cars. "Hey Logan, do you want to see … your dad?"

Logan's smile lit up, full of hopefulness. "Can I?"

I heard Marcus' laughter through the phone. "Have I mentioned how much I fucking love being called a dad?"

I shook my head. "Maybe once or twice. But you're really going to need to start watching your language, you know."

"Shit. Oh … crap. Yeah, I keep forgetting. Anyway, can I bring you guys some dinner tonight and spend a couple hours with him?"

I smiled at the hesitancy in Marcus' voice. He seemed so vulnerable and like maybe he had as crappy of an afternoon as me. Plus, Logan was excited. There was no way I was going to be the one responsible for wiping the smile off Logan's face.

"Not a problem. I'm finishing up Logan's bath, but we'll be here."

"God, thank you, Emma. Seriously, you don't owe me this, but I'm so fu … freaking grateful for you giving me this chance."

"Yeah, well just don't screw it up," I replied, not even half-joking.

I practically heard Marcus' teeth grind together through the phone and I almost regretted the warning immediately. All day yesterday he had acted like the guy I remembered—the good guy - before everything went to shit. Deep down, I knew he was a good guy, and one of the reasons I'd agreed to elope and hadn't been afraid of having a child with him.

"I won't. What do you guys like to eat?"

"Sorry," I muttered. My anger at Jack had nothing to do with Marcus. "It's been a shitty day." Before he could say anything, I cupped my hand over my receiver and peered at Logan. "What do you want for dinner Logan?"

His little nose crinkled up, as if he was really thinking hard about it. I didn't buy it for a single second and I splashed him with water, almost forgetting Marcus was still on the phone. While Logan sputtered and spit the soap and bubbles out of his mouth and off his face, I took my hand off the phone. "You'll probably be his biggest hero if you bring him a cheeseburger Happy Meal."

"And a video game dad!" Logan shouted and I heard Marcus' laughter through the phone.

"No video games," I said sternly to both of them at the same time.

"Sounds good, see you in a little bit."

We said our good-bye's, and I knew I was going to be spending the rest of the night watching Marcus and Logan jump on paper mushrooms while I pretended to be annoyed. I'd let Marcus have this time of spoiling the shit out of his kid because I knew it was partly my fault that he didn't know his son.

Sure, I thought he was a prick when his dad showed up all those years ago. But the truth, was that I could have gone to Marcus at any time and told him I didn't have an abortion. I could have chosen to be brave any day over the last five years and let him have his chance with Logan. Fear and anger kept me from it. I sighed, the guilt weighing on me.

I kept Logan—intentionally—from his dad. Even when he asked about a dad, or where he was, I lied. I hated that. I hated feeling like I'd knowingly kept my son from the one person who he wanted to know more than anyone, thinking that replacements like Tate and Jack were enough for him.

I stared at my son and fought back the tears. Marcus's admissions from the previous day about how much he wanted this family played in my head on repeat. Would Logan hate me forever for keeping his dad from him or would he forgive me when he was old enough to understand why I did it? Was Marcus in his life now, enough to erase all the pain and tears I'd caused my boy?

The only thing I knew for sure was that not knowing the answers sucked.

Eighteen

My friends ganged up on me. Apparently, forty-eight hours was enough to wallow in the misery of losing your job and your lover at the same time. Macy spent Friday night with me, listening to me cry and bitch about how shitty Jack was. I didn't tell her specifics, but she knew enough. She also told me how wretched Jack had been at work that day. If it was supposed to make me feel better, it didn't. I didn't want Jack miserable. I wanted him to open up for once and talk to me. I wanted him to want me.

The realization he didn't hit me smack in the chest and Macy stomped her foot down when I tried defending him.

"That's it." She stood up Saturday morning, brushed muffin crumbs off her pajama pants, and faced me, looking taller than her just over five foot frame allowed. "We're getting wasted tonight."

"I've already talked to Marcus," she said with a smirk on her lips. "He wants to have Logan over at his place anyway so he said he'd watch Logan while we went out tonight."

I really didn't want to go out. I had more wallowing to do. I just knew better than to argue with her. If I didn't join the party, she'd bring it to me.

"Fine."

She left, making me promise to meet her at the bar after I dropped Logan off at Marcus' later in the afternoon. While Logan watched an animated super heroes movie, I sorted the laundry, cleaned up the apartment and got ready to go out.

I was doing well, pushing thoughts of Jack to the back of my mind until I saw Macy's eggplant colored dress, the dress I wore on our first date, still hanging in my closet.

Memories of him flooded my mind even as I tried to turn them off. I sat on the floor of my closet, crying quietly knowing that Jack was terribly wrong.

His three-date-rule was still strongly in effect.

We may have screwed around a lot more than that, but as soon as something bad happened—whatever the hell it was that happened to him earlier in the week—Jack had thrown up walls faster than a rocket launching into space, even after professing his love for me.

Suddenly, getting skunk drunk sounded like a fabulous idea. A night out without having to worry about paying babysitters or being quiet in the morning so I didn't wake Logan up? Sounded like a vacation to me, and if anyone had earned one after the way this week went, I figured it was me.

I allowed myself a few more tears, promising myself that they were the last I would cry over Jack, got dressed, and then helped Logan pack an overnight bag.

Armed with a small suitcase, his pillow, and a couple of his favorite sleeping blankets wrapped under his arms, we headed to Marcus' apartment. It was just a few miles from where I lived and I nervously wrung my hands on the steering wheel the entire time at the idea of leaving Logan alone for the night.

Eventually I knew we'd have to sit down and work out a custody agreement, but Logan was so happy around him and Marcus seemed so excited to make up for lost time, that I didn't want to set anything in stone just yet.

Marcus's apartment was slightly larger than mine and much newer. His furnishings were fancier and his big screen television on a far wall rivaled Jack's. I instantly hated the comparison.

"You're going to keep him from your dad, right?" I asked abruptly and then instantly wanted to duct tape my own mouth shut. I waved a hand in apology. "Sorry … I've had a long week …"

Marcus cut me off. "You don't need to worry about that, Emma. I swear it to you." By the darkening of his eyes and the fiercely protective stance, I knew he was right.

"I know. Like I said, I've had a lot going on this week."

I watched Logan happily drift off and explore his new surroundings while trying to find something less stupid to say.

"Where do I sleep?" He asked Marcus, his eyes wide with excitement.

Marcus smiled and ruffled his hair. "Right this way, buddy."

Instantly, tears burned the back of my eyes. That was my nickname for Logan and no one else used it. Ever. I didn't know if I was pissed or sad that he was getting someone else to call him that now too. Some irrational part of me wanted to scream that it was my name and he couldn't use it. Fortunately, the rational side of me was still in somewhat control so I bit my tongue. Not soon enough for Marcus to miss the anger in my eyes.

He frowned but turned back to Logan. "I made a room for you. Do you want to see it?"

"Yeah!" Logan yelled and clapped his hands, jumping up and down like only a little kid can and hopped off down the hall. I followed, my curiosity piqued.

My jaw dropped as soon as I stepped foot in the doorway. It was amazing. Perhaps I'd need to bring up the 'don't spoil the shit out of your kid' speech earlier than I thought. With wide eyes, Logan and I both glanced around his new room in utter awe.

A bed, that looked like a tree house was on one wall and underneath were two shelves of books. Hundreds of books. Over a dozen Lego sets sat in their boxes on one of the shelves, completely unopened. A bucket overflowing with cars sat in one corner, and a stack of board games and puzzles sat on another shelf. And on the dresser, sat his very own television, complete with a new gaming system and a stack of games.

I was too terrified to look in the closet. Toys R Us had showed up and vomited all over the place. It was too much.

Logan didn't think so as he squealed and jumped. "Look mom! Daddy bought me Legos … all of them!"

"I may have overdone it," he said, smiling sheepishly. We left Logan in his room to enjoy the insanity.

"You may need to reign that in a little bit." Marcus frowned and I felt bad for chastising him, sort of. "I get it. You haven't been around him and you want to make up for it. But I guarantee you—the only thing that kid in there wants—is your love."

Marcus nodded and walked me to the door. "So what are you doing tonight?"

"I'm meeting Macy, Tate and their friend Dean out for drinks and dancing."

Marcus chuckled and ran his hands through his hair. "I can't believe you and Macy are still friends. That girl was crazy in school."

I laughed at what I can only imagine the memories Marcus was reliving. Macy had been wild and crazy in school. She ran from party to party, boy to boy, with sometimes a girl thrown in to shake things up a bit, and still managed to make the Dean's List every single semester. I often wondered why she 'settled' on working for Jack in the first place since her finance degree, grades, and sparkling personality could have gotten her a job anywhere. Not to mention that her dad was loaded and she probably had a trust fund and didn't need to work. But she was all about making it on her own while having fun in the process.

"She's calmed down … some," I admitted with a small smile as I grabbed my purse. "You have my number if he needs me. He hasn't slept away from home very much so if he gets scared, just call me and I'll come get him. I'll be here in the morning to get him. I don't want you to have to bring him back."

"Emma," Marcus put his hand on my shoulder. I didn't realize I had been rambling until I forced myself to take a deep breath. "We'll be fine. If I need help, I'll call. I promise, okay?"

I breathed again and nodded. "It'll be fine."

He laughed as if he didn't believe a single word I said. I'm not sure I did either.

"Go." He made a waving motion with his arm towards the door and I threw my hands up in defense.

"I'm going, I'm going."

I heard his laughter after the door closed and smiled. Maybe Marcus wasn't so bad after all. Besides, this co-parenting thing could be good. I'd get free nights out alone every once in a while which could only help my social life, and my monthly income would increase if I didn't have to pay Penny so much. Not that I ever had to worry about that before, but suddenly focusing on my lack of income caused my mood to plummet.

By the time I reached Sips, the club where I was meeting Macy and the guys, my mood had shifted from wallowing to planning. I had enough money saved where I'd be okay for a few months on my own, and I'd always considered going back to school. I could do this without any help from Jack. Logan and I would be just fine. At least that's what I was going to continue telling myself. Hopefully, it would sink in.

"Drink up!" Macy ordered as she slid me another shot. I threw the vodka straight back and grimaced while the alcohol burned its way down my throat. I coughed and took a swig of my vodka tonic, which didn't help much.

Macy smiled and Dean looked at me wide-eyed, concern etched all over his face.

"You had enough yet?"

I shook my head. My head had begun reeling of thoughts of Jack and the other night as soon as I saw the looks of pity on my friend's faces and I was determined to keep drinking until my mind was completely blank. I was numb … just not blank yet.

"Nope," I said, popping the p.

Macy threw her arms in air and cheered for me, almost smacking Tate in the face behind her. He moved her off to the side and set his beer on the table.

"Do we need to go kick his ass, Emma?" He asked me with all the seriousness of a big brother. Dean crossed his arms and narrowed his eyes at me, looking fierce. And slightly blurry. Maybe it was time to slow down on the shots.

I snorted. "Like you guys could do it."

I watched their faces morph into wounded ego expressions and laughed. "Seriously, guys. Look, I'm sorry. Jack was a prick, but that's nothing I didn't know was possible before I hopped into his bed. It's over and everything will be fine."

I was a rotten liar and they all knew it. I wanted so badly to believe everything really was going to be fine, but no matter how many times I repeated it to myself, it wasn't sinking in yet.

I grabbed Dean's fist and opened his fingers so he could hold my hand. "Dance with me."

I pulled him down to the dance floor, stumbling on my heels the entire way.

"You're completely wasted," he said as we got to the dance floor and began moving our hips close together.

I was. I couldn't deny it. I just wasn't drunk enough yet to forget. No matter how many times I tried to brush Jack out of my head, I kept seeing visions of him professing his love for me in the back of the limo, before everything went to shit. For a moment, I thought I had found something special. Someone special.

I turned around so Dean couldn't see tears fill my eyes as I remembered the way Jack made love to me, the way he made me feel as soon as he put his arm around my waist, and the pain I felt when he took me so roughly in his living room.

With my back to his chest, I tried to relax, wrapping an arm around the back of his neck, moving against him as I lost myself in the music. I kept my eyes open, worried that if I closed them, I would think he was Jack.

One song turned into another and soon, I was starting to feel hot and sweaty, not having any idea how long we'd been on the dance floor.

Slowly, one of Dean's hands moved up to my neck and brushed my hair to one shoulder. I felt his breath on my neck, and then my ear.

"If you weren't so completely in love with another man, I might be willing to forget that I think of you as a sister."

My eyes widened and I spun around, shocked. Did he seriously just say that to me? With a mischievous grin, Dean grabbed my hand and spun me out into a full circle. I tripped on my heels and wobbled, grabbing onto his arm with my free hand before my ass landed on the dance floor. I squealed as my body swayed to the side, and I started falling but then Dean's free hand grabbed my waist.

I laughed at my mishap and stumbled some more as he pulled me back to him.

"I'm just screwing with you, Emma. I just wanted to see you smile." He winked and tapped my nose. "Let's get you another shot."

"Drunk enough?" Macy asked as I reached our table. Tate's hands were wrapped possessively around her waist and he was licking her neck, not bother caring—or noticing - that Dean and I had come back.

"Ew," I said with a scrunched up nose at the slobber he was leaving all over the place.

Macy laughed and brushed him off. "He won't remember this in the morning."

I waved down the cocktail waitress as she walked by and asked for another round of shots and a refill on my vodka tonic. While I waited, I pulled out my phone and saw five missed calls. Panic seized me at the thought that it was Marcus needing help with Logan or something. Just as I was swiping my finger across the screen to unlock it, it started buzzing in my hand.

It was Jack.

Tate grabbed the phone from me instantly, probably recognizing the look of either fear or fury that crossed my face and held it out so I couldn't reach it.

"Hey!" I yelled, and jumped for it. Except he was so tall and his arm was so far away, I practically dove over the table and crashed a bunch of our shot glasses into the floor. Tate caught me with his free hand and steadied me so I didn't fall over again.

Everyone at the table busted out laughing, but I was pretty sure my face was purple in anger.

I held out my hand and put another on my hip. "Give me my phone, Tate."

He shook his head. "No way. You're going to talk to him and say something stupid, or take him back when he apologizes for being such a prick."

I huffed in frustration. They knew Jack fired me, and that was reason alone to be concerned about me, but they didn't know the other details. I wasn't going to explain the feral and cold way he looked at me after he got done forcefully screwing me against his couch. It was mortifying. I couldn't even bring myself to tell Macy afraid of what she would say, or do, to Jack at work.

She'd probably lace his coffee with diuretics.

My phone lit up and I knew he was calling again so I put my hands on the table and glared at Tate. "I want my phone. I'm not going to be stupid. I promise." I crossed my heart with an x over my heart and smiled sassily.

Slowly, he handed me my phone and I answered it.

"What do you want Jack?" I yelled into my phone over the noise in the club.

"Where are you?" He demanded. Seriously?

"None of your fucking business," I yelled back but started walking back toward the bathroom hallway so I could hear what he was saying to me. Tate shook his head while I walked away, clearly not believing my story about not being stupid.

"Damn it, Emma. I need to know you're safe. Where are you?"

"I don't think you have any right to know where I am or what I'm doing."

I heard him sigh through the phone and I could imagine him leaning against his kitchen counter, gripping a fistful of his hair.

"I know. I know. And I can't explain what happened. I just …" His voice trailed off and I said nothing. I stared at the graffiti along the bathroom walls like I was actually planning on calling Damien for a good time like the carving on the stall door suggested. Jack spoke again, his voice a little bit softer. "Where are you?"

"I told you. It's none of your business."

I think I heard his teeth grind together, and maybe I was pushing his buttons intentionally, but I was drunk and didn't care.

"I can tell you're wasted. I just need to make sure you're okay."

I scoffed. "Sure you do, Jack. Because you always take such good care of me. You don't need to worry about me; Dean will take good care of me tonight."

I closed my eyes, knowing I had gone too far when Jack growled a string curse words through the phone.

"Emma."

"Whatever Jack. I need to go." I hung the phone up.

I cleaned up in the bathroom and walked back to everyone at the table.

As soon as I got there, my phone started buzzing in my hand again.

"What?" I yelled, not even bothering to look at the number, but just assuming it was Jack again.

"It's Marcus. Logan had a nightmare and can't go back to sleep. I hate to ask, but can you come help?"

I swayed a little bit. A mixture of the alcohol, my argument with Jack, and worry about Logan. I put a hand on the table and closed my eyes, trying to get my balance under control.

"Emma?" He shouted through the phone.

"I'll be right there," I said and then turned my phone off. I could be at Marcus's in five minutes and already the realization of how drunk I must have sounded to Jack made me realize he was going to start blowing it up in a few minutes anyway.

Dean frowned, seeing the concern on my face.

"There's never a dull moment with you around, is there?"

I snorted. He was right. In the last two months, I'd started a passionate affair with my boss, fell in love, been faced with my ex walking—literally—back into my life, attacked by a well-known Senator, introduced ex to his son, ended a passionate affair, and lost my job. My life was anything but dull.

Having a dull and boring life suddenly sounded absolutely perfect.

"I need to get going, can you help me get a cab?" I asked. At least I was sober enough to realize being alone wasn't a smart idea.

"Tell me you're not going over that asshole's house, Emma."

I shook my head at Tate. "No, that was Marcus. He needs some help with Logan."

Macy hiccupped. "Sure … Logan. Of course that's what he needs help with."

My eyebrows pulled in. "What's that supposed to mean?"

She grinned at me and I rolled my eyes, figuring out what she meant.

"Whatever," I said with a wave of my hand. "Logan had a nightmare and can't go back to sleep." I looked at Dean. "Can you walk me outside?"

He nodded, and once a cab pulled up, he slid in next to me.

"I can get there by myself, you know." I felt a little uncomfortable with him sitting so close, remembering what he said to me in the bar. He was probably joking, but still.

"I know. I'm going to head home anyway. Just want you to be safe." He clamped his mouth shut and didn't finish the rest of his thought. Which was probably along the lines of … and not stupid.

Dean told the cab to wait when we pulled up to Marcus' building. He walked me to the elevator and down the hallway to his door - it was really more him dragging me while I held on and stumbled instead of walking - but whatever, semantics.

I practically fell into Marcus's apartment when he opened the door.

"Thanks, Dean!" I called out, but he was already gone.

Marcus's mouth dropped open when he saw me. "You're trashed."

I giggled like a girl and dropped my heels just inside the doorway. He reached out to hold me at my elbow.

"Sit here," he said and pulled out a kitchen chair for me. He left and came back with a glass of water and two pills.

"Thanks." I swallowed the pills and chugged the water, still feeling thirsty. I wanted to drop my head onto the table and pass out, but then I remembered Logan. "I'm going to see Logan."

Marcus stopped me with a hand on my shoulder. "Don't worry about it. I tried to text you. He fell asleep right after I called you. Sorry for cutting your night short."

I looked up at him and then closed my eyes to stop the room from the slow spin it had started. I shook my head and heard Marcus laugh.

"Come one. Let's get you to bed." He started pulling me to my feet.

I was so confused. I was mad at Jack, dancing with Dean, and now I was sleeping with Marcus? When did I become such a slut? I choked on my own laugh and Marcus turned to me, with a slight smile.

"I'm not sleeping with you."

"Yeah, because I like my women this wasted. I prefer to have them not acting like a sloppy fish."

Somehow, I found myself in Marcus' room and looked around. "Have you had a lot of them?"

He walked me to the bed and once I was sitting down, went to his closet. "Do you really need the answer to that?"

He tossed me a shirt from a shelf and crossed his arms.

"Answer to what?" I asked him. Did I ask him something? His room felt suspiciously like one of those merry-go-rounds I used to play on when I was kid. Those were fun.

He shook his head and laughed. "Do you need help getting in the bed?"

I looked around his room again, and then his bed, and furrowed my eyebrows. "Where's your fish?"

"What?" He asked, clearly choking back laughter.

"You said you like your women to meet your fish."

Marcus bit down on his knuckle and I watched his shoulders shake. What is so funny? I didn't know he liked fish.

"Go to sleep, drunk girl. I'll tell you all about my fish in the morning."

I shrugged. Sleep did sound really good right about now. Before I knew it, Marcus was holding me up while he pulled back the covers. Once he laid me down on the bed, he pulled his cream comforter over me and gently brushed the hair off my forehead.

Nineteen

I woke up the next morning under the softest comforter I had ever felt in my entire life and on top of smooth as silk chocolate brown sheets. I was not in my bed, and my heart rate began thumping wildly out of control. I peeked out from under the covers and closed my eyes when the sunshine from the windows pierced straight into my brain.

Where in the hell was I? And how did I get here? Was I drugged? That would certainly explain why my head felt like it was going to explode and my mouth felt like I swallowed a bag of cotton balls.

I laid back down and closed my eyes hoping to stop the pounding in my head. I was out with Macy, Tate and Dean at Sip's. Dean and I danced and he hit on me. My eyes flew open and I immediately regretted even the smallest, quickest movement. Dean hit on me. But he had said he was joking. Right? Right. Of course he was just joking. He said something about me being his sister.

I talked to Jack. I groaned and burrowed even further under the covers as I tried to recall Jack's phone call. He was angry. I knew that. And I led him to believe Dean was taking me home. And then I left. The memories came slowly back like a loosely fit jigsaw puzzle.

I left the bar in a cab with Dean. I moaned miserably again. Am I at Dean's? I looked around the room for more clues. First—I was wearing a man's t-shirt. But it was grey and non-descript and I didn't know Dean well enough to know what types of shirts he wore.

A knock on the door startled me and I crawled up against the headboard. I curled my legs up in front of me, and hoped that somehow, I could let Dean down easily. A quick glance to the side of the bed told me it was still made. It hadn't been slept in.

I sunk my head into my knees. Thank goodness.

"Yea?" I asked, when someone knocked again. My throat felt like I had swallowed a bowl full of broken glass and I cringed at the sound of my own voice.

My mouth dropped open when Marcus peeked his head in through the door.

"You awake?"

"I'm in *your* house? How in the hell did that happen?"

Marcus chuckled and stepped into his room. He was holding a large bottle of a yellow sports drink, a bottle of pills, and my phone.

"Oh god, you're my hero," I moaned and rested my head back against the headboard. Marcus handed me the drink and my pills.

"Jack's been calling every ten minutes for the last hour. He's kind of a persistent ass, isn't he?"

Marcus had no idea. I turned my phone off without even looking at the number of missed calls I had.

"What happened to me last night?" I asked after guzzling half of the drink bottle.

His shoulders started shaking as he shook his head and sat down on the bed by my feet. "I called you when you were out because Logan had a nightmare and couldn't go back to sleep. Dean brought you here and dropped you off, but Logan had already fallen back asleep. You could barely walk so I brought you in here. You don't remember?" He laughed again and I could only imagine what dumbass things my drunk-self did.

"Do I even want to know?"

"Nothing bad I swear. You were funny."

"Glad I could amuse you. Thanks for letting me stay."

"Not a problem. I have eggs and bacon cooking for Logan and me. Feel like you could stomach some food, right now?"

Grease sounded exceptionally good. "Can I use your bathroom to get cleaned up a bit first?"

He nodded and went to the bathroom and came out a few seconds later with a towel and unopened toothbrush. "Not a problem. But can I give you a suggestion?"

"What's that?"

"Call Jack before he has a heart attack. I turned your phone on last night to call Macy to let her know you were here and you had ten missed calls from him. And another handful of calls and texts this morning."

I wrinkled my nose and felt myself grow crimson from anger and embarrassment. I didn't want to call Jack. I barely remembered the phone call from the bar. Although I could figure from his incessant calling afterwards, it probably didn't end so well.

I nodded and closed the door to the bathroom. Mascara ran halfway down my cheeks, my brown hair was matted and crazy from sleeping on it, and I had lipstick smeared all over my mouth. I looked like a demented clown.

Before Jack could call or text me again, I sent him a quick text message, hoping it would pacify him.

I'm fine. Now leave me alone.

I took the few necessary minutes I needed to wash my face and brush my teeth. I was so dehydrated from the night before, I guzzled water straight from the bathroom tap as if I would never see water again.

Finally, I stopped ignoring the constant buzzing on my cell phone and answered it when Jack called again. I should have known better than think that text would do anything except irritate him further.

"Where are you?" He barked as soon as I answered. Had I been a dog, my teeth would be snarling and the hair on my back would be standing straight up I was so instantly irritated at his tone.

I bit my cheek to keep from snapping back at him.

"What do you want, Jack?" I asked, exhaustion pouring through my voice.

He sighed and I could hear him grinding his teeth through the phone. "You didn't come home last night and I want to know where you are. That you're safe."

I looked around Marcus' master bathroom and one edge of my lips tilted up. "How did you know I didn't come home?" I asked as sweetly as possible, even though I knew I was goading him. He was about ready to snap all of his control, and a part of me, liked pissing him off. Served him right.

"Because I've been sitting outside your building waiting for you ever since you fucking hung up on me. Now where are you?"

I shook my head, irritation and fury growing within me, but I refused to let him see it. "Stop worrying. I'm fine, and I'll be home later so you can drop your watch outside my place."

"Did Dean take you home?"

I pursed my lips. Why would he think that? Oh yes, I had let him believe that before I hung up on him. I knew he wouldn't be any happier knowing I ended up at Marcus's so I wisely kept my mouth shut.

"Listen, Jack, I don't really remember much of what happened last night, but I'm not exactly feeling like telling you everything going on in my life when you think you can throw me over your couch, screw me like I'm some sort of animal, not bother answering one fucking question of mine and then fire me. I don't owe you anything. And I certainly don't want to talk to you."

The sound of a throat clearing made me snap my head to the right. Marcus's eyes were wide and I instantly paled. Based on the shocked look he wore, I had a feeling he had just heard every single word I threw at Jack.

I rubbed the tips of my fingers across my forehead trying to soothe my pounding headache and hide my embarrassment.

"Breakfast is ready," he whispered. Before he turned away, I mouthed a silent thank you to him as Jack groaned unhappily into my ear.

"I know I owe you an explanation …" he began saying but I cut him off.

"And an apology. A big fat ass, I'm the world's biggest asshole apology."

"I know," he said with a slight chuckle. I wanted it to piss me off, instead it only calmed me down. I couldn't believe I was even joking around with him about this, but damn it I loved him and I knew something huge happened to piss him off so badly. Not that it made me want to instantly go another round with him, but I still didn't hate him, either.

"I'll make it up to you. But I can't explain what's going on. I just need you safe."

I rolled my eyes in the bathroom mirror before walking out to meet Marcus and Logan for breakfast.

I sat down at the kitchen table while Marcus served me up a plate of eggs and bacon. I plastered on the fakest smile I could muster given the circumstances and squeezed Logan's hand next to me while he shoveled his eggs in his mouth as fast as his little mouth could open.

"Did you have a fun sleepover with daddy?"

Logan smiled and squeezed out mushy eggs through the gap in his two front teeth. Gross. "We built Legos and he said I could stay over again."

"Anytime you want to, buddy, you got it."

We finished our breakfast with an awkward silence filling the table. Now that my headache was disappearing, I was starting to recall even more of my night.

I turned to Marcus. "Did you get fish?"

"We don't fish, mommy!" Logan said but Marcus choked on his eggs. His shoulders shook with laughter and I stared at him, wondering what in the hell I had just said.

Finally, he drank his orange juice and wiped his drool off the sides of his mouth. He shook his head, still laughing. "No, I don't have fish here."

"Why am I thinking you do?"

With a laughing smile he just shook his head. "You don't want to know. Remember anything else from your night?"

It was all kind of fuzzy. Like I was replaying my drunken memories through a hazy tunnel with holes.

"A little bit," I replied and began clearing my breakfast dishes. "We should probably get going soon."

"Daddy said I could go to a baseball game today. Can I mommy, please?"

I looked at Marcus's sheepish grin. His eyes lit up every time Logan called him dad or daddy. Guilt smacked me through my chest again.

"That's fine," I smiled at Logan and grabbed my purse. "Just bring him back to my place after?"

Marcus nodded and said a quick thanks before turning to Logan and told him to go get dressed.

"So how did everything go last night, besides the nightmare?" I asked, once we were alone.

He grinned, "You have no idea how awesome it was. To be able to have my son here, watching movies with me, and teaching me how to play Sorry."

"He suckered you into a game, huh?"

"More like five," he said and then his face turned more serious. "You get everything worked out with Jack?"

I rolled my eyes and blinked several times to keep tears from reappearing. "He fired me," I whispered out and hung my head.

Whatever reaction I was thinking Marcus was going to give, his complete lack of one, was completely unexpected.

All I saw was red. It started at the outside of my vision and sparkled like firecrackers until an entire firework show was going off inside my eyes. "You knew?"

He licked his lips and pressed his mouth into a tight white line. "I'm one of his lawyers."

Lawyers? What in the hell did he need his lawyers for?

"What's that mean?" I narrowed my eyes and could feel my nerves on fire. Except I wasn't nervous. I was full out pissed. I threw my chair back, grabbed my purse and stalked to the door. "You're on his acquisition team. How in the hell does that have anything to do with me?"

Marcus followed me with a hesitant look in his eyes. "I can't say. But just know he didn't want to. He thinks he has to."

"What am I supposed to do with that Marcus? I just lost the man … I just lost my damn job and I have Logan to take care of!" I cringed at my shouting, and that I had almost confessed to loving Jack. It made my headache split wide open and the last thing I wanted was for Logan to hear me yelling at his dad. I took a deep breathe, exhaling loudly, and tried to calm down before I strangled someone.

He looked down at the floor with his hands in his pockets and shook his head. "I can't tell you anymore, I'm really sorry. But just know that I'll be here to help with Logan in any way I can."

"Screw you, Marcus," I spat out as I opened the door and looked back. "Besides, I still have your daddy's blood money. Logan and I will be just fine. Just bring him to my place after the game."

I slammed the door in his face as soon as I saw his eyes widen in surprise.

Twenty

I missed Jack like crazy. I was upset, and hurt, and cried myself to sleep almost every night, over the course of the next week, only managing to put a brave happy face on for Logan during the day. I had to act as if nothing was wrong, for his sake, but even he noticed the lack of Jack's presence in his little life. I hated it. Seeing him miss a man who had been there for him since he was born, was almost like feeling he had lost another dad. I hated having to snuggle him and tell him we wouldn't be seeing Jack anymore.

I resisted the urge to call Jack and scream at him for not only screwing me over, but my son as well. All his promises he gave me had been shot down the drain. Logan missed him. I missed him like crazy and I hated that Jack invaded my nightly dreams. They weren't the nightmares I wanted, either. They were fantasies of his large hands on every inch of my body, pulling on my nipples and turning them into tight pink buds, and images of him entering me, pleasuring me like no man before him had ever done.

I woke up several times during the night and taken matters into my own hands, furious at myself for fantasizing about the same man who had taken my heart when I was hesitant to give it away and then stomped all over it.

It shocked me when on the following Thursday, I got a text from Martin asking me to meet him at Peet's Coffee Shop, a local and delicious coffee house in Lincoln Park. Their coffee was better than Starbuck's and it had a great little play table in the back for kids to sit at so I could take Logan with me.

I arrived before Martin so I settled Logan at the table with a coloring book and crayons, some metal die-cast cars, and took a seat at a spot a few tables away from the kiddie area. I could keep my eye on Logan, but have privacy to talk to Martin.

He showed up a few minutes later and I drank my caramel latte while I waited for him to get his drink and join me. He gave me a sad, half-smile when we greeted each other and pulled out the chair on the other side of the table.

"Jack wanted me to meet with you."

I figured. I took a sip of my drink and arched an eyebrow. "Why's that?"

Martin laughed silently and shook his head. "You're too smart for your own good most of the time, Emma. But sometimes, you're really naïve."

"Thanks for the compliment."

"If you think Jack is doing any of this, for any reason except for you, then you don't know him."

The admonishment settled like a weight in my gut. How did firing me help me? Why should I trust Jack? Was I wrong to be mad at him right now based on what Martin just said? A dozen questions flew through my mind as I watched Martin watching me, thinking about all of this.

"I wanted my job," I said quietly, but doubt had already filled my mind.

Martin nodded and said nothing, but slid a thin brown envelope across the table to me. I opened it slowly and frowned. Inside was a letter of recommendation and my severance. It was enough to cover a year of my salary. I took the check out and held it in my shaking hands, feeling suddenly more disappointed in Jack than I had the day he fired me.

Would I ever meet a man who didn't think they could just pay me off when things went south? Was this all I was worth to the men I invited into my life?

Tears pricked my eyes and I felt my nerves begin to boil in anger and disappointment.

Sliding the check across the table to Martin, I wiped the first fallen tears off my cheek. "I don't want this."

Marin sighed. "He's trying to help, Emma."

"And I've already got a bank account full of pay-off money. I don't need to add his to it."

"That's not what this is. He's trying to do the right thing, and even if you don't agree with it, just know that he still cares about and wants to take care of you."

I set my coffee mug down on the table, too harshly, and grabbed the attention of a few nearby customers. I cringed and looked at Logan. He was obliviously playing with cars on a padded foam mat and car ramp.

"You know what I'm getting really sick and tired of, Mr. Crawlson? People thinking they know how best to help me, but not telling me why I need the help in the first place."

He nodded slowly, but reluctantly took the check. I pocketed the recommendation letter in my pocket even though I didn't want Jack's help at all with getting a new job.

Martin's eyes softened and he took a sip of his coffee. "Has he ever told you about his parents?"

Curiosity bloomed in me. No, he hadn't. I'd always wanted to know how they died, but too afraid to ask, worried he wouldn't give me the answers. I shook my head.

"It was a house fire." Martin set his cup down, and clasped his hands together in front of him on the table. I sat up straighter, intrigued and frightened at the same time. "Something about faulty electrical wiring during a kitchen remodel. They were all sleeping at the time, and Jack's dad got Jack out and went back in for his mom." I wiped away a tear, knowing how everything ended before Martin finished his story. "They never came out. Steven had to tackle Jack from running back into the house to look for them."

"Oh my god." I couldn't even imagine what Jack must have gone through as a young teenager watching his parents burn alive, knowing he couldn't get to them. No wonder why he was always freaking about me being safe. It explained so much.

"Steven always told me that after that, he watched this happy young kid go to an angry teenager, pissed off at the world, but once he got his head on straight, he shut off everything else around him. Steven always thought he was trying to prove to his parents that he could be the kid they wanted, and he worked hard at it. Almost obsessively so, until you came along. You're his weak spot, Emma. The first person he has opened up to in almost twenty years."

His hand reached across the table and held mine. His hands were a little bit wrinkly, showing his age at almost sixty, but they were firm and warm. Caring. "Don't take the money, but don't second guess for a single second that he doesn't care about you. You may be the only thing he *does* care about."

"Then why did he fire me?" It was all so confusing to me. I had to know. I had a *right* to know what went so horribly wrong between us.

Martin shook his head. "I can't tell you that, but hopefully Jack will be able to tell you someday soon."

I pressed my lips together, thinking about that for a minute. Did it even matter? Regardless of the reason, I wasn't important enough to Jack for him to want me by his side when things got rough.

Finishing my coffee, I stood up and called Logan's name, getting his attention.

"Thanks for the letter, Martin. Take care." I waved good-bye as Logan and I walked back to our apartment. We turned the corner of the coffee shop and from outside I could see Martin talking on the phone, shaking his head and frowning, and looking at the refused severance check. I fought the urge to go back inside and grab the phone from him, knowing he was talking to Jack.

"I still think there's something really shady going on." Macy took another sip of her red wine and sat back down on my couch.

She was over for a girl's night while Logan was out with Marcus again. If I wasn't so stressed out from a lack of a job, and completely heartbroken over Jack, it could have actually been a nice vacation.

I had wanted to call Jack when I got home. I wanted to tell him I was sorry about his parents, sorry about his life and beg him to open up to me, but I didn't. I called Macy instead, hoping she'd be able to distract me.

"Can we please not talk about him anymore? I've heard enough about Jack today." Not really, my heart was broken and feeling even more shattered after learning about his parents. I was upset, but I also wanted to call him and crawl into his arms and just hold him. No wonder why he claimed to be broken.

Macy flipped me a look. It said I was full of bullshit and she wasn't going to push, but our conversation wasn't over.

I pretended to flip through the re-admission paperwork for DePaul University I downloaded earlier in the week. I also had a stack of paperwork for Chicago University, Marquette University, and Notre Dame. I hated the idea of running away and going out of state to finish school. I didn't want to be the girl that ran from the guy who broke her heart. I wanted to be strong and hold my own ground. Chicago was my city and I'd be damned if I let Jack and my feelings for him cause me to cower like a scared little girl in a corner, afraid to see him.

But I was, and I hated it. Everywhere I went over the last week, I saw Jack. I saw him in the parks we'd taken Logan, I saw him when I drove by businesses and buildings I knew he had bought and or sold. Everywhere I turned, reminders of him smacked me in the face and made my chest ache.

Who knew Chicago was such a small town?

"I still can't believe you're thinking of going out of state for college, though. Don't get me wrong, I'm proud of you for wanting to finish college finally, but Indiana or Wisconsin? Do you have to go so far away?"

I pushed the hair off my face and looked at my best friend's sad eyes. She hated this just as much as me, and she had the added bonus of having to see Jack every day. Something she hadn't let me forget. Apparently over the last week, he'd become even more difficult to work for and this girl's night in was for her, just as much as it was for me.

"I don't know, Mace," I said quietly and then picked up the letter of recommendation Martin had given me. It was impressive, cataloging all the work I'd done for Jack and singing my praises. If I were to send this letter out, I'd be able to get a job with no problems. Having such a glowing recommendation from Jack McMillan would surely open dozens of doors for me. And yet, I hated … hated the idea of allowing him to help me. If I was going to move on, I was going to do it my way and not take a single little bit of help from him.

"I just … I don't know. I feel like I need to get away. With everything going on with Jack, and now Marcus, I feel like I might explode."

"But Wisconsin? Really?" She wrinkled her nose into a squishy icky face and I giggled.

"I know," I said, smiling now. It was practically sacrilegious for a die-hard Chicagoan to move to the cheese state up north. "But Notre Dame and Marquette are still close enough to be able to see you on the weekends, and for Marcus to see Logan."

"How's the daddy doing, anyway?" she asked with a slight inflection I wasn't sure I appreciated. Marcus had become, friendlier, over the last week to say the least.

He started coming a little bit earlier every time it was time to pick up Logan, and staying a bit later every time he dropped him off. He said it was because he wanted to be around Logan as much as possible, and I wanted to believe it, but I had also caught a few lingering glances of his in my direction. He watched me just a little bit closer … with his eyes a little bit softer. I didn't say anything, afraid I would embarrass myself around him. I wanted to believe that he was concerned about me.

Something told me it was more than that though, and I wasn't sure how I felt about it. So I did the most mature thing possible and ignored it. Denial was my closest ally when it came to Marcus.

I rolled my eyes at Macy. "He's fine. He took Logan to a movie tonight."

"That's not exactly what I meant." She set down her glass of wine on the coffee table and leaned back against the couch. "I heard him in Jack's office today."

I shook my head. "I said I don't want to hear about him anymore."

She raised an eyebrow. "Not even if they were arguing about you?"

My hands froze on the Notre Dame campus brochure. I set it down when I noticed my hands were shaking. I did want to know. I desperately wanted to know what in the hell changed so quickly with Jack that he could profess his love for me and then throw me out like some used tramp. I knew something was going on, and I hated that everything ended with so many questions. And yet, I was too afraid to hear the truth. Maybe he just decided I wasn't worth the trouble, or that Logan wasn't worth it, and Marcus was just defending my honor or some silly bullshit.

Either way, I didn't think knowing the truth, or the rumors about what Jack and Marcus were yelling about would help anything.

"How are your wedding plans coming?" I asked, changing the subject again. It was the lamest attempt in the history of the world and Macy pursed her lips, but because she loved me, she humored me.

"Fine," she said. Then she picked up her three-inch thick binder that she used for coordinating every single possible need she could have for her wedding. Everything was tabbed and color coordinated. Pictures and prices of wedding venues, invitations, florists and potential bouquet pictures, dozens of styles of bridesmaid dresses, and everything else you could imagine were packaged perfectly into sheet protectors inside this binder. She guarded that book with her life.

She was a little bit psycho about the wedding planning, although January was only a few months away. Why she wanted a winter wedding, I had no idea. Chicago in the winter was freezing cold, windy, and downright miserable. But she got stars in her eyes and looked all fan-girl silly when she talked in a dream like voice about starting out the new year, as a new bride with a new name and the man of her dreams.

Who was I to argue with my best friend's happiness? If a January wedding was what she wanted, I wanted to help her in any way that I could. Even though I cringed when she kept showing me pictures of strapless maid of honor dresses.

I feigned a groan of frustration when she opened it to the invitation section and patted the seat next to her on the couch.

"You asked for it," she said jokingly and I moved to sit next to her. We spent the next couple of hours, drinking wine, laughing about Tate and Dean, and picking out invitations for the bridal shower and wedding, along with flowers for the wedding party.

When Marcus brought Logan home, we were well into our second bottle of wine and laughing hysterically about You Tube videos we had watched with wedding parties doing flash dances down the aisle. It was apparently all the rage in weddings this season, but Tate had two left feet and we couldn't imagine him pulling off something so cool looking.

We were right in the middle of drunkenly acting out Tate's version of smooth dancing—which looked similar to the chicken dance -when Marcus opened the door.

His jaw dropped in surprise as we sang and robotically moved, off beat, to Maroon 5 blaring through my speakers.

"Having fun?" He finally asked with a smug grin. Logan held his hand and looked up at his dad with a questioning look. He probably wondered what in the world was going on with his crazy mom. Macy and I collapsed onto the couch in a fit of laughter.

Gasping for breath through my laughter, I held my arms open for

Logan to crawl into them. "We were pretending to be Tate dancing."

Marcus chuckled and set down Logan's backpack before joining us in the living room. He turned down the volume on the stereo so we could hear him and smiled lazily at Logan curled into my lap.

"He's exhausted," he said with a nod of his head in Logan's direction.

"Did you have fun at the movie?" I asked, and rubbed my hands through Logan's hair.

"I got to wear glasses and thought the monsters were going to eat me," he said with a worried look.

"What movie did you take him to?"

Marcus shrugged. "It was just a kid's movie in 3-D. And it wasn't that bad. I'm sure he'll be fine."

"Sure, until I'm the one up with him having nightmares during the night."

"I could always stay over, just in case." Marcus said with a small teasing of his lips. But his voice was smoother than it had been before, and a little bit deeper, and I had a feeling he wasn't just concerned about Logan and his possible nightmares.

"And that's my cue to take off," Macy said with a cheeky smile thrown in Marcus's direction. I frowned, but helped her pack up her wedding binder and walked her to the door.

"I'll get Logan ready for bed," Marcus said and held his hand while they walked to his room.

"Don't do anything stupid," Macy said as she walked out the door.

I frowned. She could be referring to a dozen stupid things. I wondered which one she meant specifically.

"About school. Don't let Jack be the reason you take off. Schools in Chicago are great, if not better, than your other options and you know it. I might have to kick your ass if you take off."

I opened my mouth to respond but she skewered me with a glance. "Just think about it before you decide."

I nodded and closed the door.

Logan and Marcus were laughing in his bedroom so I went in to see them huddled together in his full size bed. Marcus was laying on his side, one arm curled under Logan, his other hand holding Logan's favorite Corduroy book.

"Crash went the lamp!" Logan said when they got to the page where the little bear knocked over the lamp in the department store. I crossed my arms and leaned against the doorway, watching Marcus read to our son and a feeling of warmth spread over me. I had dreamed of this scene for years, Marcus and I as a family, tucking our baby into bed.

Marcus's blond hair fell almost to his eyes. I remembered how soft it used to be when I would run my fingers through it when we were together. It was a little bit shorter now, and styled more professionally, but his natural light blond highlights were the same. The edges of his eyes wrinkled a little bit as he smiled at Logan while reading the story. He was older now, and so much the man I remembered, but in a way, better looking. He looked peaceful, curled up reading his son a bedtime story.

I felt tears pricking at the edges of my eyes and backed out of the room before they saw me, but when I hit the living room, I picked up my camera and tip-toed back to the room. I wanted to remember this moment and I knew Marcus would, too.

I caught both of their attentions when they heard the camera click as I took the picture. Marcus set the book down on Logan's lap and leaned in to give him a kiss on his cheek.

I smiled, happily, at the joy that flooded Logan's face and the tears returned. I was right in the middle of living out the dreams that used to torment me at night after Marcus left, and in the first couple of years after Logan was born. The memories of those dreams and the real-life events occurring right before me scared the crap out of me.

Marcus said good night and walked to the door.

He lightly put a hand on my arm and my body warmed instantly. This was a softer touch than the friendly ones he'd given me, and his eyes were more serious when he gazed down into mine. "Logan wants a kiss good night from you," he finally said and quietly left the room.

I watched him leave the room and when he was gone, I realized I was still frozen in the same spot. What in the heck just happened?

I shook off the funny feelings I felt when Marcus touched me and looked at me like that. It was just so familiar. Safe. And nothing at all like Jack.

I gave Logan his kiss good night, tucked him into bed by tucking the sheets of his bed down the length of his body and under his feet. It was our nightly ritual of tuck-tuck-tuck so he was as snug as a bug in a rug, and we giggled just like always.

I closed the door to his room, smiling at my perfect little boy. He was the best thing to happen to me in the world.

I froze again when I reached the living room. This time, there was no warmth in Marcus's eyes. He stood in the middle of the room, his green eyes looking positively glacial and held up the brochures for the colleges Macy and I had spent most of the night talking about.

"What in the hell is this shit?" he spat out and smacked them down on the coffee table.

I ignored him and walked to the kitchen, knowing I had some explaining to do, but not knowing how to start.

"Want a drink?" I asked casually, but based on the anger that flickered across his face, only pissed him off more.

"Beer. And then explain to me why you think you're going to leave the state with my kid."

I bristled at the accusation but handed him his beer anyway. "They're less than two hours away, Marcus. And I'm not taking Logan from you. You'd still be close enough to see him on the weekends."

He looked panicked as he took a long pull on his beer, almost finishing half of it with one large gulp. He wiped his mouth with the back of his hand and took a deep breath. "I just started getting to know him, Emma. You can't leave now."

"I don't know if I can stay," I said after a few minutes of quiet, but thick tension prickled in the air between us. "I don't even know if I'm going back to school. I've just been trying to figure out what in the hell I'm supposed to do now. Without …"

I cringed and stopped talking.

"Jack," he supplied. His voice was full of venom and anger as he spit the word out like it was the most foul four letter word in existence. Although, it did have four letters, so maybe he wasn't too far off the mark.

I nodded and re-filled my own glass of wine.

Marcus sounded softer when he spoke again. "You know, a part of me is really pissed off that Jack hurt you like this. I hate seeing you this broken, and sad."

Irritation rippled through my nerves, making me feel like I needed to shed a layer of skin. I didn't want to talk about Jack with Marcus and I certainly didn't want anyone telling me how broken I looked.

"It was worse after you left, if that makes you feel any better."

Marcus gasped. "Are you fucking serious right now? No, that doesn't make me feel any better! Damn it, Emma. I hate what I did to you, and I feel like shit every single day knowing that I left you—with Jack, no less to take care of what's mine."

I don't know what in the hell he had to be so pissed about, but I certainly wasn't anyone's possession. The very mention of the word 'mine' threw me back to visions of Jack and how he so adamantly declared that Logan and I were his to protect and care for. How did it get so screwed up so quickly?

"I'm not yours," I said through tears that began falling. I hated them. I hated every single tear I let fall for Jack, because I knew. I knew this was going to happen the minute I first touched him at that stupid Irish Pub. I knew I would let him in and he would crush my heart into a million pieces and that was exactly how I felt right then.

I looked down at the floor, almost as if I could see my heart beating on the tiled floor at my feet.

Before I knew it, I was wrapped in arms that at one time, had been my favorite place in the world to be.

"I'm sorry, that's not what I meant." Marcus held me while my sobs were the only sounds filling the entire apartment.

When I quieted down and stopped shaking, I realized who was holding me and slowly backed away.

"Sorry," I said while wiping my tears and giving him the most pathetic smile ever. "I just … I didn't mean to do that."

Marcus took a few steps away and rested his hands at his sides. "You know, what I was going to finish saying was that I hate that he's broken you like this. But the other part of me … the other part is glad you're single again."

My eyes widened and he held up a hand to stop me. What in the hell was he saying?

He held his arms out, and looked at me nervously. "I always wanted this, Emma. You, me, and our child. I know I fucked it up. I know I don't deserve another chance, and I definitely know now is a really bad time to even bring it up. But being with Logan at the movie tonight, and the sleepover last week? It's just not the same without you. I want my family. I want the family we—you and me—always wanted together. And you might think I'm an asshole for saying this now, but I'd hate myself if I bit my tongue and didn't tell you."

What did I say to that? I stared at him, my eyes wide with wonder and amazement at the proclamations I just heard, and just stared. I don't know how long I looked at him, feeling—who knows what in the hell I was feeling at that moment. I missed Jack. And I loved Jack. My heart was broken from the way Jack treated me. But at one time, I loved Marcus. He had been it for me and I was so sure when I was young, and twenty, that I had found the man I was going to spend the rest of my life with.

I looked at him. Really looked at the man he had become and even though I hadn't looked at him with anything more than an attraction before, now, I saw him. He made my stomach flutter as we stared at each other in my little galley kitchen. He was taller, his shoulders broader, and his jaw more square. He had that same smile. It was lazy, like he didn't care about anything in the world, but I knew how passionate he was. I knew what his hands felt like when they caressed my body softly, gently, as he tenderly made love to me for the first time and took my virginity. He cared for me. He used to, many years ago and I could see that same protective, but loving look he gave me now.

He was nothing like Jack.

Marcus … this Marcus, was safe, and he was the father of my child. Did I owe it to Logan to see if we could make something work again? Did I owe it to my son to see if we could be a family the way we had originally planned?

"Marcus," I finally said, ending our staring contest. I didn't know what I wanted to say. I didn't know if I should say okay, or get the hell out of my house, or what. It was too confusing. Too emotionally surprising, given the shitty week I had had.

My eyes grew wider, and my stomach flipped as he closed the few spaces between us and cupped my cheek with his hand. It was soft and tender, just like I remembered and I found myself leaning into the warmth he provided.

"I don't need an answer, tonight," he said softly. I tilted my head up to look at him and blinked. His green eyes were softened; just like they used to be when he looked at me in college. I remembered that look. Did he really feel the same way he used to? "I just needed you to know. But please," he said and nodded towards the living room, "don't take Logan away. Don't leave me, until you know for sure it's the best thing for everyone."

I swallowed slowly, thinking of what he was asking from me, and then I froze. Marcus leaned forward softly, aligning his firm and muscular body with mine just like he used to. It sent chills down my spine. How could I feel like this, with Marcus –the man I hated more than anyone just over a month ago? But I did, and my body responded before my heart could tell it to back the hell up.

Before I knew it, his soft, warm lips were pressing gently against my forehead. I did nothing. I couldn't move. I almost wanted to put my hands on his waist to see what he felt like, but before I could even finish the thought, much less act on it, he pulled away and smiled down at me.

"I'm willing to wait for you to figure everything out with Jack, but I also want you to know I'm not going anywhere. I just want a chance to have the family we used to want."

He lightly brushed my cheek with my knuckles and headed for the door.

I stood in the kitchen, long after he left, polishing off my bottle of wine alone wondering what in the hell just happened. His parting words left me thinking. What stuff did Jack and I have to work out?

He left me. Fired me. And I was left to pick up the pieces and figure out a way to provide for Logan and myself.

Twenty-One

"This place is pretty damn cool," Macy said with awe as we walked into SkyJump, an indoor trampoline park, for Logan's fifth birthday party. A dozen of his classmates gathered in the entryway, their parents signing release forms, while Macy and I were standing, mouths wide open at the massive room filled with one enormous trampoline. It was the length of the entire room, had red padding in between the individual trampolines, and they curved up the walls at least eight feet in the air.

It was awesome and I couldn't wait to get on them and jump off some much needed steam. Dean, Tate and Marcus had already taken off their shoes and joined Logan on the trampolines, jumping around like the big kids they were.

We bounced and jumped for an hour. Tate and Dean stopped halfway through, completely out of breath after doing flips and jumps and trying like hell to impress a bunch of little kids.

Macy and I laughed so hard while we threw ourselves off the wall, that we almost peed our pants. That was my cue to take a break along with the other guys, although Marcus and Macy stayed on, determined to get their money's worth for every single second.

My legs shook from overuse by the time I got off. I walked over to Dean, fixing my messed up ponytail, a huge smile on my face, my breath panting like I'd just run a marathon. My legs were going to be so sore by the time bedtime hit.

"That was so awesome," Dean said, while chugging a bottle of water.

"I know," I breathed out. "Who knew a place like this could be so fun. I wonder how many kids puke on it."

"Gross. Probably more than we could imagine." He took another chug of his water and then turned to me, more serious. "How are you?"

"Crappy, to be honest." I shrugged and smiled at Marcus trying to teach Logan and his friend, Spencer, how to do a back flip. I cringed, hoping Logan's birthday party wouldn't end in a trip to the Emergency Room. "I'll get over it, though."

"You still thinking of running?"

I pursed my lips. "I was never thinking of running, but sometimes a change of scenery can be a good thing. You of all people should know that," I reminded him of the night we met and he had said he went out of state for work to get away from his family's expectations and not just take what he was given.

He shrugged. "Yeah, but I had good reasons. You'd just be leaving because you're scared."

"Whatever, it doesn't matter. I sent my applications in this week to Chicago only schools." I smiled and winked at Dean. For someone who I had originally thought was going to be a stuck-up little rich boy, he had turned into a good friend over the last couple of months.

I thought he would smile back, but instead, his shoulders tightened and one of his arms went around my shoulders. I frowned.

"Jack's here." He narrowed his eyes and looked out the window to the entryway behind us. "Want me to tell him to leave?"

How did Jack even know we were going to be here? And why was he here? My hands started shaking nervously and I felt my heart begin racing out of control.

"What?" I asked with a voice so shaky I could barely understand myself.

Slowly, Dean turned me around, but kept his hand on my shoulder the whole time so that by the time I was staring at Jack through the windows, Dean was standing completely behind me, both his hands on my shoulders, holding me up.

My mouth dropped and I leaned back into him.

"What am I supposed to do?" I asked as I turned my head to Dean and away from Jack. I couldn't describe the look on Jack's face. His lips were pulled into a tight white line and his free hand was stuffed into his front pocket. His eyes were unreadable. Blank and cold and absolutely devoid of any emotion as he stared at the two of us.

"I can make him leave," Dean repeated, but I shook my head.

"It's okay, I can handle it." Dean gave me a doubtful look, but let go of my shoulders anyway.

With shaky legs, I took a few steps out of his protective hold and walked to the entryway doors to meet Jack. It was the first time I had seen him in weeks and I could feel large, angry butterflies trying to burst free from my stomach. I suddenly felt like throwing up and knew it had nothing to do with the thirty minutes I had just spent jumping around.

Jack did this to me. He always made me feel all sorts of crazy. Where before it was in awe and wonder at the man who could make me feel beautiful and desired and wanted like no one else had before, now, I was terrified. Why was he here?

"What are you doing here?" I asked as I met him outside. He stayed on the sidewalk the entire time, never once entering the place we were having Logan's birthday. He held up a gift bag in one of his hands that was decorated with Star Wars Lego people.

"It's Logan's birthday, I wanted to bring him a gift."

I crossed my arms and took a step back, refusing to take the gift he offered.

"I don't want it."

"It's not for you," he said with a frown.

"I'm not letting you give that to Logan. He's finally just stopped asking questions about why you left us … why you left him. And I'm not going to give him anything to encourage the idea that you might be coming back into his life. It wouldn't be fair to him."

"Emma …" He roughly ran his free hand through his hair. He looked down at the ground and when he looked back up to me, I saw how tired his eyes looked. Stress lined his forehead, and he wore purple circles under his eyes. He opened his mouth to say something but then closed it. I hated it when people did that.

"What?" I snapped at him and looked back to Dean and into SkyJump, wondering if anyone could see us. I had a straight view of the trampoline area so I took a few steps backwards, out of view from everyone else and gave Dean a head nod, letting him know I was okay.

"Are you dating him?" Jack asked me, his eyes narrowed in anger. I felt anger and annoyance prickle every nerve in my body. I bit the inside of my bottom lip, for just a second, trying to hold myself back from saying anything stupid and then decided I didn't care.

"None of your business." I spit at him, my eyes looking just as pissed off.

And then, I saw it. I saw the regret and pain flash through Jack's eyes as he stared me down. Did he regret breaking things off with me or firing me? I wanted to know. I had to know. At the same time, I was terrified that what I saw was just an illusion. Jack was a master manipulator with the gift of getting anyone to do what he wanted to do, at least when it came to business. Hell over the last few weeks since we'd been apart, I'd spent enough hours wondering if all I was to him was just some manipulation. He came on so strong and swooped me up, making promises he didn't end up keeping. Was I just a game to him - screw the housekeeper when he got tired of the blonde supermodels that typically clung to him?

"I'm sorry," Jack finally said, as we stood there staring at each other for who knows how long. "I'm sorry for everything … for hurting you."

"Why did you?" I asked, quickly blinking back the tears of frustration, anger and pain that I tried so hard, every day, to keep in check so no one could truly see how much he broke me.

He shook his head and took a deep breath. "I can't … I can't tell you. Just know that it was best thing for everyone, considering."

"Considering what, Jack? Why can't you just be honest with me for once and stop screwing around with my head?" And my heart. I felt my chin begin to tremble and knew I couldn't hold back the tears for too much longer.

"Just forget it," I said as I lowered my head and tried to walk around him. He grabbed my elbow as I passed him, his large warm hand that I knew with so much familiarity instantly left a burning sensation and a trail of goose bumps along my arm. When I tried to pull out of his grasp, he held on tighter; not hard enough to hurt me, but with enough force to let me know we clearly weren't done with our conversation.

"I can't forget it. And I can't forget you. Just … shit!" He yelled and pulled me to him. Without warning, my body was flushed to him, his hand still gripping my elbow and his other hand wrapped around my waist. "I miss you, and I'm sorry I hurt you. But I need you to know that I'm hurting too, and I'm trying to fix everything."

I wiggled with enough force that he finally let me go. "There's nothing to fix," I said once I took a few steps away, closer to the entrance to SkyJump, although I really wanted to throw myself back into his arms. I wanted him to make me forget my pain. I wanted his hands on me and to breathe him in like he used to let me do after he'd screwed me senseless. Memories of our time together assaulted me on the sidewalk as I stared at the man I loved.

"You ruined us, Jack. There's nothing else to say."

I turned to walk away and ran smack into a firm wall of muscle. "Are you okay?" Marcus whispered into my ear. I wrapped my arms around his waist without even thinking, or caring, that Jack was still there watching me. I nodded, although I knew my tears were already falling silently against his sweaty shirt.

"You need to leave," Marcus said, not backing down from Jack or removing his arms from mine. "You know what this could do."

Even in my emotional breakdown, I knew something was going on that I didn't understand, and yet, needed to know.

"What are you talking about?" I finally pulled back and stepped away from Marcus. He pressed his lips together and I turned to Jack who was still there, boring his eyes into mine. Pleading with me for … something.

Marcus shook his head.

"What are you two not telling me?" I demanded, my voice raising with every word.

They ignored me, but Jack turned to Marcus. "Keep your hands off her."

"Fuck you, Jack." I spat at him, but he pretended I wasn't there as he stalked angrily towards Marcus.

"You're using this to your advantage, aren't you?" He glared at Marcus and I watched these two men stand off against each other. What in the hell was he talking about? "You little shit. I will fire you if you screw me over once this is all said and done."

Marcus smirked and I cringed. It was the same evil look his dad had mastered. I had never seen him look so feral. "I don't need this job, Jack. And you and I both know you need me right now to clean up this fucking mess you made."

"And you think you'll swoop in and play the knight in shining armor instead of doing your damn job? You and I both know she's still mine."

"Excuse me?" I gasped, stunned. "I don't belong to either of you and I'm not going to stand here like some fire hydrant for you guys to piss all over. Someone better tell me what in the hell is going on, right now."

Jack inhaled through his nose, rolled his shoulders back and ground his teeth together. He didn't look at me, just continued to stare at Marcus as if he could set him on fire just by staring at him. I knew I felt the air heat by that deadly gaze.

I looked at Marcus, who looked equally angry. "It'll be over soon, and then she can decide."

Was I even there? Was I standing there, between these two men, letting them decide that I got to make a decision? My head spun.

"What's going on?" I repeated and then understanding dawned on me. Senator Whitmore's claims at the charity ball and Jack needing Marcus. Somehow, they were connected to the reason Jack fired me and treated me like shit.

"This has to do with your dad, doesn't it?" I asked. My eyes grew larger as everything started to make sense. The Senator had promised me that if he wasn't allowed to see Logan, he'd go public with a scandal to ruin Jack. Something must have happened.

I felt like I was living in a pinball arcade game as my eyes bounced back and forth between Marcus and Jack. Marcus's skin color paled in front of my eyes and Jack looked down at the ground.

"Fine," I said reluctantly and began walking towards the front door. "When either of you can be honest with me, I'll be willing to listen. But I'm pissed at both of you for lying to me and thinking so little of me that you can't tell me what's really going on."

"I can't."

"Whatever, Jack. You can do anything you want. You made your choice, and, it was a shitty one. One that I probably won't be willing to forgive you for. When you can tell me what it is you think you're trying to protect me from, I'll listen. But only because it apparently concerns me and I have a right to know." I looked to Marcus, "I expected honesty from you, too. After all the shit that lying has done to us, I had higher expectations for you."

They had the decency to look chagrined at my outburst. Whatever.

"You both can fuck off," I spit out and re-entered SkyJump.

Dean was talking with Tate and Macy, all three of them clearly concerned about me. "Is it time to open presents and do cake?" I asked, dawning a plastic smile so I could avoid explaining.

Tate went to gather the kids. It gave me a vision of what it would be like to herd cats hopped on steroids. He bounced around the trampolines trying to usher the little kids to the edge of the mats, while they all bounced around and laughed at him pretending to be a monster. Finally, he shouted, "Cake!" And I watched the herd of cats suddenly get in a straight line and run, full speed towards our little party room.

"You okay?" Dean asked, still looking at Marcus and Jack through the windows. They were clearly arguing, Jack looked full on alpha-male pissed off, but Marcus wasn't backing down either as he argued right back and shook his head.

"Whatever. They're both assholes." I turned into Dean's protective arm once again and let him lead me to the party room. We waited a few minutes, trying to get the kids' shoes back on, and have them calm down while we waited for Marcus to come back in. He eventually did, breathing heavily, his face red in anger. We sang happy birthday, ate cake, and watched Logan smile, laugh and rip open birthday presents, squealing with happiness with each new favorite toy he received.

"So what do you think is really going on?"

I scrunched up my nose and shook my head. "I don't know, Macy. I know it has something to do with the Senator threatening me at the charity ball. My guess is he found something he could use to threaten Jack with to get close to Logan."

"Will it change anything if Jack did all of this to protect you and Logan? I know how much you love him."

"I don't know," I replied and went back to cleaning up my kitchen. My entire apartment was a disaster since we had dinner and let Logan rip open all of his new toys, mostly Legos, as soon as we got back from the trampoline park. "I just wish he could have been honest with me. If he's trying to protect me, I have a right to know. You know?"

"Do you really think Marcus is using all of this to get you back?" I didn't know. What Jack said made sense, and Macy did not even know about Marcus asking for us to be a family again. I refused to tell her since she still didn't fully trust him. I wasn't sure I did either, anymore. Not with him keeping secrets from me., too.

"I feel like I owe it to Logan to try sometimes, you know? But then I realize that I just don't think of Marcus like that anymore, and I'd hate to try and just disappoint Logan again."

"You don't date someone out of obligation, Emma."

I nodded. I knew that. I just hated the idea of disappointing Logan. He had already lost so much, and had so much thrown at him recently.

"Besides," she said with a cheeky smirk. "You still love Jack."

I wrinkled my nose. I did, damn it. And I sort of hated that I did. I was reeling from the realization that maybe he had actually done all this to protect me.

"Yeah. I do."

Twenty-Two

Curiosity was beginning to kill me. I had to know what was going on, and I knew the one way I could get Jack to talk to me.

Plans made, I dropped Logan off at school early and made my way to Jack's penthouse, the one place I didn't think I would ever go again.

"Miss Emma! It's … you're here." I turned and walked towards Perry, the doorman at Jack's building. He and I had talked a lot over the last five years. He was old. Like so old he should have retired a decade ago, but he always said as long as he was able to read the numbers on the phone dials, and open doors, he'd still be working. He looked nervous as he fidgeted with his grey top and the edges of his long grey suit coat.

"Hello Perry. I'm here to see Jack." I plastered on my most friendly smile, hoping for old time's sake that he'd let me through.

Perry's expression paled and he slowly shook his head. "I'm sorry Miss Emma. Jack said you're not allowed up in the building."

I tried to hide my hurt at learning this. What other lengths had Jack gone to keep me away from him? Why would he even bother doing this?

"Well, can you please tell him I'm here? I really need to speak to him." He looked at me doubtfully and the little light bulb in my head went off. "Tell him it's about Logan, and it's an emergency."

"Is it about Logan?" Perry asked me with a mischievous smile. I smiled innocently and shrugged as he picked up the phone. "You're not going to cost me my job are you?"

"I doubt it, Perry. It'll be fine, trust me."

I watched him dial Jack's penthouse number and then stiffen once he explained I was here. He looked at me and frowned, and I knew Jack refused to see me.

I smiled sweetly and wiggled my fingers at Perry, gesturing for him to hand me the phone. 'Please?' I mouthed silently.

Reluctantly, he handed me the phone.

"Hello, Jack. I'd like to talk to you."

Jack sighed through the phone. "I can't see you, Emma."

"Okay. I'll stay right here in this lobby, or in the garage by your car, until you leave and agree to see me, or call the cops to have me removed from the building. Although I doubt that would be the smartest move considering everything else you're going through."

I could practically see him running his hands through his hair, gripping the edge of the countertop and a vein in his neck sticking out as he considered his options.

"What game are you playing right now, Emma?"

I smirked, even though he couldn't see me. "What game are you playing? Just ten minutes of your time, Jack. That's all I'm asking—you owe me this and you know it."

"Fine. Tell Perry to send you up."

"See you soon," I sang sweetly into the phone. I swear before he hung up that I heard a low growl come through the phone.

I handed the phone to Perry and allowed him to walk me to the elevator. Once inside, I took a deep breath, fluffed my hair, and tightened the belt on my knee-length grey rain coat. I kept my eyes on my reflection in the shiny metal doors the entire ride up to the penthouse, hoping I had the courage to go through with my plan to not only get Jack to talk to me and tell me what was going on, but to admit that he loved me and wanted to be with me.

It was a huge gamble. And one that I was willing to risk because after taking a long time, days and weeks to think about everything I had with Jack and lost once he kicked me out, I realized that he was who I wanted.

I had yet to let Marcus know, but it didn't matter. Logan would forever link us, and while I was thankful that we could be friends, and even though I may have been physically attracted to him, I didn't feel the same way for him that I used to. I had grown up in the five years since we'd been together. Jack was the man I loved.

Jack was the man I wanted.

The elevator dinged and I took a deep breath, waiting for them to open in the entryway of his apartment. I only hoped I could convince him he still wanted me.

"Hello," he said curtly as I stood in the doorway to his condo.

I raised my eyebrows and clenched the knot on my coat's belt with both hands to keep from fidgeting. He looked as incredible as ever in faded jeans and a long-sleeve grey fitted t-shirt. I had rubbed my hands and tongue over every single valley on his muscular stomach and chest. I missed it like crazy.

"You going to invite me in?" I asked saucily as he stood there, watching me with hooded eyes. I pulled out whatever bravado I had to keep my fears at bay and inwardly smiled when he watched me lick my bottom lip suggestively.

A quick look down showed me that he wasn't unaffected by my presence.

Good.

Slowly he stepped back from the door and I watched him erase the look of lust that had flicked across his face. I walked through the apartment and took a deep breath as I saw his couch come into view. It was the last place I had been with Jack. Where he had so forcefully taken me, not caring that he hurt me. I bit my lip to keep my tears and hurt away.

I flinched when Jack came up behind me and placed a hand on my shoulder. I turned to look at it, then him. By the look of sorrow written across his face, he was thinking and remembering the same thing I was, and he wasn't any happier about it.

He slowly removed his hand from my shoulder without saying anything, but I knew. I knew why he did it now. He knew it was the last time we'd be together and he was desperate.

Just like I was desperate now.

"I take it everything is okay with Logan?" he asked with a smirk. I ignored the deep, baritone tremor in his voice and shook my head. "Can I take your coat?"

I smiled and turned my back to him, undoing my belt. "Sure."

He hissed in a breath through his teeth as he lowered my coat to my elbows, and then he froze. I bit back a smile as he muttered a string of curse words. I slinked out of my coat and took a few steps away, so he could see the full effect, before he could slide the coat back on.

"Fu-ck," he muttered when I turned around. He rubbed one hand down his face and closed his eyes, most likely hoping he was seeing a mirage.

I looked down at my black thigh highs, lacey garter belt and matching black lace demi bra and back to him and smiled.

"Get dressed," he demanded and held out my coat.

I took a few steps backwards and shook my head. "We need to talk."

"You think I can talk when you look like that? Christ, Emma. You're not even wearing underwear." His frustration, and arousal, were evident and I didn't bother hiding my giggle of happiness. I was watching him unravel in front of me.

"You like me bare for you." I rubbed the palms of my hands against my hips and thighs, resisting the urge to cover up in front of him.

"Shit." He turned and left the room, running upstairs, faster than I had ever seen him move while I stood still, in the middle of his living room, shocked that he had run away from me. I frowned, and just as I debated whether to hang my head and slink out of there, or chase him upstairs, I heard his footsteps in the hallway upstairs and knew he was coming back down.

He held out one of his white dress shirts, staying an arms-length away from me. Frustration etched in every one of his facial features.

"No." I crossed my arms against my stomach. It only served to push my full, aching breasts up further and I watched Jack's gaze settle on them, before drifting lower to my bare skin that I knew he wanted to get his hands on. He couldn't hide his desire from me.

Even if it pissed him off that he wanted me.

"Put the shirt on." He closed his eyes and shook his head. "I can't talk to you when you're dressed like this. Put the damn shirt on and I'll talk to you."

I took it from him reluctantly and pushed my arms through my sleeves. "It's on."

I smiled when he cursed at me again. "Button. It."

I started laughing. I couldn't help it. I loved his frustration. I loved how his eyes darkened, knowing how much he wanted me. How hard he was trying to resist taking me and having his way with me. I reveled in it and I knew I could have him back. Every look he gave me showed me how much he loved me. I saw how much he desired me. His pants grew tighter as his crotch grew more uncomfortable and I giggled again. I did. Like a school girl, and I didn't care.

"You do it," I finally said, not surprised at all that my voice came out in a deep whisper.

Jack closed his mouth and I watched as he licked across the front of his teeth. With his hands balled into tights fists at his sides, I knew he was trying to resist ripping his shirt off and throwing me over his couch again.

I loved it. I loved how I could bring him to the brink of losing all self-control. I watched him debate what I said before he finally closed the space between us. He started at the lowest button and focused on each button and his fingers as if it were the most precious project in the entire world. He held his shirt and hands far enough away from me so there was no chance of his skin brushing up against mine.

I smiled down at him and looked around the living room, remembering the night he made me come, straddled on his couch, the first night he said he wanted to try dating me. I bit my cheek to keep my tears away at the memory.

"How does it feel?" I whispered as he continued to work, shakily, on the buttons on his shirt. He grunted something unintelligible and I continued. "How does it feel to walk into every room of this place and remember what it was like when I was spread out for your pleasure, Jack?" I didn't give him a chance to answer before I flung more questions at him.

"Do you remember how I tasted when you had me on your kitchen counter? Do you think of how I sucked your cocked when you were sitting at the desk in your office? Do you miss the way my thighs wrap around your waist when you slide into me and completely fill me?"

He dropped his shirt and stepped away so quickly, rubbing the back of his hair, that for a second I wondered if I pushed him too far. Had I pissed him off so much he was going to throw me out again?

I almost regretted getting carried away until he turned away and I saw that his face was flushed. His cheeks were pink and he was so turned on, his pupils were almost completely dilated, his breathing heavy.

"What in the hell has gotten into you?" He exhaled loudly, staring at me, from too far away. He looked at me as if I was a wanted but dangerous treasure. As if one simple touch would destroy him. I knew exactly how he felt as he stared at me, breathing heavily, the tendons in his neck sticking out. My pulse raced and for the first time in weeks, I felt alive.

"You did, Jack. You made me fall in love with you, to want you every second of every day, and I know you love me too. And I'm not leaving today until you make love to me like you love to do, and then tell me what's going on."

"I. Can't." He spit it out with such frustration that I knew I was close to getting what I wanted. What I needed.

"Can't or won't?" I asked with an arched eyebrow. "Don't lie to me, Jack."

I placed a hand on my hip and chewed on the inside of my bottom lip. Every one of my senses felt alive. I could smell him from across the room; practically feel his hands caress the curves of my hips and breasts. I took a large breath, knowing he could see my chest heaving. Heavy and waiting for him.

He looked tortured and I loved it. I wanted him to feel the exact same way I had felt for the last several weeks, what it felt like to be without him. He glanced back at the door and down to my coat, most likely debating kicking me out. But I held my ground, refusing to leave until I got from him what I needed; what I came for.

"You need to leave. It isn't safe for you to be here." He held out my coat, silently asking—begging - me to put it on, and I shook my head.

"Tell me why," I breathed out. I was wet, dripping, and I knew he could see it on me. I looked at him devilishly, and resisted the urge to press my legs together. Instead, I moved my feet further apart and his gaze dropped to my thighs. His lips disappeared into a tight line as he pressed them together when my fingers began undoing the buttons he had just put together. I didn't want to be hidden from him, and this was the only way I could get him to act. His eyes looked hazy, practically drunk, as he dropped his gaze to my garter belt and nakedness beneath it as I gently, and teasingly slowly placed one of my fingers against my folds and pressed it in slowly.

"Shit," he groaned and grabbed the back of his neck with both hands, lacing them together. My eyes rolled back and I moaned at the thought of pleasing myself in front of him, under his hot stare that could undo me in an instant, but I stopped myself.

I slowly moved my own finger and rubbed it once, then twice, against myself before bringing it to my mouth. Jack's eyes followed me the entire time.

I parted my lips, and slowly licked myself off my finger. It reminded me of the time he touched me in the elevator. Our first date when he didn't speak and took control. I kept my eyes on him the entire time, teasing him.

I saw the moment he lost control; the moment I had him.

In three quick steps, Jack was in front of me.

"Fuck it," he muttered and grabbed my hand from my mouth and placed it in his. I closed my eyes and moaned as his hot mouth finished licking the juices off my finger. I was hot, and ready to explode as soon as his lips touched me.

He used his free hand and grabbed my hips, pulling me flush against his body as he devoured my fingers that touched myself. I pressed my hips into him, feeling his hardness through his jeans and threw my head back.

"Jack," I whispered or moaned or screamed. I had no idea and I didn't care.

Without warning, he removed my hand from his and pushed two of his thick fingers into me. I jumped up onto my tiptoes from the force of his entrance and laid my head against his shoulder.

"Always so wet and tight for me. God I've missed you, Emma." He moved his fingers exactly how he knew I liked it, rough and fast, with no sense of slowing down anytime soon.

My breath grew ragged. I panted against him and inhaled his sexy scent. I licked his neck, wanting him, needing him. I wanted to sink right into his skin so I could always be with him.

I felt my body begin to shudder, my orgasm growing quickly and fiercely in a way that only Jack could do to my body.

"I know, baby," he whispered right before locking his eyes on mine. I could feel how much he wanted me with his erection pressed against my stomach as his fingers screwed me.

He attacked my mouth just as my orgasm hit, plunging his tongue unforgivingly into my mouth, devouring me, plundering every place in my mouth as I moaned and cried out. He swallowed my cries and still kept up his vicious assault on every nerve.

He pressed the heel of his hand against my clit just as I was coming down and it threw me into a second orgasm. My insides clamped down viciously on his fingers inside of me, trying to milk them and he groaned like a wild animal as I came apart and gave him all I had to give. His hand around my waist tightened, holding me up.

Thank god, because my knees were so shaky I thought I would collapse at any second, but he just pushed up with his hand still in me and drew me even closer to him. I felt consumed, completely taken over. I melted into his body as I screamed out a second time, Jack murmuring softly into my ear and licking my neck. My entire body shook from the release.

Twenty-Three

We stayed there until my shocks subsided and he slowly pulled his hand from me.

I looked up to him, and saw all the love he had for me, reflected in his eyes and I took a deep breath. I fought back the tears that wanted to fall, knowing this wasn't anything more than what I planned for.

I wanted to ignore it. I wanted to jump up and wrap my legs around his waist letting him carry me upstairs like I could tell he wanted.

Instead, I took a step back and looked away, regaining my self-control.

When I looked back at his eyes, Jack reached for me, but I took another step back and shook my head. I blinked my eyes once, then twice, removing every emotion I had for him. Just as he had done for me.

"Emma," he said in a voice that bordered on panicking. His breathing quickened faster than normal and not from what we had just shared. But still, I didn't move to him.

I walked around the couch to avoid his touch and his lustful gaze. With my eyes still on him, I removed his shirt and picked up my coat.

I wrapped it around my half-naked body re-doing the knot, and then brushed my hair off my shoulder.

"Marcus wants me back," I said as emotionlessly as possible even though my own heart was breaking all over again as anger, then jealousy flashed across his face. "Do you want another man touching me like that, Jack? Another man making me come and scream his name?"

I knew I was playing with fire. Jack could kill Marcus and then destroy him in a single second. I also knew this is what it would take to show him exactly what he was losing.

"Because if you can't stand it, if the thought of another man's hands on me drives you as insane as I think it does, then you need to get your head out of your ass before you lose me completely. I can forgive you for how shitty you treated me, and how you fired me. Because I know."

I paused and watched him take a deep breath, clearly debating whether to grab me and haul me upstairs, or scream at me, or … something. The vein by his temple popped out as if he was literally about to blow his fucking lid.

"I know you love me, and I know that scares the shit out of you. But you need to have more faith in me. I can be strong and I can deal with a lot of bullshit to fight for what I want. I want you, but I don't want you if you're not willing to fight for me or if you're going to give up, and toss me aside the first time trouble comes our way when you promised—you promised to protect us. I won't stand for that. I just wanted to remind you what you're missing."

"Emma," he warned frantically, taking a few steps towards me, but I backed up, knowing if he got his hands on me again I would be lost in him completely.

"Marcus will fight for me. He will stand by me …"

"Fuck Marcus!" He yelled, panting.

It was evil. I knew it. It was like poking an angry lion with a stick and I was just asking to get my head bitten off, but it had to be done. I just hoped it didn't back fire completely.

I winked and picked up my purse. "That's always an option."

I turned and left, rushing down the stairway without bothering to wait for the elevator knowing he could chase after me with that threat lingering between us.

"You got the shit beat out of me," Marcus hissed at me when he came to pick up Logan for another sleepover.

I cringed and shrunk away from him, feeling bad for a moment before I remembered he was lying to me, too.

"You deserved it," I calmly stated and began picking up the useless college applications strewn all over my coffee table. I had made my choice on schools and the rest were pointless.

"I can't believe you put me in the middle of this shit."

For a moment, I felt bad again. Bad enough to wrinkle my nose at Marcus's swollen black eye. I went and grabbed a bag of peas from the freezer and tossed it towards him.

"Thanks," he muttered and sat down on the couch. "What did you tell him?"

I blushed as I remembered exactly how that conversation went with Jack.

"Never mind, I don't think I want to know."

I chuckled a little bit and shut my mouth. "I didn't think he'd beat you up. I just told him you wanted me and I was considering it."

I dropped my eyes, feeling slightly ashamed of myself for using Marcus like this.

"I'm sorry," I whispered finally. He stared at me like I had two heads. "That wasn't fair to you. Or I at least should have warned you, but I just can't be with you Marcus. Too much has changed and I don't feel the same way about you anymore. I'd love to be a family with you, but I don't love you anymore. I love him."

I hadn't heard from Jack in over twenty-four hours since I high-tailed it out his apartment the night before, but based on the black eye Marcus was sporting, I had clearly impacted him.

Slowly, Marcus nodded reluctantly and sighed. "I know. I know you do. And I think I just wanted what we used to have without realizing we're now totally different people."

"I think we can be friends, though." I sat down next to him, slightly nervous he might smack me for being such a shit to Jack and getting him beat up. "That will be the best for Logan."

He nodded and tossed his frozen bag of peas in my kitchen sink. "I get it," he said and leaned down and gently pressed his lips against my cheek. "I love you, though."

I smiled and winked. "I love you, too. I always will. And I'm really glad you're back in Logan's life. He's been a completely different kid since his dad showed up."

I pursed my lips and bit back my tears. "You're a great dad, Marcus."

I saw his own eyes begin to water up but he did some sort of man sniff to clear them away. "Thanks, Emma."

"Can you tell me what's going on yet?" I had a sinking feeling that I wasn't going to hear from Jack until whatever bullshit he was dealing with was done. Regardless, I was finally better than I had been in weeks. I should have been, after the mind-blowing orgasms he gave me yesterday.

But I threw my cards down and laid my hand out for Jack to see. He knew I wanted him and the ball was in his court, so to speak. I was determined to wait for him; to trust that he loved me and was doing something to protect me, and I would stand by his side figuratively, since I couldn't be there literally.

And if, when all was said and done he still didn't want me? Well, I had already made decisions about my future and what was best for me and Logan. Jack could be a part of it, or not, but Logan and I were going to be just fine regardless.

He shook his head and frowned, just a little bit. "I can't. But I suggest you keep your eye on the news later this week." He flashed me a wink and walked to the door. "Shit's gonna get fun."

I jerked my head back just as Logan came out of his room, backpack in hand, filled with clothes to stay at his dad's for the night.

I pulled him into a hug and gave him a slobbery kiss on the cheek as he tried to wiggle his way out of my arms. "Not a chance, Logan. I'm never letting you go."

He laughed with me, and then kissed me back. "I love you mommy."

I set him down on his feet and kissed him again. "I love you, too. Have fun tonight."

They both waved to me as they walked out the door, leaving me alone to try to figure out what Marcus said.

I was finally sick and tired of watching the news almost twenty-four hours a day. The only thing I saw were reports on hurricanes hitting the south, earthquakes in India killing thousands of people, the economic collapse causing the highest unemployment rates in history, and dictators killing hundreds of children and women in Uganda.

None of that shit sounded fun.

Listening to the depressing stories of things going on in the world, made me happy that the worst thing I was dealing with was the fact that Jack still hadn't called.

Whatever was going on, he'd decided not to let me in. I hated it.

But I had cried the last tears I would over him. We were together for just a couple of short months and I refused any longer to sit at home, drinking wine alone after Logan's bedtime, and staring at the news ticker waiting for whatever was supposed to happen; happen.

Whatever Marcus alluded to the week before didn't happen, and it was time for me to move on.

Which is how I reluctantly found myself in a bar, connected to one of McMillan Holdings hotels, frowning into my long island ice tea with Dean while we watched Macy and Tate practically copulate on the dance floor.

The only bright side was that The Nadas were back in town for one last summer show and I was finally getting a chance to see them for the first time in years.

"Have they always been like this?" Dean asked with a scrunched up looking face while we both stared at them. It was gross, and I'm sure neither one of us wanted to be staring at them making out on the dance floor, but there we stood. Rubbernecking like you just have to do when you pass a car accident on the highway. We just couldn't look away.

"Yep," I replied and took a large gulp of my drink. "It's too bad you weren't around when they first started dating. Most nights I felt like I should just join in their fun since Tate was always in our dorm room anyway." I turned to him and winked. "Do you have any idea how small the dorm rooms are at DePaul?"

Dean's eyes went wide. "Did you … join in?"

I laughed. It was the first genuine time I'd laughed in weeks and I wished in that second, that I could look at Dean and see the hotness right in front of me, instead of a pseudo-brother. I wiggled my eyebrows and smiled coyly, "I will never tell."

Dean shook his head while laughing. "That's just wrong, and hot, all at the same time. I'm not sure what to do with that information."

"You can get me another drink." I waved my empty glass in front of him and turned back to the dance floor and the folk rock band on the stage while Dean took his cue. You couldn't watch The Nadas live and not have a smile on your face and your feet tapping out the beat. I loved them.

Several songs later, Macy and Tate were finally taking a break, waiting their turn in line at the bar, when Dean returned with my drink and awkwardly draped his arm across my shoulder. He pulled me closer into his neck and when I turned toward him, he looked down at me and lightly kissed my temple.

"Jack's here. Want me to play the new boyfriend and make him jealous all over again like the night of our first date?" His mouth was pressed so close to my ear, I'm sure it looked like he was kissing me to the casual observer.

At least this explained his sudden affection toward me. I debated for a split second before I smiled up at him and kissed his cheek.

"You don't have to do this. I need to get over him."

"He doesn't look like he wants to get over you anytime soon." He nodded and slowly relaxed his hold on me and I followed his nod in the direction he indicated.

Jack stood several tables away. Dozens of people were crushed in between us and I heard the music playing on the stage to my far right. I think I even vaguely remembered that Dean was still next to me, holding me like we were together.

He leaned forward and whispered in my ear again, "Come on, tell me it won't be fun to play with him just a little bit more. The man still clearly wants you."

Dean was right. Even from the distance that separated us, I could see the tension in Jack's shoulders. His eyes pierced into me so completely, it felt like he was standing right in front of me.

Dean's hand tightened on my shoulder and he pulled me closer to him. And when he did, I watched Jack's lips pull together and his eyes darken. He noticed the gesture, even from the distance and I almost wondered if steam was going to come out of his nose he looked so angry. Like a bull ready to charge the matador, and Dean was the red cape.

I smirked at him and then turned around and back into Dean's embrace just as Macy and Tate joined our table.

"You two look cozy," Macy sang teasingly as I sipped my drink.

"Jack's here. Dean's trying to make him jealous on my behalf, and before your head spins around; he's behind us."

"You trying to get your ass kicked like Marcus did?" Tate asked.

Dean smiled and kissed the top of my head. "Nah. Just thought I'd help her out. And if it has the added bonus of making *the* Jack McMillan feel like shit," he shrugged and continued, "I'm all for it, man."

"Your funeral." He set down his beer and grabbed Macy's hand, an unspoken invitation to get back out on the dance floor apparently. Macy clearly understood because she giggled like we were twelve and let Tate lead the way.

"They're good together," Dean observed once they walked away. "You know he asked me to be his best man?"

"You going to walk down the aisle with me, then?" I asked while wiggling my eyebrows.

"The fuck he is." A very familiar, and completely pissed off Jack spoke from right behind me.

I turned to Dean, momentarily widening my eyes, and saw his twinkling with mischief. I loved that he was willing to play this game for me. But Tate was right, we took it too far and Dean could possibly die.

At the very least, be incapacitated for a while.

Neither option sounded good to me so I slowly turned to Jack, while allowing Dean to wrap his arms around me just a little bit tighter.

"You need to leave." Jack bit it out as a command and I instantly felt my heels dig into the floor. I took a deep breath trying to calm myself down because when Jack was in front of me, even when I wanted to be pissed at him for hurting me, all I could think was how sexy he was and how much I loved him.

It made me feel all sorts of warm and tingly all over as his eyes roamed up and down my body, taking in every inch of my high heeled brown leather boots, short frayed denim skirt and tightly fitted one shoulder tank top.

Seeing Jack's eyes fill with lust as he finally reached my long curly locks that fell down over my breasts and then my eyes … made me so glad I was dressed the way I was. I could practically see him thinking of all the things he wanted to do to me in those boots and my lower stomach warmed. My legs pressed together, not even remembering that Dean's hand was still wrapped around me and he could feel it.

"Calm down," he whispered into my ear and I felt my cheeks turn pink from embarrassment.

"You need to leave. Now," Jack repeated.

I smiled and turned my head toward the stage. It went against every instinct I had in me to play this Dean's way. I wanted to curl up against Jack. I wanted to breathe him in, touch the ripples of his chest and feel him move against me. Instead, I forced myself to lean back to Dean.

And then I shook my head. "No. I like this band."

Jack's fist clenched and I saw the tendon in his neck pop out a little bit. I bit my lip to keep from my smiling when I saw his eyes flash a feral anger in Dean's direction who, if I was correct, had stiffened slightly under Jack's furious gaze. His eyes held a realm of fury I had never seen before and never knew existed.

A lesser man would have shrunk back, or run away, under that kind of stare. I watched Jack glare at Dean for several minutes, and I swore, even though the music was loud, that a low growl actually escaped his lips.

It was then that Dean leaned towards my ear and whispered, "I'm going to go before we push this too far and he kills me. Plus, I think you've proven your point."

"I'll give you two a few minutes," he said, nodded at Jack before heading out to the dance floor with Macy and Tate.

Twenty-Four

After what seemed like an eternity of Jack and I glaring at each other, he finally spoke first. "You trying to make me jealous?"

He crossed his arms and arched an eyebrow.

I wanted to smack him, and then I wanted to lick him. His neck, his jawline, all the way back to the sensitive part behind his ear that I knew drove him absolutely wild, because hot damn Jack was just the sexiest man I had ever seen or touched. And even angry at me, or me angry at him—and I still was—he was just perfection wrapped up in an even prettier package. Instead, I smiled sweetly, hiding every annoyance and sexually frustrated feeling. "I already told you. I like this band."

"And Dean?"

God I hated that he couldn't tell me what was really going on. I hated that he didn't trust me enough to let me in. But I really enjoyed getting even, even if it was originally unintentional, by playing coy and letting him seethe in jealousy. Immature? Maybe. Deserved? Definitely.

I just turned my head and smiled at Dean on the dance floor. That boy could move, and for the second time that night, I knew Dean was going to make some woman incredibly happy one day. If he could move his hips like that on the dance floor, I could only imagine how he moved them in bed.

"It's really none of your business anymore, is it Jack?"

"Damn it, Emma." He took one more step closer to me, closing the space between us and whispered more harshly into my ear. "Have you stopped for one fucking second to think that I'm doing all of this to keep my promise to you? Don't show up here, in a hotel and bar I own, with some other guy's hands all over you and pull this game with me."

I exhaled slowly.

"What promise, Jack? The one where you promised you'd fuck up? Because there were a lot of promises you made to me so you might have to be just a bit more specific."

"The one where I promised I would keep you safe from all of the Senator's bullshit because you're mine and I will protect it at all cost, but you have to put a little bit of trust in me."

"You fired me!" I hissed back at him. "And you've shut me out. If you want to protect me, then tell me what's going on."

In one quick second, Jack's arm wrapped around my waist and I was pressed against his chest. We were both panting heavily, our chests rising and falling at an incredible pace and all I could think about was how amazing he smelled. His cologne mixed with just … him.

I breathed in heavily, and allowed my forehead to rest against his chest and relax. In that one second, everything was perfect all over again. The lyrics in the background, the only other sound I heard above our beating our hearts.

You can run away, but you can't hide
You duck and dodge, keep it all inside
With a whisper, a wink, a spin of the wheel
At the end of it all, it's no big deal
Only love is real
Only love is real

I just wanted Jack to let me inside, and to realize that all I needed was his love. But then he did, and I wanted to vomit.

I felt Jack inhale a large breath and then his free hand brushed my loose curls behind my ear. "He has pictures and a video … of us."

Holy shit! My head snapped up and met Jack's eyes. All the color drained from my face as I stared at him wide eyed. "What do you mean?"

With his eyes closed, Jack's face scrunched up in a look of disgust. "Remember that night on the roof?" He choked the words out and I knew instantly what night … and what roof he was talking about.

"How?" My own voice sounded scratchy and barely audible. Oh my god. How in the hell could he have pictures of that night?

"It's all I can tell you, but just fucking trust me that I'm handling this in the only way I can. And the only way that will keep you, and Logan, safe."

"Brian?" I asked, even though I wasn't sure I wanted to know anymore.

He took another large breath and shook his head. "Rehab. I told him if he didn't go, I was cutting him off for good. I'm done covering for him, but I wanted him to have one last chance to get help. He's down in Florida."

I let that sink in for a few minutes before I slowly pulled away. I reached up slowly, to feel Jack but at the last second he took a step away and glanced around. Slowly the pieces were beginning to click together. He really had done all of this to protect me.

With a safe amount of distance between us, Jack pulled his hands from me and placed them in his pockets. He rolled his shoulders back and erased his emotions, business look finally stamped back in place. But his eyes told another story. I saw the passion and desire he still had for me.

"What I need you to do is stay away from any place that can be connected to me. You can't come to my place again, or any club or building with McMillan involved. And I need you to stop letting other men paw all over you before I end up screwing up everything I've just put weeks into. You got me?"

Slowly, I nodded. I hated it, but I got him.

A slight smirk of his lips was the only indication he gave me that he saw me. Then he turned toward the dance floor, found Dean, and nodded his head in my direction.

"Everything okay?" Dean asked cautiously when he approached us and slowly went to put his hand on my shoulder.

He stopped, wisely, when Jack took another step forward and moved his hands from his pockets.

With the same feral look he gave Dean earlier, he unleashed it again as he spoke deeply. "I'm going to forgive you for touching Emma earlier because she didn't know what the hell was going on." Quickly, his eyes went to mine before he looked back to Dean. "But now she knows enough to know that I'm serious as hell when I tell you that if I see your fucking hands on her again, or your lips anywhere near any part of anything that belongs to me, you will regret it every day for the rest of your very short and very painful existence."

Dean very quickly pocketed his hands in his jeans and rocked back on his heels. "Understood."

I bit back a laugh.

Jack's eyes came back to me, and while he was still distant, they were at least slightly softer when he glanced at my mouth before moving up to my eyes.

He smiled lightly. "I need you to tap your shit down and trust me. And trust that this will be over soon and I'll explain the rest."

"Okay, Jack."

"Good." He looked to Dean with a visibly pained expression. "Get her home. And keep her safe."

As we walked away, I heard Jack shout, "And keep your hands off her."

I laughed and from behind me, I knew Dean was doing the same. "He's an intense asshole, isn't he?"

He really had no idea.

"Sorry!" Logan shouted with glee as he picked his card from the top of the pile. We were in the middle of our fifth and never-ending game of Sorry!.

I moaned into my hands and cried out, "You're killing me kiddo!" He really was. How a five year old could kick my ass in Sorry! I had no idea. But he did, almost every single time. Currently he had three of his blue guys at home, while I had all four of mine—make that three, now, spread throughout the board.

My phone rang on the kitchen counter, but I ignored it. I hadn't spent nearly as much time with Logan as I was used to. With him spending more time with Marcus and having sleepovers, I was missing my favorite little man.

Logan simply laughed and filled his mouth with a handful of popcorn, half of which ended up in his lap and on the floor, while he moved his last piece from Start and kicked my red little piece back to home.

"You know, buddy," I said teasingly while wiggling my eyebrows. "Someday you're going to beat me so bad, I'm not going to play anymore.

It was a lie and he totally knew it. Smart little kid that he was.

He shrugged a shoulder and wrinkled his nose, a move so similar to Marcus that it now made me smile. It really was amazing how much of a mirror image he was to his dad. "Dad will play."

"Ouch!" I said and reached across the coffee table, tickling him.

I don't know what brought on the feeling, but suddenly as we were laughing and rolling over the floor, a tingle went down my spine and my head snapped up.

And my jaw dropped at what I was seeing on the television.

Oh my god. Marcus was right. Shit was about to get fun, and I couldn't believe what I was seeing.

Completely forgetting about Logan or the game we were playing, I sat back down on the couch, vaguely heard my phone ringing on the kitchen counter again, and turned up the volume so I could hear what was going on.

I had the television muted while Logan was awake, but I had to hear this.

Because on the screen, on a stage in what looked like a press conference, was Senator Whitmore, and behind him, Marcus. He looked grim and all sorts of pissed off as he stood still as a statue with his shoulders tense and hands shoved into his pockets. A scowl on his face showed he was not happy with whatever the hell was going on.

As soon as the volume was high enough to hear, Logan turned to the TV.

"Hey, that's daddy!"

"I know buddy," I shushed him, rudely, but was too enraptured in the scene taking place to apologize. "Go put your pajamas on, Logan."

"But mom!" he whined, as soon as I heard something that surely couldn't have been anything about leaving office come out of the Senator's mouth.

Oh my … shit.

"Now, Logan." I shot him my most serious don't-mess-with-me look and turned back to the screen as he walked down the hall.

It was just in time to hear the Senator's closing remarks. "I ask that you respect my family's privacy as we get used to finding our new normal outside of our public office. To my constituents and the voters and others who have supported me for the last twenty five years while I've been in office, thank you for helping me make Illinois the great state it is today."

He closed his eyes briefly before turning his head to Marcus. He nodded once while Marcus stayed as still as he had been the entire time. Had I not known that they didn't have any sort of relationship to speak of, it would have looked almost resigned, and like a father needing comfort and support from his son.

Instead, he looked defeated, and as the Senator's—or now former Senator's jaw tightened—I saw the briefest flash of anger and malice he shot towards Marcus. Whose expression didn't change. Not one single bit.

Marcus may have refused a relationship with his dad, but damn, in that second, I knew how much he had learned growing up a Whitmore and I thanked God that he wasn't the man his father wanted him to be.

But that realization and thankfulness did nothing to stop the sudden rampage of questions flooding my mind. What in the hell did Jack get on the Senator, that was powerful enough to not only stop the photos of me and him from being released, but caused him to step down from his beloved throne of power midterm?

I was still sitting there, watching the newscasters and political analysts discussing Senator Whitmore's decision to step down when Logan came out dressed in his pajamas.

"Why was daddy on TV?" he asked, rubbing his eyes and trying to stifle a yawn.

"He was just working, honey." I scooped Logan up in my arms just as my phone began ringing again. I stopped in the kitchen to see Macy calling.

Assuming she had seen what was on TV as well, I decided to ignore her call until Logan was in bed. I was going to need wine, or something stronger, to talk to her about this.

Senator Whitmore stepping down from his Senate seat, but I didn't know why. This was huge.

Would this fix things between Jack and I? Did I want it to? Of course I wanted Jack back. But did he have to end a man's—granted, an asshole of a man—career in order for that to happen between us? Was I worth that?

Shaking the thoughts from my mind, I leaned down and gave Logan a kiss on his temple.

"Come on, buddy. Bedtime."

"Can I call daddy and tell him I saw him on TV?" He asked with wide-eyed wonder.

Shaking my head again, I carried him down the hall. "He's busy working. We'll call him tomorrow. Okay?"

He wrinkled his nose and I pretended to bite it off, causing all sorts of laughter. "Fine."

"You talk to Marcus, yet?" Macy asked after our initial 'what-in-the-fuck-did-we-just-we-see' conversation starters were completed.

I ran a hand through my hair and then took a sip of my wine. Straight from the bottle again. Why dirty a glass when you don't have to?

"No. Although I thought of calling him."

"What about Jack?"

"I haven't heard from him." I said with a bit sharper tone than I intended. Thankfully, Macy loved me enough to let my slight bitchiness slide.

"I can't believe Marcus was on stage looking pissed as all get out. It has to have something to do with Jack. Why else would he be standing up there with his dad?"

She was right. To the few of us that knew my connection to Marcus and Jack, it was just a little too slick to have Marcus standing there with his dad like the supportive son, when we all knew how much Marcus despised his dad.

Besides that, even Macy couldn't deny how much he absolutely adored Logan. If Marcus was standing by his dad's side, it was all for show. It had to do with protecting Logan at the very least.

"I don't know," I said with my voice trailing off and staring off out the windows.

"What happened last night at the club? You never told me."

I snorted. "That's because you couldn't remove your mouth from

Tate's face long enough to take a breath, much less have a conversation."

"I know, I know … I'm such a slut with my fiancé. But we already knew that, so tell me what happened."

"Nothing. He came over, got pissed that Dean was touching me and kicked me out." And told me there were some photos of us having sex on top of one of his hotels.

"That's it?" She asked doubtfully.

My face flushed as I thought about the way he touched me. His strong hands on my hips when he pulled me to him when Dean had walked away and he whispered roughly into my ear about the photos and the desire I saw in his eyes when he pushed me back away. His eyes roamed and drank in every inch of my body. I could almost watch his struggle to stop himself from unraveling my silly braids and messing them up in his hands the way he always did when he played with my hair.

"You gonna answer me?" Macy's laughter brought me back to reality and I forced another swig of cheap red wine down my throat.

I cleared my throat as her knowing laughter rang through the line. "No, I don't think I am, Mace. Listen, we can talk all night about what this is about, but the truth is, until I hear from Jack—if I hear from him—none of it means anything to me."

"All right. But call me when you know." I was just about to hang up the phone when she spoke again. "And just so you know, Jack has been so freaking miserable the last few weeks, and I know he's totally crazy about you. This will all work out and you guys will be back to having hot crazy sex before you know it."

"How do you know we have hot crazy sex?" Did I even want to know how she knows that? Probably not. "Never mind," I say as she starts laughing through the phone. Who in the hell knows what she heard during phone conversations Jack and I had while he was at work. "I'm going to turn in. I'll let you know if Marcus tells me anything, K?"

We hung up and just a few seconds later, my phone rang again.

"I am not talking about my hot sex with Jack, Macy." And then my jaw dropped, my mouth went dry and I immediately reached for my wine bottle as the sexiest laugh bellowed softly through the line. Every nerve ending in my body instantly came alive as soon as I heard Jack's soft laughter. That's what I get for answering the phone without checking the caller ID first.

"Hot sex? That's what you tell Macy we have?" He paused for just a moment. "It's a bit more than that, isn't it? Somehow I don't feel like you're giving me enough credit."

He was so right. Hot sex didn't begin to describe the moments I'd shared with Jack. Passionate, fire-starting, orgasms exploding so powerfully I saw stars and passed out. That was much more in line with the sex Jack and I had. And then the tender moments of him making love to me slowly but still forcefully as he slid into me and filled me so completely that I thought I would burst from the inside out.

The very thought made me shiver, and thank god that Jack wasn't standing in front of me to see my body turn to mush and my legs start shaking nervously as I remembered the first time he told me he loved me while he was buried deep inside me in that limo.

Shit, that limo night was amazing.

And gone. Which I had to remember.

"What do you want Jack?" I asked, probably a bit more breathlessly than I should have been so like the classy girl I never claimed to be, I took an even larger swallow of my cheap wine and set it forcefully down on the counter.

"I need to see you." He said it so matter of fact; I thought I had missed some important part of the conversation. He sounded like he was asking me to take care of his dry cleaning, or handing me over his grocery list and my stomach dropped to my knees at the very thought that all passion, all want and desire—and even love—he felt for me, really was gone now.

"When?" Man I hoped my voice sounded as emotionless as his did when I answered.

Twenty-Five

"Now." He said it softly and just a few seconds later, I heard a soft knocking on my apartment door.

"I'm busy right now." A slight smile tilted one corner of my lips and I tried not to move a single muscle knowing Jack was just a few feet away from me, on the other side of the door.

I looked down at my rumpled clothes I had been in all day long and decided I at least had a few minutes to change into something else a little better for an encounter with him this late at night.

Moving slowly so I didn't giveaway that I was in fact, at home and doing nothing besides drinking alone, I shuffled quietly down the hall to my room.

"You're not busy. And if you are, you need to get home so I can see you."

I tsked twice. "I'm not sure you get to boss me around anymore, Jack." But I was smiling, and the humor in my voice gave me away immediately.

He didn't miss a thing.

"Open your door, Emma." His voice was just a little bit tighter, a little bit tenser and I knew I was running low on time before he started flipping out on me. Five minutes, tops.

"I'm not at home, Jack." I removed my pants, slowly sliding my panties down with my nasty and faded black yoga pants. I don't know what in the hell came over me but my fingers paused just briefly at the apex of my thighs and I could feel how turned on I was.

Jack did that to me, always. I didn't even know if there was a future for us, but just hearing the smoothing timbre of his deep voice coming through my phone as I wiggled out of five year old sweat pants was enough to turn me on.

"Don't mess with me, tonight, babe. It's important. Now open your door."

I detected the slightest amount of humor in his voice and laughed just a little bit.

"You have about thirty seconds to get to this door before I start banging on the door so loudly it wakes up your neighbors and Logan; and then you'll have to waste your entire night getting him back to sleep."

I smiled. "Ah, but then you wouldn't get to talk to me like you so desperately want to."

His frustrated growl came through the phone. I moved it away from my ear and threw on my robe. The one he hated. The one he had told me he didn't want me wearing ever again.

"All right, all right," I feigned irritation and began moving toward the door. "I'm coming."

"Not yet."

The line went dead and I froze, just staring at the phone in my hand while I saw his name blinking on the screen.

I stumbled over my feet and blushed at his innuendo.

I wanted to be mad. I wanted to scream at him for being such an ignorant ass and hurting me so badly.

Except mostly, I just wanted him. Flaws and all, I just wanted his hands on me—at least one more time.

My cheeks were flushed and my body was warm when I opened the door and received one more surprise for the night.

Jack looked disheveled as he leaned against the doorframe to my apartment. His silver tie was roughly pulled away from his darker grey dress shirt that had the top button undone. The shirt was wrinkled and his suit jacket looked like it had spent the last four hours crumpled into a ball and shoved into a plastic garbage bag. His hair was mussed, and for the first time it wasn't in that sexily perfect way I loved so much. But what I noticed most was the dullness in his eyes and the tiredness that surrounded them. His piercing dark brown eyes just look blank.

It wasn't in the emotionless, professional blank way where he could just stare right through you and you knew he didn't give a shit one way or another what he thought of you.

This time, he just looked … sad. And maybe a touch scared.

He stood up a little bit straighter as I opened the door and with one hand that was behind his back, held out one cala lilly.

"Someone told me I sucked at this whole dating thing. I thought this might help."

God I'd never seen Jack look like this. His voice wavered a little bit as he pushed off the door frame and stood, timidly, in front of me.

I wanted him. I loved him. I just needed answers first.

Slowly, I pulled the calla lilly from his fingers and inhaled the sweet fragrance.

"Come on in." I turned from him and began looking for a vase. Not finding one, I emptied the red wine from the bottle into a couple of glasses, filled the bottle with water and stuck the lilly in there.

"Nice," Jack said with just a touch of humor.

I handed him a glass of wine and set my new faux vase in the middle of my table. "I'm a classy girl, what can I say?" I winked and moved to my couch, waving him over as I passed him. "What'd you want to talk about?"

He looked uncomfortable, almost nervous as he stood next to my small and chipped wooden kitchen table. His hands were in his pockets and he rocked back and forth on his heels, not making eye contact with me. In fact, he was looking at every single thing in my small and hand-me-downed apartment except me.

"Logan sleeping?" He finally asked and brought the wine glass to his lips. I watched him swallow slowly, becoming more antsy with what he really wanted to say, and trying to resist the urge to wrap my hand around his tie and wrinkle it up.

I licked my lips and just nodded. I didn't miss the hazy look he had in his eyes as he watched. I wasn't trying to turn him on right now. It was just a nervous tick, but it made me smile and feel all sorts of warm inside knowing he was that affected by me.

Who was I kidding? I loved it.

"Did you see the news conference that went on earlier?"

I nodded again, a small smirk forming on my lips. "I did. My sympathies go out to the Senator and his family during this time of transition."

Jack shook his head but I didn't miss the gleam in his eyes. "Smart ass," he muttered and slowly began walking towards the living room. My apartment was small, allowing him to reach a chair that suddenly seemed much too small once he sunk his large frame into it. It looked like a children's chair and he was the giant. "Do you want to know why he stepped down?" He looked at me with a questioning gaze.

I was thinking of Jack in that tiny chair and thinking of Goldilocks and the Three Bears. 'This chair is too big, this chair is too small, this chair is just right …' I frowned into my wine glass and slowly set it on the coffee table. I must be drunker than I thought if the only thing on my mind right now, with Jack back in my apartment and not yelling at me was nursery rhymes.

I sighed heavily and looked to Jack, remembering he had asked me a question.

"What?"

"How drunk are you?" He frowned.

I wrinkled my nose. The room wasn't spinning yet, but my tongue felt slightly larger and thicker than normal. "Just a little bit," I finally deduced, hoping my words weren't slurring. "You were talking about the Senator."

I tightened my robe across my breasts and held my hands there a little bit longer than necessary feeling my nipples harden. Jack's eyes dropped to my hands and a small smirk lifted on one side of his mouth, his dimple appearing.

God I loved that dimple. I wanted to lick it.

"Jack … the Senator?" I asked, just barely breathing even though I could feel my own pulse racing.

He shook his head as if clearing it and brought his eyes back to mine. And I waited, while he figured out what to say. Somehow, I didn't even care anymore. I loved him. And I knew he loved me. I just wanted this shit behind us so we could figure out where to go from here.

"He had the pictures." Jack cleared his throat and looked at me apologetically. "Somehow he paid off a security employee—who has now been fired—to release them. He showed me the video and pictures and demanded I stopped seeing you or else he would release them to the public."

I hated seeing the remorse in Jack's eyes. They weren't for himself, they were for me. He had to have known I was stronger than that.

"I wouldn't have cared, Jack."

His head snapped to mine. "I cared, Emma. There was no way I was letting that shit get out and have you be a fucking laughingstock all over the country. That's exactly what would have happened. I promised to take care of you.

"I didn't want moms at Logan's school talking about you—or anyone thinking less of you because I felt the need to screw you on the roof. It was my mistake in the first place, and mine to clean up."

He quickly moved and sat next to me on the couch, adjusting us so we were facing each other. Far enough away where we weren't on each other, but close enough to where I could feel the heat from his body. It seemed to emanate from every pore of his body and I saw his pulse beating a little bit too fast on the vein in his neck as his eyes dropped to the skin just showing above my robe.

"Why did he resign?"

"Marcus had his mom's suicide note that talked about all of his affairs." He stopped and shook his head. "She mentioned over a dozen women in her note, Emma. Marcus has held on to that thing since he found her when she died. He eventually showed a copy of the note to his dad and said he'd go public and ruin his dad's career and reputation if he went public with the shit from our video. We've been fighting with him for the last month, Emma. Senator Whitmore pulling his punches, and calling our bluffs. Marcus finally had a meeting with his dad tonight and had a reporter show up. He held up the note to tell the truth about his mom when the Senator finally caved."

"I don't get it," I said shaking my head. "Wouldn't seeing that note be enough reason to get him to back down from showing the videos and pictures of us. Why force his hand into quitting?"

Jack smirked. "That was Marcus's own personal vendetta with his dad and he finally had the winning hand. He forced him to quit because he blamed his dad's position as Senator as the reason why he forced you to leave so many years ago and what gave him the opportunity to screw around on his mom for so many years. I didn't know that was going to happen until we showed up tonight."

I swallowed slowly. "You were there?"

"I figured we'd show up, scare him with the reporter and he'd finally cave. I also had some legal documents for him to sign that says he can't contact Logan until he's eighteen."

I frowned.

"It's the best I could do. Logan will be an adult then and able to make his own decision about seeing the older Whitmore, but Marcus's dad can't contact him in anyway until then."

I exhaled slowly. The realization of everything he'd done, falling down on me. A faint smile touched my lips. "Because of you …"

Gently, he put his hand on my cheek and I melted into the warmth he offered me. When he pulled me so I was facing him again, I swear I saw tears in his eyes before he blinked them back.

"I'm sorry I was pissed and I took it out on you. That day …" His voice trailed off and I knew exactly what day he was talking about. "I'm just fucking sorry. It's a shitty excuse. I was pissed and stressed and needed to feel you one more time. I met with him the day before and found out that he had people watching you since Logan's been born," he skewered me with a glance, "which you neglected to tell me before. But regardless, I had to know what shit he was trying to pull and when I found out you were being tailed by some goons he fucking hired, I almost lost it on him."

"Jack …" I said softly but he started talking again.

"I've never loved anyone since my parents died. I've never cared about anyone until you and Logan. I was so wrapped up in what I was feeling for you that I would do anything to keep you safe. The only thing I could figure out was cutting all contact so there was no point in him showing those photos." He swallowed and his voice choked out the words a little bit. I moved closer, almost curled into his lap, wanting to be near him. To feel every inch of him when he closed his eyes and took a deep breath.

"It almost killed me to do that to you, baby. I promised to protect you regardless of the cost, and I hated pushing you away, but it had to be done. I figured if we weren't associated anymore then the Senator would lose his pull with the pictures and video."

I got it. I understood everything the instant he told me in the club about the pictures.

"It's okay, Jack," I said and rubbed my hands through his hair. I wanted to get closer, but I couldn't. There was too much between us, too many clothes and it didn't matter that I crawled up into his lap and pressed my cheek against his. It wasn't close enough.

"I never stopped loving you."

He began pressing his lips against my cheek and laughing softly when he saw the goose bumps that followed his trail of kisses; softly, barely touching my skin but still lighting a fire and leaving a trail of proof of how much I wanted him.

"I don't deserve you." He whispered against my ear when he finally reached it and I pulled back slightly.

He was so dead wrong. But I had one more question.

"Have you talked to Brian?"

Jack shook his head. "I called the counselors a couple of times but they keep saying he's not ready to talk to me. There's just too much history that's passed between us, but I keep hoping once he's clean—if he stays clean—we'll be able to talk."

"I hope so, too." I leaned in and kissed him softly on the lips. Jack exhaled as I pulled away and I felt some of the tension leave his body. "How long will he be there?"

"Until he demands to leave, or three more months whichever comes first, but I've heard he's doing really well." He pushed me back a little bit and my eyes widened at the distance he put between us. "How can you not fucking hate me right now? I treated you like shit and yet you're hear listening to all of this and caring about me and Brian." He shook his head and closed his eyes like he couldn't believe how someone could love him so much to see past their faults.

Maybe he didn't get it.

I grabbed his cheeks with both of my hands and pulled his face to mine.

"Because I love you, Jack. And love isn't always rainbows and unicorns. It's work. And sometimes it's ugly and nasty, but when you love someone, you press through all the bullshit because you remember how good it can be."

He leaned forward, resting his forehead on mine. "I don't deserve you, Emma. But I swear," his eyes pierced me and I saw how much he loved me. "Give me another chance, and I promise not to fuck it up ever again. I love you, Emma. Take me back and I promise I will make it up to you and will never push you away again."

I didn't know if it was a promise he could keep, but I knew Jack's love for me was real. Any type of relationship with Jack would feel like a rollercoaster. I would always feel the absolute thrill of being at the top where you think you could conquer anything, and we would have our heart splattering plummets at the very bottom. But he loved me, and he loved me fiercely. He also loved Logan

That alone would make the ride completely worth it.

It took me about a half second to agree and he knew the moment I did because he smiled and his eyes dropped again to my hideous robe.

His smile increased and I laughed softly, knowing what he was thinking.

Slowly, he reached out and rubbed the edge of my robe, just above my breasts. My breath caught in my throat as he touched me for the first time in too damn long.

He brought his eyes to mine, one eyebrow raised. "Haven't we talked about this ugly thing?"

I pursed my lips, biting back my smile. "I'm not sure it's yours to critique anymore."

Jack licked his lips and rubbed his tongue across the front of his teeth. "You've been mine since our first kiss and you always will be."

"Always?" My breath hitched in my throat.

He nodded and I smiled. In an instant, I was in Jack's arms, being carried down the hall.

He tossed me on the bed and all I could do was stare at him wide eyed as he began unbuttoning his shirt, a feral and wild look in his eyes as he watched me remove my robe.

"Always." His eyes darkened as I took off my robe and he climb slowly, predatorily over me. He lowered his mouth to one of my breasts and sucked it until it hardened into a pink nub. Soon we were a mess of hands, furiously roaming each other's bodies. We stroked, pulled, grasped at each other, our moans and the sound of skin slapping together the only things I could hear.

"I need you," I cried out as his fingers teased my clit. "All of you."

He leaned forward, panting just inches from my mouth and smiled wickedly. "I'm one fucking lucky man to have you. I won't ever forget this chance."

His mouth descended onto mine as his hand left my body. His hips pulled back until I felt the tip of his cock sitting at my entrance. My hands gripped him, pulling him into me. I arched into him, wiggling my hips against him, getting used to the feel of him inside me again.

It was perfect. The feel of him on top of me, his body surrounding me, the way he moved inside of me, his scent permeated everything in the room. Jack owned every inch of me.

I was in heaven as he slowly began moving again. His eyes stayed on mine, peering down on me with nothing but love in them.

"Jack?" I whispered, almost against his mouth when he was so close to me.

His raised eyebrows asked the question 'what?'

"I love you."

"I love you, too. Always."

"Always."

Twenty-Six

Almost four months later …

My cheeks felt like they were plastered into a permanent smile. I had been standing at the front of the church for almost two hours, smiling and posing for the camera. The heat wasn't working properly and my body felt frozen.

I was sure that when Macy got her pictures back from her overly excited photographer, my lips would show a slight tinge of blue, and my bare shoulders would be bright pink from frostbite.

"Say cheese!" Her photographer cheered and clicked away at least a half dozen times. I looked down at Logan, dressed immaculately in his little tuxedo that matched the groomsmen and groom and cringed.

"Logan," I hissed quietly so as not to interrupt the photographer; again. "Look at the camera."

His eyes moved to mine. He was standing in front of the group while I was in the back next to Macy. "My feet hurt," he whined and all the guys laughed.

"I understand your pain, man," Tate said and patted him on the shoulder. "Just hang on a little bit longer, okay?"

Logan frowned but nodded.

Twenty minutes later, the pictures were finally done and I was in a back bridal room, with Macy, her younger sister and two of her cousins, waiting for the time when she would walk down the aisle.

We were drinking mimosas, and wearing plastic bibs to ensure we didn't spill on our dresses. We looked absolutely ridiculous, but I had to hand it to Macy's mom for the idea.

"You ready for this?" I asked Macy, completely joking. Her and Tate were completely in love and if any couple could stand the test of time it was them.

She brushed an invisible piece of lint off her dress and smiled. Her brown eyes got all fuzzy looking, like they always did when she thought of—or looked at—Tate. You could feel her peace and excitement from a mile away.

"I've never been more ready. How about you? Are you ready for school next week?"

"You're about to get married and you're asking me about school?"

She rolled her eyes. "I'm starting to freak out. Quit being a bitch and take my mind off of it."

Who could blame her? Even if we all knew her and Tate were perfect together, I'd be nervous too if I was getting ready to confess something like that in front of hundreds of people. "I feel nervous, but that's probably because I'm going to be older than most law students, but Jack's been really supportive."

He was actually my biggest supporter next to Macy and my parents. They were thrilled when I told them I was re-admitted to DePaul School of Law when they came to visit for Christmas, and stayed with Jack, Logan and me in Jack's condo where we were now living together. Jack didn't waste any time in taking advantage of the second chance I gave him months ago. We were spending every night together anyway, so it only made sense, and now that there were no longer any secrets between us, we only continued to grow closer. We had moved in right after Thanksgiving at Jack's insistence the only thing he wanted for Christmas was me, in his bed, every day. How could I say no?

Macy grinned. "Just think, next year this could be you." She laughed when I made a face. Moving in with Jack and going back to law school were big enough adjustments to handle for a new year. Not that I didn't see myself with Jack forever, I did. I just wasn't in any big hurry to rush things now that we were finally feeling stable in our relationship.

"We'll see," I said noncommittally and heard a knock on the door.

Dean poked his head in when Macy's sister, Peyton gave him the all clear. "You ready to get this show on the road? It's time."

Macy heaved a large sigh, exhaling loudly and slowly, calming her nerves. "More than anything."

"Then let's roll, woman. If you keep Tate waiting any longer he might throw up."

I smacked Dean on the shoulder as we filed out of the room and down the hallway to the entrance of the sanctuary.

I watched the first three bridesmaids walk down the aisle, and when her sister hit the halfway mark, I turned to Macy and kissed her cheek.

"I'm so happy for you," I whispered and watched her fight back the tears.

It took me about a half second to find Jack in the church once I started walking down the aisle to the sound of Pachelbel Cannon in D. He stood near the front on the bride's side, right next to the aisle. His smile grew larger as I walked closer. I knew I should have been focused on the front of church and making my way towards the altar and taking my space with the other women, but just like always whenever Jack was around, my eyes could only focus on him.

He blew me a kiss as I passed him, and reached out, lightly brushing my hands with his. My body tingled instantly and I had to force myself to keep moving. If it wouldn't have been Macy's wedding, I might have dropped my flowers and jumped into his arms. He always had that effect on me and I hoped it wouldn't change.

Once I was standing at the altar, I winked over at Tate and Dean and then turned to the front, and watched Logan make his way down the aisle, carrying a white silk pillow with two fake rings. The real ones were hopefully safe in Dean's pockets. As much as Macy and Tate wanted Logan to participate in their ceremony, none of us trusted my five year old to keep their wedding bands safe. Logan paused when he reached Jack, and I smiled. Both of us were drawn to the enigmatic man and it made my heart feel full that Logan had so many grown men in his life to look up to.

At Jack's prodding, Logan finished the walk and plunked down on the bottom step with an exaggerated sigh. Many in the church laughed while my cheeks warmed with a heated blush. Before I could reach down and admonish him, Jack was right there, wiggling his fingers toward him. Logan happily went to him and sat down on Jack's lap.

That's why Jack was seated so close to the front, we had a feeling this would happen. Just before the music changed, I heard two soft "clunks" and turned to Jack. He nodded at Logan who I assumed was perfectly happy, now being able to final rid himself of the uncomfortable shoes he'd been forced to wear for hours.

The music began a new song, the doors opened again, and I smiled broadly, as Macy entered the back of the church, her arm firmly linked in her dad's. I watched her, awed, at the joy and love firmly planted all over her. Tate's expression mirrored hers as he took a few steps down the stairs to meet Macy and her dad at the end of the aisle. The only sign of any nervousness was the slight way Tate rocked on his heels, but they disappeared as soon as the pastor began and Tate was able to take Macy from her dad. The men hugged firmly, patting each other once on the back, and Tate led his bride to the front where the pastor continued the ceremony.

The words were the same as any other wedding I had ever attended, but my eyes still filled with my own happy tears when Macy began reciting her vows with tears in her eyes. Tate gave her a soft and encouraging smile, wiped away her tears with the pad of his thumb, and whispered how much he loved her. My mind wandered to the statement Macy made just before the ceremony. Would I be ready for this in a year? Jack and I had a great relationship and I loved him more than anything.

While Tate recited his vows, I couldn't avoid the feel of two dark brown eyes on me anymore. I slid my eyes to Jack, who was sitting in the church pew looking as commanding and sexy as ever. It helped that Logan was curled up in his lap, resting his head against Jack's chest and looking like he belonged there. I expected Jack's eyes to be filled with lust, like they usually were, but I was wrong. Instead, his eyes flickered to Tate and then back to me, his eyebrows raised just slightly. His gaze was soft, full of a love for me that went beyond what I normally saw, as if he was asking me the same question Macy had. Seeing the affection written all over Jack's face, I knew my answer.

I was most definitely ready for anything Jack brought my way.

"I'm ready to get you home and devour you," Jack whispered against my neck, his tongue trailing along the nerves in my neck and instantly igniting fireworks inside me. We had been at Macy and Tate's wedding reception for two hours now. We had eaten dinner, cut the cake, and spent the last hour dancing every single song in each other's arms. To my surprise, Marcus had come and picked up Logan after the wedding so we could enjoy the reception together. It was thoughtful of him, and when he had offered to take him home, I was once again reminded of how lucky I was. Logan had an incredible dad in his life, and we were all figuring out how to be friends and parent him together.

I shivered under Jack's touch, something that was all too familiar to both of us, and he laughed softly against my skin. He pulled me to him tightly, and I felt his erection press against my stomach. He wasn't kidding about wanting me. It made me want to unzip my dress and let him have his way with me in the middle of the dance floor.

I pulled back from him slightly and looked up, our noses briefly brushing against the other, and licked my lips. "What are you waiting for?"

His eyes filled with want and his desire. "Do you have anything else you need to do?"

"Just say good-bye to Macy and Tate."

Jack's hand was in mine, pulling me off the dance floor before I finished the sentence. I bit back a laugh as I watched him, suddenly hurrying to get out of here, when just moments before he was in complete control. Secretly, and sometimes not so secretly, I loved it when he acted like this. He went from running a corporation and being calm and collected all day long, but a simple touch from me and his eyes went wild with hunger. I loved that I could make him feel just as unraveled as he made me feel.

Macy and Tate were talking to some co-workers of Tate's when we interrupted them. Jack didn't even bother apologizing to anyone in the group as they watched him make an appearance. The men instantly looked at him with an awed respect and the women's eyes immediately fell to his chest, and then the erection in his tuxedo pants that was only slightly hidden by his coat. I didn't fault them for looking one single bit. He was magnificent. And all mine.

"Have a great time on your honeymoon," I said into Macy's ear as we giggled like school girls. We would never stop being immature enough to giggle over sex.

I hugged Tate and Dean as well, and offered a good-bye wave to Dean's date, Harper. We had met a few times before and I liked her. She was quiet, a little bit shy, but she was slowly opening up to our loud group. They had been dating for just over two months now and it made me happy to see Dean dating someone. It also helped Jack's jealousy where Dean was concerned to finally see Dean have his hands on someone else, and away from me.

After our good-bye's, Jack whisked me into the waiting limo. The door was barely shut by the driver before Jack had me pulled onto his lap, straddling him once again. It instantly brought back memories of how far we had come since our first limo ride. I leaned in and kissed him. It was pure heated passion as our lips pressed together, his hands flying to my hair, yanking out all the pins that had been holding it up off my neck. My blonde curls fell in waves down my back as I rocked against him, eliciting a groan from both of us.

"I love it when you're so turned on for me," Jack growled against my lips. My hands moved from his neck and began working to rid him of his coat, vest and shirt. I needed to feel his skin against mine. I wanted to feel the prickly hairs on his chest brush against my chest and tickle my breasts.

"I need you," I moaned into him and then squealed when Jack threw me off his lap and onto the bench. He wasted no time in hiking my dress above my hips, kneeling on the floor of the limo in front of me. His index finger trailed slowly, and painfully, up the back of leg. "Do you remember the last time we were alone in a limo?"

His brown eyes turned dark, thinking of exactly the same thing I had done only minutes before. I nodded, not trusting myself to speak as his finger trailed higher. A wicked grin erupted on his face, showing off his dimple when his finger brushed lightly against my pussy.

He slowly pressed his finger into me and I rocked toward him, hungry for more. My eyes rolled back and my head flopped onto the back of the seat.

"It was the first time I told you I loved you." Jack's tongue flicked out on my clit and I gasped. I hadn't felt him move closer to me and the warmth against my skin was shocking. "I will tell you that every day for the rest of your life, and I hope you never forget it."

I opened my eyes, looking at him under half-hooded lashes and moaned when his tongue licked my clit again. He inserted another finger and pressed into me, pushing and twisting his fingers as he rocked against me. My hands flew to his hair as I held him in place, unashamedly.

"Jack," I moaned breathlessly.

"Hmmm?" He had a smirk on his lips that I wanted to smack and then kiss the hell out of.

"I need you."

His fingers continued working in me but Jack knelt closer to me, his lips—tasting like me—brushing against my mouth. "I need you, Emma."

I rocked against him as my orgasm began building and moaned against his mouth. The walls of my pussy began to spasm on Jack's fingers.

"I will always need you. Tell me how much you love me."

I cried out as my orgasm hit and Jack silenced my cries with my mouth, his tongue devouring every inch of the inside of my mouth. He pulled back slowly as I came down, and smiled.

"Tell me you love me," he repeated, much more softly.

"I love you. And I'll always need you." I mewled as his fingers left mine and I pressed a gentle kiss to his lips, my fingers interlocking behind his neck, holding him close. He nodded once, and fixed my dress as the limo pulled up in front of his—our—building; our home.

"Hey mom … mom … MOM!"

I jumped awake at the sound of Logan's shout. With eyes wide open, I brushed the hair out of my face and then frowned. Was I still dreaming?

Logan was smiling happily at me, standing next to my side of the bed, dressed in his tuxedo. I didn't need to roll over to know that Jack was still lying in bed next to me, his arm wrapped around my waist and preventing the sheet from falling down and giving Logan a glance of my naked breasts.

I turned to him anyway. He looked perfect; too perfect for the first thing in the morning, and I still hadn't processed why Logan was in his tux. Jack was dressed in cotton pajama pants and a long sleeve gray Henley shirt. His eyes laughed at me.

"What am I missing?" I asked, groggily.

His head nodded towards Logan. I turned back to my son, still standing next to our bed, and my eyes widened.

He was holding his ring bearer pillow proudly in front of my face and when I frowned again, he shoved it up closer to my eyes so I could see exactly what was sitting on it, and why he and Jack looked so excited.

"Daddy Jack has a present for you and he wanted me to give it to you." A tear escaped my eyes, like it usually did at Logan's new name for Jack. Marcus was dad, and Jack was daddy Jack. It was perfect.

Shock filled my eyes and I turned back to Jack slowly. He moved me, sitting me up against the headboard on our bed, making sure I stayed covered. My arms wrapped around the sheet on my chest as Jack moved and straddled my hips. His eyes turned serious as he reached over to the pillow, extracting the gift and holding it up to me. My eyes followed his every movement and my heart stopped.

This couldn't be happening. Already? Did Macy know this was going to happen? Is that why she made that statement yesterday? Did my parents know? I couldn't imagine Jack asking my dad for permission to marry his daughter, but at the same time, I wouldn't put it past him to show my dad that respect either.

I breathed out slowly, my eyes flickering between Logan and Jack. My two men. Oh my god, this was really happening.

"Tap it down, babe," Jack whispered softly, with a grin on his face.

I laughed, beside myself. I couldn't believe this.

He held up the sparkling ring in between us and his smile fell, his expression turning serious and pensive. My jaw dropped. The only thing I could see were his brown eyes, boring into mine, and a massive amount of sparkling diamonds. An emerald cut diamond sat high and proud in the middle, larger than any diamond I had ever seen, all around the band were more emerald shaped diamonds, set down into the band, and the sides were filled with round cut diamonds. Diamonds. Everywhere.

All the blood drained from my head. If I had been standing, I might have passed out.

Jack cleared his throat. My eyes flew back to him and away from the offensive amount of sparkling ice he held in between his thumb and forefinger. He smirked, seeing the shock written all over my face.

"I've loved you for years, Emma, I just didn't know it. You are my strength, and you and Logan fill my heart with an amount of joy and love I never knew possible before you walked into my life almost six years ago. You have given me a second chance at showing you how much I love you, and I want to make sure you know every day, for the rest of our lives, how much you mean to me. Marry me."

I choked down a laugh at his command. He wasn't even asking, just demanding.

Tears fell down my face and a smile erupted. My entire body flooded with goose bumps in the happiest kind of way. I turned to Logan who smiled.

"Say yes, mom!" He dropped his pillow and clapped his hands together, cheering me on, with pure exaltation.

I ruffled his hair and turned back to Jack. His eyes held a tiny amount of humor and nervousness.

"Of course I'll marry you," I whispered, barely able to get the words out as the tears fell down my cheeks. He brushed them away before sliding the ring on my finger. I thought he was going to lean in to kiss me, but at the last second, his arms reached over and he pulled Logan onto our bed, placing him in the middle of us and wrapped both of his arms around us.

Loving us, protecting us. If it was possible for a heart to burst with love and admiration for someone else, mine would have exploded on the spot.

He leaned forward, pressed a kiss on Logan's forehead before moving to me and pressing his lips against mine. It was a chaste kiss, given our company, but when he pulled back and leaned his forehead against mine, I saw Jack's own eyes glistening with tears.

"I will love you, always, and I will never hurt you or push you away again."

I swallowed slowly. It was a promise he had made to me every day for the last four months since we got back together, and it meant just as much hearing it for the hundredth time as it did the first.

"I know," I whispered and leaned up so I could give him a kiss. "I love you too."

"Always?"

I nodded and glanced down at the ring on my finger before turning my eyes back to his. "Always."

About the Author

Stacey Lynn lives in Minnesota with her husband and four young children. She spends her day taking care of the kids and loving her family. At night she's curled up with a book and a blanket, or her laptop, writing down all the stories she hears in her head.

For more information about Stacey Lynn and her upcoming books visit:

Facebook:

http://www.facebook.com/staceylynnbooks

Twitter:

@staceylynnbooks

Website:

http://staceylynnbooks.blogspot.com

Thank You

I had an absolute blast writing this book, and it wouldn't have been accomplished with the help of so many people cheering me on, and a few gin and tonics along the way.

To my husband. Your male insight was invaluable. Thank you for taking the time to read yet another one of my books and to offer your helpful advice along the way. For my kids, who will NEVER EVER be allowed to read this … there is nothing you could ever say or do that would ever make me stop loving you. All four of you own my heart.

To my parents. Your support of all of my crazy endeavors has always been encouraging. Thank you for supporting my dreams and helping me reach them. Please … do NOT read this book. Especially you, dad.

To Brooke McHose, Natalie Gerber, and Amanda Halverson. Thank you all for beta reading Don't Lie to Me and for giving me your support, for helping me with the plot and for cheering me on! I owe you all huge hugs, and more.

To Autumn with The Autumn Review. Thank you doesn't seem big enough for all the help you've given me and this book. I truly appreciate all the time and effort you put into helping this book better.

Kim Person with Shh Mom's Reading. You've said a hundred times that you need to learn to say 'no,' but personally, I'm so glad you said 'yes' to me. Thank you for organizing my cover reveal and my blog tour! You are an amazing woman and this book wouldn't be in the hands of so many readers without your help.

To all the blogs who participated in the cover reveal and blog tour, I can't thank you enough for taking a chance on this new author. You are all amazing!

To you—the reader. Every note, review, message, or Facebook post I receive makes me smile and cry happy tears. So many of you supported me with my first book and I have been overwhelmed, daily, by the amount of messages I have received. Your words and excitement for reading and enjoying the characters in my head that won't stop talking make all the sleepless nights and hair pulling days absolutely worth it! Thank you for reading and reviewing this indie author's books!

To my Father in Heaven. I'm so thankful that you love a wreck like me and that your mercy and grace is new every morning.

4815943R00155

Printed in Great Britain
by Amazon.co.uk, Ltd.,
Marston Gate.